Hard Wheat, Cayman Liberty

And other stories

Second Edition

By

Donald Skiff

© Copyright 2015

ISBN-13: 9781517766269
ISBN- 1517766265

Contents

Introduction 6
Hard Wheat 8
   Chapter One - 2014 9
   Chapter Two - 1970 44
   Chapter Three - 1950 51
   Chapter Four - 1975 54
   Chapter Five - 1985 56
   Chapter Six - 2014 58
   Chapter Seven - 1980 61
   Chapter Eight - 1982 63
   Chapter Nine - 2014 64
   Chapter Ten - 1990 66
   Chapter Eleven - 2014 69
   Chapter Twelve - 2009 75
   Chapter Thirteen - 2014 77
Cayman Liberty 79
   One – The Boat 80
   Two – Liberty in George Town 81
   Three - Eyes 86
   Four – The Tour 94
   Five – Claudia 96
   Six – Journey Home 102
   Seven – The Past 105
   Eight – Cape May 106
   Nine – New York 109
   Ten – Connecticut 113
   Eleven – New York 117
   Twelve – New York 127
   Thirteen – New London 133
   Fourteen – Greenwich Village 140
   Fifteen – Train to New York 151
   Sixteen – New York, Again 154
   Seventeen – New London 173

Eighteen – At Sea 177
Nineteen – Oregon, Two Weeks Later 178
Twenty – San Francisco 182
Twenty-One – Washington..................................... 191
Twenty-Two – California.. 200
Twenty-Three – San Diego Harbor........................ 211
Twenty-Four – Seattle.. 213
Twenty-Five – Seattle, Some Years Later............. 214

Hood Canal 218
One 219
Two 222
Three 232
Four 234

The Smile 237
One 238
Two 242
Three 244
Four 244
Five 246
Six 251
Seven 255
Eight 262
Nine 263

The Kerchief 275
One – Current Time 276
Two – About 1950 276
Three – Current Time 304

Touching 306

Do-Over 317
Track One... 318
Track Two 320
Track Three.. 322
Track Four 323
Track Five 325

Acknowledgments

The inspirations for these stories were probably buried in my unconscious, in some cases for years, emerging in those hazy moments lying in bed after awakening but before being able to rise and face another day. For years I've been curious about where my stories come from. Once begun, however, they have benefited from advice and suggestions by my friends and relatives. Foremost has been Judith, my wife and lover, who reads nearly every word I write before anybody else.

My group of friends in *Writers Unlimited* have heard and read all these words and offered valued comments and suggestions. Their sharing of their own writing has inspired me to continue and to work harder to express more clearly what I want to say.

This second edition is the result of comments and suggestions by good friends who read the first edition and expressed frustration that at least one story (The Smile) begged for expansion. In particular, thank you, Mark.

"Cayman Liberty" was a separate story not intended originally for this collection, but on subsequent reading seems appropriate.

Introduction

One of the ideas that have become clichés in our culture is that the past and the future do not exist; there is only the present moment. It takes a lot of effort to become aware of the *now*, moment by moment. Without that awareness, we tend to live in some other time—and risk missing the present experience altogether.

It's true enough that we can't do anything about the past. Regret or nostalgia can perhaps affect our present, but they cannot change what has been. What we think or do or feel now can affect our future, but we seldom consider—or even know—all of the consequences of our present actions.

Each of the stories here is about the past. The characters did what they did, made the decisions and launched the experiences, to the best of their abilities at the time. The ultimate outcomes, even now, are uncertain.

About Cayman Liberty: The life of a man, like the life of a ship, is limited in time. From the day that they first appear on this earth, they both experience the processing of aging.

A ship has no choice in what it experiences, other than its built-in functionality. "Life," we might say, simply happens to it, without consciousness of experience or purpose.

We like to believe that a man can choose how he is to live, at least after a manner of speaking. Even though he inherits certain traits, and accumulates others from his early experiences, we assume that he can alter the path of his life at least a little bit, sometimes greatly. Culture—and especially society—assign him responsibility for his behavior, and by extension, his fate. He is at liberty to live his own life.

Still, things happen to us all, regardless of our purposes and prior decisions. Sometimes we can only try to change the way we see things, and even that is not always possible.

These stories are fictional. The characters and events portrayed do not represent any actual people or events. Any resemblance is purely coincidental.

Don Skiff
October, 2015

Chapter One - 2014

It didn't make sense. The blue and red flashing lights in his rear-view mirror annoyed him more than anything else. Al knew he hadn't been speeding, and he was a half-hour past the last little town on the interstate. He took his time coasting to a stop, allowing the Prius to get a little more gas mileage. He'd managed to get over 48 on that last leg, something that gave him some satisfaction. Little else did lately.

He rolled down the window as the officer approached. He knew that he'd be asked first for his license, but he wanted the guy to have to wait for him to dig it out of his pocket. When it did happen, he pretended to fumble, to take more time as the officer held his flashlight on him. "I wasn't speeding," he said.

The patrolman took his license and examined it carefully. "This you?" he asked.

"Who does it look like?"

The young officer did something to the tablet in his hand, then looked directly at Al. "Where are you headed?"

"Montana. Visiting my son in Butte."

"You're from Indiana?"

"That's what my license says, doesn't it?" He enjoyed seeing the scowl appear on the patrolman's face.

"Sir, would you step out of the car, please?"

Al sighed. *Okay,* he thought, *I deserved that. I shouldn't have smart-mouthed him.* He got out of the car and allowed the door to close. The little alarm in the Prius beeped to tell him he'd left the car without shutting it down.

At least the guy didn't treat him like he was a gangster running from a bank holdup. He looked Al over from a few feet away. "Do you know someone named Gladys Gibson?"

That shook Al a little bit. "What about her?"

Hard Wheat

The patrolman watched him carefully as he said, "It seems she's dead."

Al wilted. *No wonder she didn't answer her door!*

Al Vincent had rolled up the gravel drive to the old farmhouse, thinking about Gladys, his ex-wife, and how much she would have aged, as he himself had in the past thirty years. He hadn't even seen a photograph of her in twenty years; Eliot hadn't talked much about his mother when he had visited Al last year.

A late-model van sat in the yard next to the house, but there was no sign of life. Al had knocked on the door. In the late afternoon, maybe she was asleep. Finally giving up, he'd returned to his car and written her a note that he'd been on the way to see Eliot in Butte, and decided to drop by. Going back to the door, he stuck the note in the crack and started back down the steps from the porch.

That's when the other car had pulled up next to his, and a young woman got out, looking suspiciously at him. He didn't know her.

As they passed, Al said, "Nobody seems to be home. I left a note." He went on to his car and got in. The woman was standing on the porch, watching him. He didn't want to talk to anybody. He turned the car around in the yard and drove out to the highway.

He was disappointed. Ever since he'd gotten the doctor's pronouncement about his imminent lack of a future, he'd thought of Gladys in a different way. The years of bitterness following their divorce seemed stupid now. They'd been so close in the beginning; they had both told all their friends that they'd be together forever, and Al had believed it to be true. After Eliot had grown and gone off into his own life, Al and Gladys didn't have much to talk about any more, and eventually they split up. But Al remembered those years when Gladys was young and vivacious, and he still had feelings for that young woman. At the end, they both knew they couldn't live together any more. He didn't know how she felt about him in recent years. She'd remarried and had a daughter, but Al had never seen either of them since. Eliot had told him that his mother had divorced again, but hadn't said much else, other than, "I can't imagine you two together. You are so different."

They hadn't seemed so different, back in their early years. Yeah, she had done all the talking; he didn't find much to say about anything, actually, but he'd enjoyed the way she had arranged their life together, deciding where they should live and who they made friends with. She had seemed to love him, taciturn as he was. It wasn't as though he never said anything; he just didn't have much that needed to come out.

So he'd planned this trip to see their son in Montana and to go by Fargo to stop in to see her, let her know that she always had a place in his heart. It wasn't something he would be able to say easily, but he had been determined to connect with her at least this one last time. The doctor had given him three to six months. He wanted her to know that he felt something for her, for those first years.

It was cloudy in the west as he drove on. He wished he'd brought some music with him; there was nothing on the radio in those desolate plains.

Al didn't like leaving the Prius sitting there on the side of the highway, but the patrolman didn't give him any choice. As they drove back toward Fargo, Al wondered what had happened to Gladys. He felt like crying, but took deep breaths to keep it down. The officer wouldn't talk to him about it, just that he needed to be taken back to see what the facts were.

Hard Wheat

At the highway patrol station in Mapleton, he had to sit on an uncomfortable chair in an otherwise vacant office. Another officer came in and talked to him, asking him about his relationship with Gladys and where he was going and why he had been to her house. Al answered truthfully. "I didn't see her at all," he said. "How did she die?"

"We don't know that yet," the officer said. He filled out a form and told Al to read it and sign it. The form didn't have anything on it but bureaucratic nonsense, plus some notes someone had made about Al, describing him and what he had said. Al signed it.

A female officer came in and asked him if he needed anything. She gave him an old magazine. "Something to do," she said, in that funny Scandinavian lilt they had in North Dakota.

"I could use a whiskey," Al said.

She just smiled at him and left the room, closing the door.

Al leafed through the magazine, something about farm life. "Shit," he muttered, and tossed it aside.

Even though it had been many years since he and Gladys had had anything to do with each other, he felt a lump in his chest thinking about her being dead. Dying was no big thing to him—he'd be there pretty soon himself—but he grieved a little bit for Gladys. He wished they'd had that one last talk. Some things he'd never said to her, but wanted to before he died. He pictured her the first time he'd seen her; it was after church back in Indiana, and she was wearing this funny little hat with fake flowers on it. He'd thought she was so beautiful, and he liked the way she was always laughing.

There was some commotion outside the office he was in. Several police were talking to a young woman—it was the woman who had driven up to Gladys's place as he was leaving. She glanced at Al through the glass, but the officers herded her away. *She must have told them she'd seen me there,* he thought. *How'd they track me down clear out on the interstate?* Of course, he'd left the note for Gladys, and that had his name on it. *It wouldn't take long with their computers.*

After a long time, the female officer came back in with a sandwich wrapped up in butcher's paper. "They think she just had a heart attack," she said. "They'll probably let you go."

Al didn't say anything as he ate the sandwich. The woman stood and watched him, waiting with him.

"Who was the girl?" he asked finally.

"The woman's daughter. She lives here in town."

"She think I killed her mother?"

The officer looked away for a moment. "She was pretty upset."

"Guess I should have talked to her," he said. "I was there to talk to Gladys—we've been divorced for thirty years—and I didn't want to talk to anybody else."

Another officer came in. "They think it was just a heart attack," he said. "You can go, but we might need to talk with you some more. Can you stay around for a day?"

Al grinned. "You trust me that much?"

The man smiled a little, then said deliberately, "Will you stay in town for a day?"

Al shrugged. "My car's out on the interstate. Where can I go, anyway?"

The woman said, "There's a motel down the street. I can take you down."

"We'll send a truck out to get your car," said the man.

"You're not charged with anything," said the woman. "They just might want to ask you some questions."

Al grinned again. "You didn't have any trouble finding me the first time. You probably could again."

"Yeah," said the man.

The female officer drove Al to the motel in a police car, and waited while he registered. Outside, he asked her, "Any chance I could talk with her daughter?"

She smiled. "Do you know her?"

"No. I knew about her, that's all. It's been thirty years since we divorced."

"Her name's Heather. Heather Gibson. She works in town," she said. "I'll ask her."

Al went into the motel room. The place matched his mood; smell of disinfectant, cheap wood paneling, tiny TV facing the bed. He turned on the television and flopped on the bed. Every channel spewed crap. He muted the sound and stared at the ceiling.

A knock on the door got him up. It was a man in work clothes. "Your car is right here," he said, pointing outside. "You got the key?"

"Yeah," said Al. He followed the man outside, and retrieved his bags from the back of the car. "Any place to get a drink around here?" he asked the driver as the man got into his truck.

"There's a bar in town. Hagge's over on Olsen."

"Thanks."

Al carried his bags into the room, set them down without opening them, and sat on the edge of the bed. The whole trip was suddenly different. It was like nothing made sense. Going to see Eliot would now be something else, something other than a way to say goodbye. If he were to die now, it wouldn't be a big thing. Eliot would be upset, sure. But what would it mean to him now to go there and say, "Hey, I'm at the end of my journey, and I wanted to tell you I love you," when Eliot would be grieving over his mother?

Eliot had always blamed him for the divorce. The kid had gone off to college, and came home for Thanksgiving to find his father moved out, gone back to Indiana. Al had tried to explain to him on the telephone that he and Gladys had just lost the love they used to have. It wasn't the same without Eliot to hold them together, but the boy closed him off for years. Al assumed that Gladys had said the same thing to him, but he wasn't sure. She hadn't written to Al, and their phone conversations back then were weird.

Sometime later, Eliot had made up with him, and said he just hadn't understood. But their relationship was never close after that. Al had gone out to Montana to visit him a few times, but Eliot had seldom reciprocated. They talked on the phone once in a while, and exchanged a few letters and then emails.

Al decided that he should call Eliot to let him know about Gladys. He needed a drink first.

The bar was a typical small-town place, with pool tables in a back room. Country Western music blared from speakers all around the place. There weren't many customers. Al ordered Wild Turkey and a water chaser.

A hand on his arm made him turn around. It was Heather, Gladys's daughter. Her eye makeup was smeared. "I'm sorry," she said, so softly he could barely hear her. "I didn't know who you were."

Al downed the shot. "I'm sorry for your loss," he said. Looking around, he asked, "Is there someplace we can talk?"

She shook her head. "Fran told me where you were. I just had to say I'm sorry I got the police after you."

"Anything I can do?"

"No, I got friends who are taking care of Mom right now, but I got to go back over there."

"Can I come see her?" Al was close to tears. This pretty little girl *was* Gladys's. She looked like her, like Gladys did forty years ago. *How could she have a daughter this young?*

"The funeral parlor will have her ready by Friday. We'll just have a little service—she didn't have a church. Sure, she would want you to come." Heather turned toward the door, then looked back at him.

"You're at the motel, ain't you?" When he nodded, she left.

Heather looked *so much* like her mother did forty years ago. Same curly red hair. The feelings he had been having since learning of Gladys's death, the remembering how she had looked and talked and laughed, all sort of focused on Heather. She was the Gladys he had fallen for, back in Indiana. Al thought about her for a long time before finally going to sleep on the lumpy bed.

In the morning he went over to Hagge's again, where the smell of pancakes and sausages had replaced the beer and pot smoke from the day before. Some guys in hard hats were talking loudly at a table, and Heather was behind the counter. The bartender from the previous day was in the kitchen, behind the stainless pass-through.

Heather was watching him. Her eyes were red-rimmed and sad looking.

"Anything I can do for you?" Al asked quietly when she was close by.

She just shook her head and wiped the counter with a rag.

"You have family around here?" He marveled at how much she reminded him of the young Gladys.

She shook her head again and said, "Friends."

Al felt that lump again in his throat. He swallowed and sighed. "If you want, I could be kind of family."

She turned away from him, then wiped at her face with a corner of the bar rag.

"I was once family to her." Saying that almost brought his own tears.

She turned around. "Thanks," she said softly.

"Why are you here? You ought to have some time off."

"I have to work." She nodded back toward the kitchen. "He's got nobody else."

Another customer entered and sat at the counter. "Hi, Heather, the usual?" Al looked at him out of the corner of his eye, then at Heather. She didn't respond, but wrote something on her order pad, tore the sheet out and clipped it to the rack over the pass-through. The bartender/cook took the slip silently, watching Heather and the customer.

The customer, a guy about as old as Al, in weathered overalls, looked at the cook quizzically. The cook shook his head, then turned back to the grill. Heather went into a back room.

Al moved to a stool close to the customer. "Her mom just died," he said quietly.

"No shit!" the other man whispered. He went around behind the counter and leaned close to the pass-through. "Why'nt you close down?" he asked, still whispering.

Al barely caught the reply, "I will, for the funeral on Friday."

The customer came out from behind the counter just as Heather reappeared. He took her hand and said something Al couldn't hear. She leaned her head against his shoulder for a moment, then went to her station. The cook set a plate of food on the pass-through and slipped the order under it. Heather moved the plate to the counter without saying anything.

Al studied a menu. When Heather glanced toward him, he said, "Coffee and toast with peanut butter?"

She set a cup in front of him and dropped two slices of bread into the toaster. Just then the men from the table gathered at the end of the counter next to the cash register. They were still talking among themselves, oblivious to the drama. Heather rang up their sales and impaled the slips on a spike next to the register. When they left, she retrieved Al's toast and set it on the

Hard Wheat

counter with a jar of peanut butter, giving him a weak little smile.

Al wrote his phone number on the sales slip and put a bill on top of it. By the time he had finished, other customers had come in. He left the money and the sales slip and walked out.

Just as he was about to start the Prius, a patrol car stopped next to him. The female officer rolled down her window. Al did the same.

"You talk to Heather?" she asked.

He nodded. "She's busy."

She looked steadily at him for a moment. "She gets off at three."

Al nodded, and the patrol car moved on down the street.

Small towns, thought Al. *People know each other. Take care of each other.* He started his car and drove toward the highway patrol station. *But they aren't family.*

It wasn't as though he'd forgotten he was dying. The girl felt like *family* to him, something that he had long ago forgotten, and now it seemed more important to him than his own death. He wondered if Eliot knew Heather. *Of course he must. They share a mother.*

Parked in the highway patrol station lot, he dialed Eliot's number. There was no answer, so he left a message: "Eliot, I'm in North Dakota. I was on my way to see you, but I need to talk to you." Then he went inside the station.

"Anything new about Gladys Gibson?" he asked the woman at the desk.

She looked at him carefully. "You are …?"

"Her ex-husband."

"The coroner's report hasn't been issued yet, but they think she died of a heart attack."

Al explained that the officers the day before had requested him to stay around. The woman looked through some papers, and said, "I think you can go now."

"Actually," Al said, "I'm going to stay for a few days—at least until the funeral."

She wrote something and replied, "I'll tell them."

Al walked back to his car thinking about how bizarre the situation seemed. Here he was, in a town so far out in the boondocks that the only place to eat was a bar. He'd seen a school somewhere, but not even a used-car lot. There must be a grocery store—it was twenty miles to Fargo—but he hadn't seen one.

After a misunderstanding, he was free to go on his way to Butte, but he was choosing to stay because of a young woman he wasn't related to, but who somehow felt to him like family. Her mother—his ex-wife—and he hadn't spoken in many years, and now she was dead. He, himself would likely be dead in another few months. There was something surreal about it all.

Maybe that's why it didn't matter much to him. The only part of it that seemed to be important was Heather. What could he offer to her? Why should he be concerned? Yes, she was attractive—he wasn't dead yet. But something about her reminded him of his youth, of Gladys and how stricken he was with that young woman, when life seemed to stretch endlessly into the future. Was he trying to recapture life? Deny death, somehow? *The mind,* he recited to himself, *isn't mostly rational. We only think we can be objective, because we make up reasons for what we feel.* He was grieving for life, and lecturing to students in his classroom.

His phone rang through the car's Bluetooth. It was Eliot. Al switched the call from the car's speakers to the phone at his ear.

"Hey, Dad, what's up?" Eliot was middle-aged, but he sounded young.

"I'm in Mapleton," Al said, not sure how to continue. "Your mom died."

Hard Wheat

There was silence on the other end. Finally, Eliot asked, "When?"

"Not sure. They found her yesterday."

Eliot stammered. "What—what happened?

"They think she had a heart attack. Heather found her."

"Dad, what are you doing there?" Then he stammered. "I mean—I didn't—I didn't think you had even seen Mom in years."

Al related his experience. "I just wanted to talk with her one last time."

Another long silence. "I don't understand, Dad. Did you know she was going to die?"

"I'll explain later. I thought you might want to know about your mom. The funeral is Friday."

"Sweet Jesus!"

"I can pick you up in Fargo, if you want. I presume there are flights."

Eliot's voice sounded dead. "Guess I'd rather drive. I can be there tomorrow sometime."

"I'll tell Heather."

"You know Heather?"

"Yeah. You may hear from her. I 'spect she'll call you."

"Dad," Eliot said haltingly, "I still don't understand why you're there."

"Tell you when you get here."

Al clicked off and stared into space. *Why AM I here?*

He drove slowly around the little town. There were a lot of empty lots; it had once been bigger. Several old homes had been fine residences a long time ago. He found a community center, which was closed, and an auto repair business. The water tower seemed fairly new.

Curious (and bored), he opened his iPad and found the town website. At least they were part of the Twenty-First Century. Barely, he decided.

At about two P.M., he made his way back to Hagge's. Heather was still there, sitting at a table with a couple of people. She returned to her post behind the counter before she seemed to recognize him. Her eyes still looked sad.

He scanned the menu that was propped against the napkin holder. "Would you recommend your fish sandwich?" he asked.

"Caught it in the creek out back just this morning," she replied with a straight face.

Al grinned. "You've used that line before."

Her expression didn't change. "That what you want?"

"Sorry," he said. "Yeah, that'll be good."

When she turned back from clipping the order at the pass-through, she said, "Coffee?"

"Yes. I'm sorry. I don't know what to say to you."

"We can talk after I get off at three," she said.

"I'd like that. I've been driving around town all morning."

He nodded to the cook, who was watching him through the pass-through. Then he turned on the stool enough so that he could see the middle-aged couple Heather had been talking to when he entered. They were also watching him.

They all probably know who I am, by now, he thought. *Small town.*

When Heather served his sandwich and fries, he smiled at her and began eating without saying more. She wiped down the counter and straightened the bottles behind the counter. Country Western music played softly.

When he finished the sandwich, Al carried his coffee to a corner table where a newspaper had been left. He leafed through it, struggling to focus, wanting to leave, wanting to talk to her, wishing time would go faster.

He suspected that Bloomington, Indiana, where he had grown up, wasn't much different from this place, but the endless wheat fields and prairie here had always depressed him. He and Gladys had moved out here when Eliot was a small boy because Al had been offered a job in a new food products company. That job hadn't lasted ten years. They had stayed because Eliot had friends and wanted to finish high school here.

Al wondered, now, how much of his dissatisfaction with the marriage had to do with the depressive environment. Gladys had insisted on staying in North Dakota where she felt "was home, now." At the time, he had even wondered if she was interested in another man. It was always easier for her to make friends.

When he'd heard that she had remarried and had another child, Al was only mildly interested. He lived a different life for thirty years, remaining single by choice, returning to school and then teaching.

Surprised by a movement, he looked up to see Heather standing next to him. The restaurant was otherwise empty.

"I can talk now," she said simply.

Flustered, he picked up his lunch check and went to the cash register. She rang it up and impaled it on the spike. They left together.

"You want to drive, or walk?" he asked.

"Drive out of town," she said. "There's no privacy here."

On a narrow country road next to a creek, he pulled off the pavement and shut down the car. They sat for a while, wordless.

"I've seen pictures of you," she said finally, "but you didn't have a beard."

"How are you doing?"

"Okay."

"Can I do anything?"

She thought for a moment. "Mom had some old stuff you might help me go through." Then she added, "After the funeral."

"Eliot is on his way here." Al was fumbling for words.

"I know."

"You talked with him?"

"Yeah."

Al sighed. "I hope I'm not intruding," he said. "I'm just a stranger to you."

"No," she said. "I appreciate your being here." She turned to face him. "You were always kind of a mystery man to me. Mom had a couple of pictures of you in her album, but she never talked about you."

"We were very happy for a long time," he said.

She shook her head. "Mom never seemed happy. Dad tried, but he finally gave up, he said."

"How old were you when they split up?"

She smiled. "I was a uh, *difficult* teen ager."

"Tough age to lose a father."

Heather nodded. She was silent for a long time, then said, "She got crazy. I finally had to leave, myself."

Al frowned. "What do you mean?"

She looked directly at him again. "Crazy. She threw things."

"Hmm," he said. "Hard to live with."

She traced a seam on the dashboard with her fingertip. "Am I going to get like her?"

Al had a sudden impulse to take her into his arms and comfort her, but he sat motionless. "Why do you say that?"

"Sometimes," she began, "I used to get so mad at her. She wouldn't listen to me. *She never listened to me!*"

He waited a few minutes before asking, "You let your dad know?"

She looked at him, tears forming in her eyes. "I'm mad at him!"

"He'll want to know."

She leaned forward until her forehead rested on the dashboard. Her shoulders shook.

"Feel abandoned, huh?" Al placed a hand gently on her shoulder, then withdrew it when she suddenly sat back.

"I wanted to go live with him," she said, her voice choked with emotion. "I couldn't take her anymore."

"Where does he live?"

"Iowa. That's where he's from. By the time I asked him, he said he had another family."

"You been feeling alone for a long time."

"He stopped sending money when I graduated from high school." Her voice became flat. "When I moved out from Mom's, I had to find a job right away, 'cause she wouldn't give me any."

"Stay with friends?"

"Yeah. Mabel and George, that couple that was in there when you came, they're from the Lutheran Church. They had a daughter graduated a year before me, they gave me her room for a while."

She absentmindedly picked at the dashboard with a fingernail. "But they wanted to tell me what to do, what time to come home, and like that."

Al smiled. "You rebelled."

She returned the smile. "I'm a handful," she said. "I don't take shit off of anybody."

Al felt a little apprehensive, and tried to change the subject. "You said your mom was always unhappy."

"I guess I'm like her."

"When she was your age, she was always laughing."

She looked up at him. "Tell me about her."

"She was only nineteen when we met. She was always so bright and cheerful. Everybody loved her."

"This was in Indiana?"

"We lived in Bloomington. It's a college town, and there were a lot of young people there. She had lots of friends. I fell for her—just like that." He snapped his fingers.

"She told me once about going to college, how cool it was."

Al sighed. "Yeah. She was a freshman, but when we got married, she quit."

Heather looked at him.

"Yeah," he said, hanging his head and nodding. "She got pregnant."

"Wish I could have gone to college."

"You can."

"Don't know how."

"What would you like to study?"

"I don't know. It just sounds like fun, going to classes and stuff."

Al's phone rang. It was Eliot, who said, "I'm stopping over in Bismarck tonight. Be there tomorrow morning sometime."

"Heather's with me. We're getting acquainted."

"Good, Dad. Give her my love."

Al looked at Heather and pointed to the phone and then to her, raising his eyebrows. She shook her head.

"Will do," he said into the phone, "Call me when you get here. No telling where I'll be."

When he clicked off, he looked at Heather. "You two get along?"

"He's sweet," she said. "He took my side when Mom was on a rampage."

"He said to give you his love."

"I heard everything."

Al grinned.

"Tell me more about her." Heather had turned in the seat to face him.

"She liked to read, and she loved flowers. We had this little apartment right on ground level, and she planted flowers all around the patio."

"She still does—did." After a pause, she asked, "She sing?"

"How'd you know?"

"She told me one time that she used to sing all the time. She sang to me when I was little, but then she stopped. She just bitched about everything."

Al nodded. "Yeah, I know."

They sat silently for a while, then Al said, "I remember one time when we just started going together, and we drove down to Cincinnati to hear Tony Bennett and dance at Moonlight Gardens. It was very romantic." He laughed. "And on the way back my old car lost its clutch and we had to be towed to a garage. We had to spend the night in a crummy motel. Her parents were really pissed."

Heather laughed. Then she began to sing, *"Because of you there's a song in my heart ..."*

Al laughed again. "Yeah. You know that old Tony Bennett song?"

"She sang it to me when I was three."

Al sighed, and turned his head away. He could picture the young Gladys singing to her child—she probably sang to Eliot—and that song meant much to her and to Al. It was *their* song.

"I need to go over there," she said. "To her place."

"Your car's at the café?"

"Yeah.

The next morning, Al had breakfast at Hagge's, and hung around, waiting for the call from Eliot. He read the day-old newspapers and Googled things on his phone.

"Is there a place around here where I can get a WiFi signal?" he asked the cook, who had been watching him.

"The community center, around the corner. If they're open."

He walked the two blocks to the community center, to find that it would open in a half-hour. He spent the half-hour walking the streets of Mapleton, looking at old houses and buildings that had once been businesses.

In the time he had lived with Gladys, he had seldom come to this little town, preferring Fargo, where there were stores and offices and better restaurants. People had said that Mapleton had once rivaled Fargo as a thriving city, but it was no longer evident.

Even so, the streets brought up happier memories. The elementary school looked the same as when they had brought Eliot in for his first year. Gladys had reassured the boy that he'd find friends there. "They will be your age, and will want to play the same games. You'll even learn some new ones!"

She had smiled at Al. "Daddy has to make some new friends at work, too."

"Mom," Eliot had asked, his face serious, "will you have to make new friends here?".

Al had laughed. "Your mom never has trouble making friends, wherever she goes!"

Eliot had hugged his mother's thighs. "Everybody loves Mom," he had said.

Al and Gladys and Eliot had always lived in the old farm house about halfway between the towns. She liked the rural feeling. The farm itself had been sold off to nearby farmers, so they were surrounded by fields of hard wheat. He had been lucky enough to pay off the mortgage before he lost his first job; after that, he settled for lesser work in retail businesses.

Eliot finally called, interrupting his reverie. He was just getting off the interstate. Al directed him to the motel. "I'll meet you there."

They sat in Al's Prius and talked.

"Do you want to go out to her house?" Al asked.

"Not yet. I need to hear about why you came to North Dakota."

Al told him what had happened. "I was coming to see you, and decided to stop here to talk to your mom, that's all."

Eliot looked at him. "Dad, I'm skeptical. I thought you and Mom hadn't been in touch with each other in years. Why now?"

Al sighed. "Well, I've had some news about my health, and decided it was time for me to tie up some loose ends in my life."

"What news, Dad? C'mon, be straight. What news?"

"I have a problem in my pancreas, and it's metastasized—it's all over." He put his hand on his midsection. "They give me three to six months."

"Jesus!"

"So I thought it was time to make things better between your mom and me. I was on my way to Butte to tell you, and stopped here. She didn't answer her door. Must have just died."

Eliot turned back and looked out the windshield without speaking.

"Heather happened to be there, but we didn't know each other." Al laughed. "She called the cops, 'cause she thought I might have had something to do with her mom being dead."

"But it was a heart attack, she said."

"They didn't know that right away. They caught up with me on I-94."

Eliot looked back at him. "I'm sorry, Dad."

"Yeah. Me, too."

"I've been intending to come see her for six months." Eliot stopped and took a deep breath. "I wish—well, now it's too late for both of us."

"She deserved better," Al said quietly.

"Yeah." Eliot ran his fingers over the dashboard. "How's Heather taking it?"

"She was pretty upset. She apologized for calling the cops on me." He chuckled. "In the middle of losing her mother, she apologized to *me!*"

"I should go see her. Wanta come?"

"No, you go ahead. She said she was going over to the house. We had a good talk a while ago. She needs comforting."

"Okay. You got a spare bed in your room?"

"Yeah. Let's drop your bags in there, and you go to the house."

After Eliot left, Al got another key from the motel office. Then he lay down and slept.

Driving to the familiar old farmhouse, Eliot thought about the last time he had been there. Heather had been throwing her clothing into her old car, and Gladys was standing on the porch, ranting at her. "You're just like everybody else in this family—you're leaving!"

Eliot managed to persuade them both to go back inside and sit down with him to talk.

"I can't take it anymore!" Heather said. "She blames me for everything that happens to her. I come home feeling happy, and in two minutes we're fighting again—about nothing!"

Gladys suddenly buried her face in her hands. Eliot put a hand on her shoulder. "Mom, what's going on?"

She wiped her face with the back of her hand. "I guess I'm just not good enough to be around anymore."

He looked at Heather and sighed.

"I'm an awful person!" Gladys moaned. "I drive people away."

"Mom, you're not an awful person," he said. "Why are you so angry at yourself?"

Nothing he said to her seemed to make any difference. She lay on the sofa, moaning.

Heather stood up without speaking. She looked at Eliot and slowly shook her head. Then she went out the door.

Eliot caught up with her as she got into her car. "I know," he said, "she gets like this sometimes. Give her some time, can you?"

"I'm not going back into that house," said Heather.

"Okay, take a break from her. Give her some space, but stay in touch. Can you do that?"

"She needs help. I can't help her."

"I know. I've tried to get her to get counseling for years, but she won't do it."

Heather started her car.

"Heather," he said, "take care of yourself. You have to do that. But don't abandon her, please?"

"Well," she said, "*you* try living with her!"

He sighed. "I can't live with her either. But let's not just give up. She has some good days, too."

Heather touched her fingertips to her lips, and then touched his cheek. "I'll call you," she said, and drove away.

Heather was sorting through papers in her mother's old desk when the doorbell rang. She had a file folder in her hand when she opened the door.

"Hi, little Sis," Eliot said.

She pulled the door wide so he could enter, then threw her arms around his neck and sobbed. He held her for a long time until he felt her relax.

A woman Eliot didn't know came out of the kitchen. "You're her brother?" she said, extending her hand.

"He's my rock," Heather said, wiping her eyes. To Eliot, she said, "Maddie's a friend. I'd have lost it except for her."

After Maddie returned to the kitchen, Heather took Eliot's hand and pulled him toward the living room. "Come and sit. I've missed you."

"I just left Dad." Eliot sat on the sofa, Heather on an overstuffed chair facing him. "He told me how you two met."

She gave a little laugh. "Poor guy. The cops pulled him over on the interstate."

"I'd forgotten—you two never met before."

"He's been great. I haven't been making much sense."

"Feels weird," Eliot said, "like he's part of a different life I used to be in."

She laughed. "He was telling me about the old days, when he and Mom were first together."

"Tell me—how are you holding up?"

She shrugged. "I go up and down. It's like I've lost my moorings—is that what you say?"

"Okay, Kid," Eliot said, "you really have lost your anchor, even if you and Mom didn't get along. She was still there, and still your mother."

"Crazy old lady."

"You tell your dad?"

Heather made a face. "He didn't want me. He didn't want her. Why would he want to come now?"

"He's still your father."

She sat staring at something on the other end of the sofa. "I get birthday cards from him—from his wife, actually. That's it."

Eliot sighed. "I know what you mean."

She looked back at him. "But your dad keeps in touch, at least, doesn't he?"

"With me, he does. I don't think he ever sent Mom a birthday card since he left here."

"Why'd he come now?"

"He's dying, and he wanted to see her one last time."

Heather looked shocked, and tears formed in her eyes. Eliot reached across to touch her hand.

"I'm sorry. I shouldn't have told you like that."

"My whole fucking family is disappearing!"

Hard Wheat

He gripped her hand more tightly. "I'm not disappearing, Heather," he said quietly.

She moved from the chair to beside him on the sofa. They embraced and she cried silently on his shoulder.

Relaxing her grip, she sniffled and said hoarsely, "You always were there in my corner, Big Brother."

"What do you need now?"

"Just got to get through the next few days," she said. "Mabel and George—you met them, they're from the church—they arranged for the funeral. I didn't even know what to do with her body."

"We've got your back, Little Sister."

She kissed him on the cheek, then laughed. "You'll shave before Friday, won't you?"

Eliot laughed and rubbed his jaw. "Thought I'd let it grow, like guys all do now."

She tilted her head and smiled. "Like your dad?"

"Mine's not gray like his."

Her face grew serious. "You like your dad, Eliot?"

"Yeah, I do—now. There for a while I didn't."

"Why?"

Eliot looked down at his hands. "He left. I was away in college, so it wasn't like he left me. But *you* know ..."

"Mom wasn't easy to live with," Heather said. "I didn't blame my dad for leaving. If only he'd stayed connected to me."

Eliot said, "I've been pretty reluctant to get involved with someone, you know, romantically, 'cause maybe I'd just bail when it got tough. Just like them."

"Fathers leave." Heather sighed deeply.

"Why do you think that is?"

She laughed. "Cause mothers get crazy?"

"Doesn't say much for marriage, does it?"

She sighed again. "Is that how it always goes?"

"From what I hear, Dad's family was pretty close. So was Mom's." Eliot shrugged. "They both lasted a long time."

"I don't want to get married," she said. "I don't trust anybody."

"That sounds pretty harsh."

"I don't want to end up like her."

"I used to think it was Dad's fault," he said. "He wouldn't stand up to her."

"She was a control freak. She couldn't stand anybody else's ideas."

Eliot sighed and looked out the window. "She was pretty unhappy. Maybe it was built in." Then he looked at Heather. "Have you thought about your future?"

She shook her head. "My future is two or three days. I don't want to deal with any more than that."

"Yeah. Well, after that, if I can help, you call me, okay?"

Heather smiled bleakly at him.

"What can I do now?" he asked.

She looked over her shoulder toward the kitchen. "Maddie has been cleaning the kitchen. Mom left it in a real mess. After the funeral, I spect folks'll come over for a while, and I don't want it looking like a pig sty."

"I can help. Let's go out and see."

Al was asleep when Eliot knocked on the door to the motel room. Dosed with whiskey to ease the pain in his gut, he managed to open the door to his son.

"Sorry to wake you up," said Eliot. "Are you okay? You look like shit."

"Comes and goes. How's Heather?"

"She's a real trooper. She and a friend have been cleaning the house for the funeral."

"Not going to be at the house, is it?"

"She's expecting folks to drop in after."

Al flopped back onto the bed. "Been doing a lot of thinking," he said.

"'Bout Mom?"

"How much she changed over the years. I came up here because I'd been remembering how she was when we were young, before you came along. She always had a book in her hands."

"I remember she used to sing a lot." Eliot kicked off his shoes and leaned on pillows on his bed.

"That's who I grieve for, right now," Al said. "I thought maybe we could talk about those times. I don't have anybody else to share those memories with—'cept you, but I mean even before." He stopped, feeling something in his throat.

"Dad, we had some good times, you and Mom and me. I remember when we first came up here from Indiana. We were in that old Studebaker, all three of us singing while we were driving along."

They were silent for a long time.

"Your mom wasn't happy up here—at first she was, but then she started complaining."

"I remember you asking her if she wanted to go back to Indiana ..."

Al broke in. "She said she wouldn't make you leave school."

You got into these terrible fights. I had to get out of there."

"But then when you left for college, she still wouldn't go."

Eliot looked at him. "I was really pissed at you."

"Why? I could never figure out why."

"I don't know. She cried all the time." He turned and looked at his father. "You always gave in to her. You'd fight, and then you'd throw up your hands and, like, 'whatever', and leave."

"Yeah." Al looked at the ceiling. "She always said I was passive-aggressive. I guess I was."

"I think she just needed somebody to hold her down—somebody to hold her—and make her ..."

"What was Rich like?" Al hadn't thought much about Gladys's other husband. He was as abstract as a statistic, somebody Al had just heard of, never met.

Eliot laughed. "He was like you, in a way. I guess Mom needed another punching bag."

Al suddenly doubled over from pain in his abdomen. Eliot sat up. "You okay, Dad?"

"It'll pass."

"You need a doctor?"

"Too late for that." Al gradually relaxed. The whiskey was wearing off.

"Dad." There was concern in his voice.

"I'll be okay in the morning."

Eliot drove both of them over to Hagge's in the morning for breakfast. Heather greeted them with a wide smile, but was busy with customers. After they had eaten, she sat down briefly at their table.

"We'll go over to the house," Eliot said, "and straighten things up a little."

"Key's under the planter on the porch."

"You get off work tomorrow?"

"Yeah. Aron's closing the bar in the afternoon for the funeral."

"Nice of him."

She half-smiled, not knowing if he was sarcastic. "He's a good guy." She went to the cash register to check customers out.

At the farm house, Al remarked about the BMW minivan in the yard. "She must have had some money."

Eliot punched him lightly on the arm. "I know you used to send her money after Rich left. He probably did, too."

"It wouldn't have bought that thing."

Eliot shrugged. "She didn't have a mortgage to pay on, at least."

They walked around the house. Al pointed to a power line from a pole to the old barn. "That didn't used to be there," he said.

Eliot grinned. "Thirty years ago."

The barn was locked. They peered through a very clouded window, but couldn't make out anything inside, so they returned to the house.

The inside of the house smelled like an old farmhouse, Al decided. They went from room to room. "I remember most of this furniture," he said.

"I guess she put all of her money in the BMW."

"I hope Heather can get enough out of this place to pay for college."

Eliot looked at him. "She wants to go to college?"

"Yeah, I think she does. She said she thought it would be fun."

They laughed.

Al found a vacuum cleaner and began running it on the old rugs. Eliot washed windows.

Later, Al pulled open some drawers full of papers, but closed them again. "Not my business," he said.

"Heather seems capable of figuring out her finances," Eliot said, spraying glass cleaner on an old mirror.

They puttered around the old house, picking up and straightening, until Eliot said, "Getting hungry?"

Al looked at his watch. "She'll get off work at three. We can eat there and bring her back. I'd like to see more of the barn and check out that pump house."

Eliot grinned. "For somebody who hasn't set foot in this place in thirty years, you seem pretty interested."

Later, Al, Eliot and Heather went out to the barn. When Heather unlocked the door, Al suddenly remembered how it looked when he and Gladys had first entered it. There was still a faint smell of hay and old

wood, even though he could see new wood here and there. One room had been closed off;
Heather had to find a key on the big ring of keys she'd brought out from the house. "I've never been in here," she said. "Wonder why she had it all locked up."
Inside the large room were tables all around, on which flats of plants sat. The room was quite dark, the windows apparently painted with whitewash.
Eliot found a light switch. The room was flooded with bright blue-white light.
"Wow," Al said. "She must have been growing plants for a florist."
"She always did like flowers," Heather said, not especially interested.
"Looks like they need water," Al said, but Heather was already going out the door. Eliot shrugged and switched off the light and they returned to the house.
Later, the three of them sat in the old parlor, drinking beer out of bottles.
"I miss her," Heather said thoughtfully. "Crazy as she was."
"I keep thinking about the good old days," Eliot said. "We had some good times, way back."
Al sighed. "I came here the other day, remembering how she was a long time ago. Being in this house again brings back some of that, but it also reminds me of the rough times when I couldn't figure out how to connect with her."
"I saw her a week ago," said Heather. "She was crabby as ever. When I found her on the floor, though, all I could think of was her singing to me, twenty years ago." She took a long draw from her bottle, and they sat in silence for a time.
"How long's it been since you moved out of this place?" asked Al.

"Bout five years, I guess. I moved out and back in a couple of times. Every time, she'd try to get me to stay, and then we'd have another fight and I'd leave again."

"I remember the last time," said Eliot. "You called me, bawling your eyes out."

"I was *so mad* at her!"

Eliot touched her arm. "Heather," he said quietly.

When she looked at him, he said, "Do you want me to call your dad?"

She looked down.

"I'll call him," Eliot said. "Do you have a number?"

Heather went into the dining room where the desk was, and came back with a battered old appointment book. "It's probably in here," she said.

Eliot found a number and dialed. When the party answered, he said, "Is Rich there?" Then he walked back to the kitchen to talk.

Al smiled at Heather, who shook her head slowly.

When Eliot returned, he said, "He couldn't come, but he said he'd write you."

She nodded.

Al stood up. "Anybody else want another beer?"

The funeral was set for 6 P.M. the next day. Several women worked at the farmhouse, getting it set up for company. Eliot went to the funeral home with Heather early in the day to make last-minute arrangements. Al stayed in the motel, resting.

Gladys was to be cremated. The funeral director took charge of the service; Heather had politely declined the Lutheran minister's offer to conduct it. "She was never religious," Heather told him.

"We will hold her in our prayers anyway."

"Thank you."

Heather had found some old popular songs that Gladys had among her records, and they were played softly as people began to congregate in the little chapel.

Eliot and Al stood on either side of Heather as she greeted those who approached. There was no casket in the room.

Heather kept a serious face, without seeming to be close to tears. Several visitors, however, held her hand tightly and sobbed on her shoulder. She introduced Eliot as "my brother" and Al as "Mom's ex." No one inquired about Heather's father. Al recognized Mabel and George, the couple from the restaurant, who greeted Heather without showing emotion other than sympathy for her.

When it seemed that everyone who was coming had been seated, the director said to Heather, "Would you like to start?"

She nodded, and took a seat in the first row before the podium. The music faded out, and the director began by reading a poem by Maureen Killoran:

> We come together from the diversity of our grieving,
> to gather in the warmth of this community
> giving stubborn witness to our belief that
> in times of sadness, there is room for laughter.
> In times of darkness, there always will be light.
> May we hold fast to the conviction
> that what we do with our lives matters
> and that a caring world is possible after all.

He assured the audience that "Gladys Gibson's life matters," and told a little bit about her life, the details of which Heather had provided earlier.

Heather read from a page of notes that shook noticeably as she spoke, mostly about her early life with Gladys—"she used to sing to me"—and about the flowers that used to grow around the house and the books that accumulated in corners.

Mabel then stood and spoke about how difficult it must be for a woman to be a single parent and how important it is for the community to "gather in the strays and those among us who are hurting."

Several people stood at their seats and offered a few words in recognition of Gladys, who "stood tall in her suffering."

When everyone who wanted to speak had had their turn, the director closed the ceremony with a poem by Samuel Butler:

> I fall asleep in the full and certain hope
> That my slumber shall not be broken;
> And that, though I be all-forgetting,
> Yet shall I not be all-forgotten,
> But continue that life in the thoughts and deeds
> Of those I have loved.

Afterwards, he announced that those who wanted to go to the home of Gladys and Heather for a few refreshments and conversation, there were maps on the table by the entrance.

Eliot drove Heather to the farmhouse, with Al following. A number of other cars trailed behind.

Maddie and another young woman were already at the house, setting out food and drinks. Soon the place was full of subdued voices. Heather seemed at ease but not smiling much. Mabel and several other women took over the tasks of greeting visitors and making sure they found food, drink and someplace to sit.

Al hung back, watching Heather and nursing a beer. Eliot seemed to hover. He pointed out to Al a few visitors that he had met on one of his visits to Gladys. Al didn't see anyone he knew, nor did he expect to, after thirty years.

Voices at the door caught his attention. A scruffy-looking man was trying to explain to the woman who had opened the door that he needed to pick up something from the barn.

Eliot intervened.

"I'm sorry for your loss," the man was saying, "but I need to pick up some of my property that Gladys was keeping for me."

"What kind of property is that?"

Just then, Heather joined them at the door and introduced herself.

"Ma'am," the man said, "Your mom had some things that belong to me out in the barn. I know that this is not a good time for you to have to deal with business, but it's important that I collect my things. Won't take but five minutes, and I won't bother you with it at all."

Eliot looked at Heather, who shrugged. "I'll go out with him," he said, "if you'll give me the key."

Heather found the ring of keys and handed them to Eliot. Al followed Eliot to the barn, while the man returned to his truck and backed it up to the door.

The man seemed nervous as he pointed out the tables full of flats in the locked room. "Those are all my plants, and they need watering and care. I'll take them all to my place."

"You're a florist?" Al asked, having already guessed what the plants were.

"Yeah, you might say that," the man answered with a slight smile.

"And you'd rather nobody said anything about all this." Al looked steadily at him. Eliot stood off to the side, the ring of keys in his hand, not saying anything.

Another man appeared out of the cab of the truck, and the two strangers began rather hurriedly loading the flats into the back of the truck. In a minute they had driven out of the property.

Al noticed that the license plate on the truck was thoroughly obscured with mud.

Eliot looked at Al. "That stuff is probably worth a lot of money."

"I doubt that Heather would want to get involved. Better to just let it go," Al said.

"I can't imagine Mom dealing with marijuana."

Al laughed as they walked back to the house. "Now we know where the BMW came from."

"What'll we tell Heather?"

Al shrugged. "He was a florist, and he came after his plants."

"If the cops had found out about that stuff," Eliot said, "she'd have lost the house—and the BMW."

"He must have heard about Gladys dying, and was afraid he'd get caught in a bust if somebody found out she was growing pot. I hope the guy is smart enough to never come near this place again."

Eliot shook his head. "Never would have guessed."

To Heather's quizzical look, Al said, "He got his flowers. He was afraid they wouldn't get watered and might die."

She turned and left them, talking with another woman who was collecting dishes.

After everyone else had left the farmhouse, Heather and Al and Eliot sat in the living room with drinks.

"You think I didn't know what they were?" asked Heather, expressionless.

"Nobody said anything at the time," said Al.

Eliot laughed. "What did you think you were going to do with them?"

Heather, still expressionless, said, "Burn the damned barn down."

"What!?"

"No way I could have done anything with them. Give me a little credit."

Al laughed. "The smoke would have brought people from twenty miles away!"

"Volunteer fire brigade would have taken an hour to get here."

Eliot emptied his glass. "But they wouldn't have left until it was all gone. Be a shame to waste a perfectly good barn."

Heather said, "She had always grown plants and things that she never talked about."

"Hmmm," Al said, "Didn't look like you knew the fellow who collected it all."

"No." She laughed. "Something familiar about him, though."

"She had some men friends after Dad left," Eliot said. "I never actually met any of them, although when she was working in Hagge's she seemed to have friends there."

Al looked at Heather. "Did you know she had worked at Hagge's?"

"Oh, yeah. That's how I got the job there, actually. The owner knew Mom pretty well."

"That how she met Rich?" Al swirled the ice in his glass. He was uncomfortable mentioning Heather's father.

"That's what she told me."

Heather stood up. "You two aren't going to stay at the motel, are you?"

Al and Eliot looked at each other.

"There's room here, you know." She went to the kitchen and returned with the bottle of vodka they had been drinking from. "I don't want to be here with her ghost tonight."

At Heather's insistence, the two men returned to the motel to get their possessions and check out. Eliot stopped on his way back from the motel to buy groceries. She found fresh sheets and made up beds for them both. "Those beds haven't been used in years," she said. She seemed to enjoy being a host.

Chapter Two - 1970

Gladys Vincent watched at the foot of the driveway until the school bus was out of sight, then walked back to the house.

The farm house was surrounded on three sides by plowed fields. The usual crop, hard spring wheat, had just begun to show its sprouts. She liked the smell of the earth. Standing alongside the old house, she breathed in the spring air.

A voice made her turn around. A young man was coming out from behind the barn, mud from the field sticking to his boots. "Morning, Ma'am."

"Where'd you come from?" she asked.

He gestured in the direction behind the barn. "I been checking the field, looking for low spots."

"Some places are pretty wet," she said.

"Won't yield much." He picked up a stick and began digging at the mud on his boots.

The morning sun was behind him, and she squinted to see him, finally shading her eyes with her hand. "Kinda late to be thinking about that, isn't it?"

"Yeah. We were too busy last month." He circled around her so that the sun wasn't directly in her eyes.

"Thank you," she said. "You live close?"

"South, 'bout a mile." He gestured vaguely again.

She and Al had chosen to live out here in the country because they thought that rural life would be more leisurely. They hadn't counted on the extra time it takes to go anywhere—to the stores, to school, to Al's work.

Gladys was feeling lonely, especially in the mornings after Eliot had gone off on the school bus. "Like a cup of coffee?" she asked, then added, looking at his boots, "I can bring it out."

"Much obliged." He almost saluted, dropping his arm in mid-gesture as though he had just realized what he was doing. His hand swung out and slapped his jeans.

Gladys smiled and went inside for the coffee. The man sat on the edge of the porch, still picking at his boots with the stick.

"You put anything in it?" she asked as she brought two mugs out. The screen door slammed behind her.

He shook his head.

"I don't even know who owns all that," she said, looking out at the field.

"Big agribusiness," he said. "They hire my old man, and he gets me to help out."

"Lemme guess—you just got out of the service." She smiled at him.

"How'd you know?"

"You damned near saluted me." Gladys lit a cigarette and inhaled deeply.

He laughed and looked down at his cup of coffee. "Habit."

"You don't say much, do you?" she said, still looking at him over her cup. She held out her pack of cigarettes to him.

He grinned and shook his head. "Good coffee."

They chatted for a while, and he began to relax more. "You like to grow flowers," he said.

"One reason I like it out here. Things growing all around me."

"Your husband's not a farmer?"

"No, he works at Consolidated Food, over in Fargo."

"Got kids?"

"One boy. He just left on the bus."

The man set his empty cup on the porch. "I better be gettin' back," he said, starting around the house. Then he stopped and came back. Gladys wrinkled her brow, still smiling.

"Ma'am, I need to say this." He wiped the back of his neck with his hand. "We're just talking. But you're pretty far out in the country."

Her frown increased, the smile now gone. She crushed out her cigarette with the toe of her shoe, then picked it up.

"I mean," he said, "you might need to be careful with strangers." Then he laughed. "I'm sorry. None of my concern, is it?"

She laughed. "I've got a twelve gauge, just inside that door." She dropped the cigarette butt into a can by the door.

"Figures," he said, and disappeared around the house.

Gladys thought for a few moments before taking the coffee cups back into the kitchen. He was right, of course. She ought to be more careful of strangers. But it was fun to talk to somebody over eight years old.

That evening at the dinner table, she told Al about the stranger, speaking very casually. He looked up from his plate. "He from around here?"

"I don't know. He said he lives south of here about a mile."

"Be careful, Gladys," he said. We don't know the folks around here very well yet."

"I think he just got out of the army," she said. "He started to salute me, and then caught himself." She laughed, and Eliot, who hadn't said anything, laughed with her and saluted very formally.

"Maybe we should get you a gun for protection."

"I told him I had a twelve gauge."

"Call me if you see him again." Al wiped his mouth on his napkin. "Good to be careful."

As Gladys began clearing the dishes from the table, she said, "I get lonely out here sometimes. Maybe we could get another car, so I could do the shopping and things."

"He just walked up, across the field?"

She stopped and looked at him. "About a car?" She frowned. "He was looking for low spots, where the wheat won't grow."

Al frowned. "What he said, anyway. What'd he look like?"

"Kinda tall, good looking, dark hair, clean shaven. Very polite."

"I'll ask around."

She made a little gesture. "I'm sure he's okay," she said.

In the days following, she looked across the field behind the barn once in a while, hoping to see the stranger again.

The next month, Al bought a used pickup truck in Fargo and drove it home. "You gotta learn how to drive," he told Gladys.

"I can drive, silly," she said, laughing.

"Okay, let's see you. C'mon." He led her and Eliot out to the truck in the yard.

"Oh, it's a stick shift!" she exclaimed when she opened the driver's door.

"Get in, and I'll show you how it works."

Gladys climbed tentatively into the cab. Al went around to the other side. Gesturing to Eliot, he said, "You go sit on the porch."

"I want to come!" said their son.

"Later," Al said, and climbed in next to Gladys.

He showed her the operation of the clutch and gear shift lever. "Okay, push the clutch all the way in and start the engine."

In the next half hour, Gladys learned how to drive a manual shift vehicle, stalling the engine countless times and causing the truck to lurch across the yard. Eventually, Al got out and told her to drive. Then he took Eliot inside the house, from where they watched her through a window.

"She'll cuss and cry, but she'll do it," he told his son. "That's how I learned to drive."

They watched Gladys finally go down the drive and out onto the county road. An hour later, she came into the house looking tense and haggard. Al poured several ounces of whiskey into a tumbler and handed it to her. Ten minutes later, she managed to smile.

By coincidence, Gladys encountered the stranger again in front of the grocery store in Fargo.

"Ah," he said, "the twelve-gauge lady!"

She laughed and blushed. Some passersby turned to look.

"And she makes a mean cup of coffee!" he said.

She smiled at him. "Have you found all the low places in the fields?"

"Yes, ma'am. After the harvest, we'll bring in some equipment and level them all out."

They sat on a wooden bench in front of the store and chatted until Gladys stood up and said, "I have to get some groceries and go fix dinner for my family."

"My time is kinda loose," he said. "If you need any repairs done around the house, just let me know. I can do carpenter and electric and plumbing—whatever you got."

"Thank you. And how do I find you?"

"My name's Larry Arnes," he said. "Here, let me get you my phone number." He disappeared inside the store and came out with a slip of paper, which he handed to her. "If I'm not there, my mom will be."

Gladys drove the pickup truck home feeling more secure about the man, and vaguely excited.

That evening, she told Al about the encounter. "He might be able to help us," she said.

"At least," Al said, "we know who we're dealing with."

"I can use somebody with a tiller in that vegetable patch."

Al laughed. "Never figured you for a farmer."

"I need something to do around here besides wash windows."

It wasn't long before Gladys found a reason to call Larry Arnes. "Can you rig a gutter and downspout so I can collect rain water?"

"You bet."

He arrived two days later in a pickup truck. "I came out last night to measure, but you weren't home," he said. "You want the gutter on the west side, right?"

"Yes. There's a ladder in the barn, and an old barrel. I don't know if it will hold water or not."

She went back inside to start a pot of coffee, singing to herself.

Two hours later, he was already finished working, and she was disappointed. "Stay for some lunch?" she asked.

"No, ma'am," he said. "I got to help my old man s'afternoon."

She walked out around the house with him. "Will that thing hold water?"

"Should, after it gets full once," he said. "Wood needs to expand. You could fill it with a hose if you want."

"That's a long way from the spigot at the pump house. My hose isn't that long."

He walked to where he could see the distance. "I can bring one over."

"That'd be nice. What do I owe you?"

"Have to look up the price on the gutter. I'll tell you tomorrow when I bring the hose."

So began almost daily visits by Larry Arnes to the farmhouse. Sometime there was no work for him to do, but the coffee pot was always ready.

"Eliot will be out of school the end of the week," she told him one day. I won't have much time to sit and talk."

"You fix omelets?" he asked. "My folks got chickens. I could bring a mess of eggs tomorrow for lunch."

The next morning, Gladys felt a strange sadness as she chopped onions and peppers. Eliot would be fun to have around during the summer, but she would miss the long conversations with Larry. Guiltily, she realized that she hadn't told Al about how often Larry visited. With Eliot home, she'd feel odd about having the man around so much. Her son would certainly mention it while Al was present.

"Got a taste for these in France," Larry said, savoring her omelet. "You make 'em good!"

"Wait," she said, "don't finish yet." She took a bottle of white wine from the refrigerator. "Needs wine to be French," she said.

An hour later, she led him into the living room, where she served coffee and brandy.

"I'm not going to be worth a damn to work the rest of the day," he murmured.

She looked at him steadily. "Eliot's going to be here every day," she said. "I won't be comfortable with you when he's around."

He set his cup down. "You mean I shouldn't come anymore."

"I'm sorry."

He reached across the space between them and pulled her by the hand to him. Gladys offered no resistance.

After Larry left, Gladys went immediately in to take a shower. Then she opened windows and cleaned up the kitchen to erase any sign that he had been there. A small spot on the sofa took her careful attention to get rid of—even as she fondly considered how it had gotten there. The faint discomfort inside her, the result of Larry's vigorous love-making, she almost treasured.

For a moment, she felt like singing. Then, gradually as she thought about Al coming home for dinner, her gaiety became a heavy weight in her breast. *What have I done?* she thought.

She didn't meet Eliot at the foot of the drive. Remorse took over her mind. As though stunned, she sat in the living room until her son came through the door. He was singing.

Even as she prepared dinner, Gladys's thoughts kept going back many years, to another of her mistakes.

Chapter Three - 1950

She and Timmy were best friends. They were also first cousins, and saw each other frequently. Five years older than she, he taught her the times table even before she entered kindergarten.

The cousins lived in the next block in Bloomington. Gladys, at five, knew they were cousins, but she didn't know anything about whose side of her family they were related to. The families often took trips and had backyard barbeques together.

When they all got together at one house or the other and the hour became late, Gladys and Timmy were put to bed upstairs until the adults were ready to leave. When they went camping, the two children shared a tent, each one, of course, in a separate sleeping bag.

Gladys came to love being with Timmy, and he enjoyed entertaining her with games he'd learned at school. For a number of years, it was a convenient arrangement for the adults in the two families. They were so accustomed to the two children being together that they didn't anticipate the inevitable changes.

Hard Wheat

Timmy began inviting his friends from school to family gatherings. He was usually considerate of Gladys's feelings and let her tag along. Their parents encouraged this, for Gladys still didn't have friends of her own. Because of Timmy's growing maturity and sense of responsibility, he was assigned the role of babysitter, allowing the adults to go out dancing or to movies.

One evening, with the parents gone, Timmy and Gladys found some magazines stored in the back of a drawer—magazines with photographs of unclothed women.

To Gladys, the photos were a curiosity; to Timmy, they were something more. He had just turned fourteen.

As young children, they had seen each other unclothed a number of times. They had even gone skinny-dipping in a lake, with their parents cheering them on.

"Will I look like that when I grow up?" She asked him on that particular evening.

"You'll get hair down there," he said, pointing to a photograph.

"Will you grow hair there, too?"

"I already have some," he said.

"I want to see."

Timmy insisted that they go upstairs to the bedroom. "We don't want the neighbors to see us."

In the privacy of Gladys's bedroom, they showed each other their young bodies. At first, Timmy was embarrassed because he'd sprouted an erection. Gladys found this fascinating.

Their conversation proceeded to the topic of function, Timmy describing to the extent of his knowledge how men's and women's bodies joined in sex. Closer examination left them confused, however. Clearly, his penis would not fit into her vagina.

For her, it was a question that could wait until she could ask her mother. For him, an immediate and insistent urge kept the subject primary in his mind. He was holding his erect penis in his hand. "Feel it!" he said.

Gladys grasped his penis. "It's hot!" she exclaimed.

"Hold it tighter! Squeeze it as hard as you can!"

"Doesn't it hurt?"

"No!"

They were seated cross-legged on her bed, facing each other. Suddenly, Gladys felt warm liquid squirt from the end of his penis, and Timmy gasped. "Don't stop!" he cried. His body stiffened, and he toppled backward onto the bed, his head striking the wooden footboard. He lay moaning.

Little Gladys was terrified. She was sure she had squeezed him too tightly and injured him. The fluid on her hands was thick and sticky like blood, but white. She watched Timmy breathing heavily.

She screamed. "Mom!"

Timmy sat up, sweat pouring from his forehead. He grinned. "Shhh!" he cautioned.

"I'm sorry!" she cried.

"It's okay," he said, still breathing hard. "It's supposed to do that."

"Ugh! Gross!"

They hurriedly cleaned themselves up as much as they could, dressed and threw the soiled towels down the laundry chute.

"Don't tell anybody what happened," Timmy said with his hands firmly on Gladys's shoulders.

"Why?"

"Just don't! We're in big trouble if you do."

Back downstairs, they returned the magazines and switched on the television.

Timmy was asleep when their parents arrived.

"Which one's the babysitter?" laughed Gladys's mother.

The incident remained a secret between Timmy and Gladys. In the next year, their experimentation grew more practiced. By the time Gladys finished high school, she had few questions about sex.

Timmy went off to college. But their secret left a mark on her that took years to fade. A mark she was reminded of when her class was assigned a book by Nathaniel Hawthorne, *The Scarlet Letter*. Hester Prynne's shame became Gladys's shame. She tried to bury the feeling, and to bury the resentment she felt toward Timmy for abandoning her.

The mark—and the memory—all but faded in the following years, but like some old wounds, never really healed. From time to time, she plunged into depression and anger, but never revealed her secret to anyone.

Chapter Four - 1975

Al noticed a change in Gladys, at first subtle, but growing into impatience with him and their son. She smoked cigarettes constantly. He tried to talk to her about it, but she had lost that easy chattiness that endeared her to him. More and more, she seemed to get angry about trifles. She didn't share as much with him about her day while he was at work.

She complained often about the North Dakota weather, especially in the winter. "I don't remember it getting this cold when we moved here," she said.

"We don't have to stay in North Dakota."

She didn't reply.

Eventually, however, she closed the question by insisting that Eliot ought to be allowed to finish school with his friends.

Al, seldom revealing his feelings, began to withdraw even more from Gladys. When his job suddenly ended, he spent more and more time in Fargo, "looking for work," and felt less and less connection to Gladys and Eliot and their home.

He first got a job as a bartender in the pub that he had frequented, being trained by the woman who had listened to his complaints as she wiped the bar and rearranged the bottles. She was also married, but they managed to have a brief and unsatisfying affair. Their relationship as mentor-protégé went smoother without sex, and soon he found other bartending jobs in town, which gave him a sense of superficial human connection without the demands of real intimacy. He could listen to people's troubles without revealing his own.

Eventually moving to retail work in a bookstore and a tractor sales office, his personal life became hidden inside his shell.

At home, he and Gladys developed a kind of truce between them, talking only enough to get through their very private lives.

Gladys had withdrawn emotionally from Larry after the first brief fling, even though they arranged occasional visits. He seemed equally satisfied with a relationship without commitment. They met when Eliot was in school, mostly at the farmhouse but occasionally drove to nearby secluded wilderness places where they made love but talked little.

Larry gave Gladys a feeling of connection, however hollow. He paid attention to her in little ways—enough to remind her of what she desperately needed. "Your neck seems stiff. Here, lemme massage you." His hands were strong.

When she begged off sex because of a headache, he stroked her forehead gently until she fell asleep. He brought her special treats that his mother had cooked for her husband.

He never spoke of his military experiences.

She thought of these trysts as glimmers of love. Sometimes she yearned for more, while often feeling that they were all she deserved. When she thought of her marriage, resentment masked her guilt.

One day, Eliot returned from high school early and found Larry's truck in the yard. He left immediately without going inside. Nothing was ever said, by him or by Gladys, if she knew that he had been there.

More and more, Eliot felt the antagonism between his parents, and escaped when he could to friends and extracurricular school activities. Suspecting his mother's infidelity, he assumed the same for his father. He was glad to finally escape from the home situation to go to college. He wasn't surprised, later, when he read in a letter that Al had returned to Indiana.

Chapter Five - 1985

When Al left, Gladys found work at Hagge's bar and grill in Mapleton. After what seemed a long time, Al began sending her money, but it was not enough to live on. There, she could also be with people. Her relationship with Larry continued to be occasional but distant, their intimacy merely physical.

A woman alone in a small town becomes known. Men patronized the restaurant during the day and the bar at night. Gladys's old bubbly personality began to re-emerge with the male attention.

One man in particular began frequenting the establishment. Rich wore no ring, something that Gladys immediately noticed. Soon he was coming in shortly before the end of her shift, and they would go for drives through the stands of hard wheat. "Down in Iowa," he said, "it's like this with corn. You can drive for hours without seeing a tree. Just corn."

"You grow up there?"

He laughed. "Tama County," he said, "right in the middle of corn country."

Gladys liked his laugh. Even though he was a little older than she was (unlike Larry), she found him attractive. He was quiet, but seemed to respond readily to what she said.

One day, as they were parked in a rare roadside picnic area, he said, "You know, I have a hard time making long-range plans. I've gone from place to place all my life."

She felt something inside, anticipation, that she hadn't felt in a long time. She looked into his eyes.

"I think," he began, fumbling for words, "that you and I could make it together."

It wasn't exactly a proposal. Gladys knew little about this quiet man—except that he didn't appear to be married. She smiled, waiting for more.

"Something else," he said carefully, "I need certainty."

"What does that mean?" she asked.

"I've traveled around a lot in my life, and I've met a lot of people." He was silent for a while, looking through the windshield. "I can't handle doubt about somebody." Looking at her intently, he said, "I need to be the only one in your life."

A slight frown knit her brow. "My ex is gone," she said. "He's gone from here and he's gone from my life. My son is in Montana. I'm sure he will never come back to live."

It was only later that she thought of Larry, with whom she had spent the night in her farmhouse a few days previously. She decided that she could live without him in her life. Rich was offering her, she felt, what he was asking from her—security.

Rich moved in less than a week later, and the first few weeks were, like most new relationships, delightful. She didn't know anything about his finances, except

Hard Wheat

that he drove a late-model car and seemed to have money to spend. He said he was working for a big farmer, keeping the equipment maintained.

Gladys kept her job at Hagge's. She was careful about how she talked with other men when Rich was present. Only once was she casually flirtatious with a customer, and saw Rich's face darken.

"You didn't tell me you were getting married," Larry said to her one day, sitting at the counter in Hagge's

She smiled. "Didn't know until the other day."

"Guess you won't be needing a handyman around the place anymore."

Gladys smiled again. "Looks like it."

"I've missed you."

She shrugged and wiped the counter down, saying nothing.

Gladys and Rich married a few weeks later, holding their reception in Hagge's. In a short time she found she was pregnant. She sang love songs to her baby.

Chapter Six - 2014

Morning sun shone through the kitchen window, glistening off the plates that Al and Eliot dried. Heather rinsed a glass and handed it over her shoulder to a waiting hand.

"Good breakfast," said Eliot.

Al slid a plate onto a stack in the cupboard. "I like potatoes fixed like that," he said.

"Mom taught me," said Heather, turning her face to smile at Al.

"She was a good cook."

Wiping her hands on a towel, she sat down at the table. "Tell me about her—about the woman you married."

Al looked at Eliot, uncertain.

Eliot laughed. "Go ahead," he said. "I want to hear what she was like at that age."

Haltingly, Al began: "I can remember only pieces of those days. Her mother was a great gal, open and interested in everybody. She encouraged me when Gladys got moody sometimes."

Heather stood up. "Wait a minute. I want to get something. Might refresh your memory." She went into another room and returned with an old photo album.

"That's Grandmother's album," Eliot said, taking it and opening it to the first page. "These are pictures of our ancestors," he said, laughing. "I don't know most of them." He turned a few pages and then stopped. "There are some pictures missing."

The three gathered around the old book. "I remember some of the ones that are gone," Eliot said. "There's Mom's family, with some cousins."

One group photograph had been defaced, someone scratched out of the group. Eliot looked at Al. "That must have been Uncle Timothy," he said. "And the missing pictures—they all had Timothy in them. I remember seeing them a long time ago."

"Why would he have been taken out?" asked Heather.

"Don't know. Mom never talked about him." Eliot turned more pages slowly. "There's Aunt Evelyn and Uncle Dan. Uncle Timothy has been deleted from history."

"I remember something about Timmy," Al said. "He went to college in Ohio. I only met him once or twice."

"Here's you, Dad," Eliot said, pointing to another photograph. "You look uncomfortable."

The three of them laughed.

"Your mother outshone me," Al said. "I was such a klutz."

Eliot looked at his father. "She had you twisted around her little finger."

Hard Wheat

"I believe it," said Heather, without looking up.

They poured over the album together.

"What else do you remember about her?" asked Heather, looking at Al.

He sighed. "She was always singing," he said. "She had a good voice, and she knew the lyrics to all the popular songs. There was a radio program, 'Your Hit Parade' that she listened to all the time."

Eliot said, "That old Tony Bennett record she had—she practically wore it out on our phonograph."

"Then she got kinda moody sometimes," said Al. "She'd get into a blue funk, and just sit on a chair in the kitchen, drinking coffee. I'd come home from work and you'd be playing by yourself in the living room, and she'd be sitting there, smoking cigarettes and drinking coffee."

"She was always like that," said Heather. "Whatever happened, it was always in the kitchen. I remember the smell of coffee."

"I remember once," said Al, "coming home from work, and you were—you were just a baby. That was in Bloomington. You must have been in your crib."

He rubbed his forehead. "Can't remember shit anymore," he said. "Anyway, Gladys was curled up in a little ball on the sofa, crying. I couldn't get her to tell me what was wrong."

"Post-partum depression?" Heather laughed.

"Don't know." Al sighed. "Pretty soon, though, she was back to normal." He looked at Eliot and smiled. "Sorry—I don't remember you then. I was pretty self-centered."

"Did she say she wanted any more kids?" Eliot asked.

Al grinned. "Well, before we were married, she said she wanted a lot of children. She loved babies. She used to babysit for some neighbors. They had a big family."

The three of them sat lost in thought.

"After we moved up here, she got moody, and sometimes she was real short with you." Al looked at Eliot. "I remember thinking that we oughtn't to have any more children, the way she was with you."

"When I was in high school," said Eliot, "she used to scream at me—at both of us."

"How about a drink," said Al.

"You go ahead," said Eliot. "I gotta drive back to Butte in a little while."

To Heather's look of dismay, he said, "Sorry, Little Sister. I have a job. But I'll call you the first of the week. Whatever you need, we'll work it out."

Al poured whiskey in a glass, and then offered the bottle to Heather. She set it down on the table and began going through the photo album again. Without being conscious of it, she sought clues to the life of the woman who had been her mother.

Chapter Seven - 1980

Gladys slid into bed beside Al, trying not to wake him. She lay on her back, staring into the dark.

"Where you been?" he mumbled.

"Thought you were asleep," she said.

"Waiting for you." He reached a hand across her belly.

She sighed. "I'm exhausted."

Al withdrew his hand. "What's goin' on, Glad?"

"Nothing. Just tired."

Al turned away from her and went to sleep.

The next morning, Al poured himself a cup of coffee and a bowl of dry cereal. Gladys was upstairs, pleading with Eliot to get out of bed. "You're going to miss your bus!" she shouted.

In a few minutes, Eliot stumbled down the stairs, dressed but not fully awake. Gladys followed him down.

"Eat some cereal," she said impatiently. "Your books are by the front door."

Eliot poured cereal into a bowl and added milk. As he hurriedly ate, Al watched him. "It tastes better if you have time to sit and eat," he said.

Eliot, mute, continued to eat. Gladys straightened his collar and smoothed his hair. Then she took a cigarette from a pack on the table and lit it.

Al noticed the ash tray, heaped with cigarette butts. "This is gross," he remarked, and emptied the tray into a garbage bag under the sink.

Gladys glared at him, but said nothing.

Al rinsed his cup and cereal bowl and set them in the sink. "I have to leave," he said.

Gladys watched him go out the door. Eliot looked from the door to his mother.

"Let's go!" she yelled. "You'll miss your bus!"

As they began their walk down the drive to the road, they saw Al's car turn onto the road toward Fargo.

"Mom," Eliot said, "could you not walk me to the bus?"

"Why? You ashamed of your mother?" She was annoyed.

"The kids tease me," he said.

"Well, what if you miss your bus?"

He shrugged. "I'll just come back home again," he said.

Her voice grew sharp. "If you'd get up in the morning when I call you, you wouldn't miss your bus!"

"Mom, I've only missed it once!"

"I need to know that you're safely on your way."

Eliot looked at her, frowning. She stopped and let him continue down the driveway.

"You're late," she said to Larry an hour later.

In an exaggerated gesture to soften her mood, he looked at her out of the corner of his eye. Then he said simply, "Had to help Dad with something."

She lit a cigarette, the lighter shaking in her hand. "I need a drink," she said, turning toward the house.

He followed her in.

Chapter Eight - 1982

"Dad," Eliot said on the phone, "I was thinking I would come down next weekend, during winter break."

"Be good to see you, Son."

"How's Mom doing?"

"Since you left she's been moping around. Think she misses you." Al sighed.

"You guys still fighting?"

Al chuckled. "No, we're doing all right. She just gets into these moods."

"I hate it when you fight."

"I know you do, Eliot. I'm sorry. You know how she hates the winter up here."

"We've got three feet of snow up here in Butte already," said Eliot. "They do a pretty good job keeping the highways plowed."

"Our roads are mostly passable right now," said Al. "I think you can make it all right."

There was a silence, then Al said, "She misses you."

"Dad," Eliot began.

"You come. We'll be on good behavior. Promise."

"Eliot called," Al said to Gladys that evening. "He called first to say he was coming down next weekend. And then he called back and said they were forecasting a big snow Thursday."

"So he's not coming."

"No."

Gladys turned back to the magazine she was reading. "Dinner's in the oven. Be about a half hour."

Al poured himself a large whiskey. "Gladys," he said, flopping unsteadily onto the sofa, nearly spilling his drink, "I'm getting tired of your being angry all the time. Can we talk about what's going on?"

She didn't look up from her magazine. "Nothing's going on," she said.

"Goddamn it Gladys! Can you at least look at me?"

She put down the magazine and faced him, expressionless.

"Ever since Eliot left for Butte—no, it's been way before that—you've been acting like I'm the garbage collector."

"You haven't exactly been Prince Charming, you know." She met his eyes, but showed no emotion.

"Well, can we call a truce? I can't live like this."

She became defiant. "What do you want from me?"

Al sighed and drained the glass. Softly, he said, "We used to like each other."

"You used to be nicer to me."

He threw up his hands. "What?" he shouted. "What do you want?"

Gladys stood up and went into the kitchen. "Dinner is about ready." She said, "Will you set the table?"

Al stood, splashed some more whiskey into his glass, and went into the kitchen

Chapter Nine - 2014

Heather looked out the window. "I only remember her being nice when I was little, before I started first grade. Then, it seemed like every day when she picked me up at school she was in a bad mood."

Eliot leafed through the photo album absentmindedly. "She did seem happy with Rich for a while," he said.

"You said he was a marshmallow," Al said, "like me."

Eliot laughed. "Dad, I never called you a marshmallow."

"Yes you did."

"Well, you did let her have her way in everything."

Al looked down at his hands. "I just felt like I could never please her."

"I thought when she married Rich that she had gotten all the anger out of her system," said Eliot.

Al sighed. "All the anger at me."

Eliot put his hand on Al's. "Wasn't just you," he said. "I couldn't do anything right, either."

"My dad was pretty nasty to her, there at the end," said Heather. "Called her a whore."

Al got up and went to the sink. Filling a glass with water, he sat back down, deep in thought.

Eliot watched him. "What?"

"I don't know," Al said. "I wondered sometimes if she was having an affair. I almost said something to her once, but I thought it would just set her off again."

Eliot looked at Heather. "You ever think anything like that was going on while you were still here?"

She shook her head. "Might have put her in a better mood," she said.

"One time," Eliot said, "I came home from high school and there was a strange pickup truck in the yard. I just turned around and left again."

Al and Heather looked at him.

"I didn't want to know," said Eliot.

"She say anything to you later?" asked Heather.

"Nothing. Never a word."

She sighed. "Our mother was a complicated human being," she said.

"When did she start growing pot in the barn?"

Heather shrugged.

"Those electric lines to the barn are pretty new." Eliot got up and paced. When the others looked at him, he laughed. "I've been sitting too long."

Al looked at Heather. "Do you remember when the lines went in?"

"Must have been after I left home. I don't remember the pole being there before."

"Heather," Eliot said, "what else can I do for you? I need to get back to my classes."

She stood up and embraced him. "You're my rock," she said. "I'm so glad you're here."

"You okay with handling the financial stuff?"

"George—remember, you met him at the funeral—he's a lawyer. Yeah, I'm okay."

The three of them walked to the front porch, and Eliot went on to his car. Heather dashed after him and embraced him. Al stood on the porch watching them.

Chapter Ten - 1990

"You're growing a beard?" Gladys asked as Larry climbed the steps to the front porch.

He grinned. "Mom hates it," he said.

She led him through the door without speaking. Inside, she turned to face him. "Let's see if I like it," she said, and put her arms around his neck.

They stood together for a long, passionate kiss.

"I guess it's okay," she said.

"I'm gonna have to shave it off again."

"Why?"

"I'm going back in," he said.

Her face showed shock. "To the army?"

He looked down. "I'm not doing any good here. Can't find a regular job." He waved toward the window. "I'm not cut out to be a farmer."

Donald Skiff

"But Al's gone back to Indiana, and Eliot's in Montana!"

Larry went to the refrigerator and returned with two bottles of beer. "Been thinking about this for a while," he said.

She wailed. "What about me?"

He pulled her close to him and kissed her. "Let's talk about it later," he said soothingly.

Later, lying on her bed together, she pleaded softly with him. "Don't go!"

"Well, maybe," he said. "A fella over in Argusville wants me to go into business with him."

Relieved, she said, "Well, doesn't that make more sense? What kind of business?"

Very casually, he said, "Well, it's agriculture, actually."

"You're in the right place for that! What will you be growing?"

He paused. "Well, I can't really talk about it just yet. You know, until we get it going."

"Wouldn't that be better than the army?" She caressed his bristly chin.

"Have to see if it works out."

He turned and fondled her breast. She relaxed and closed her eyes.

A moment later, he stopped what he was doing.

"What's wrong?" she asked.

He rolled off of her and sighed.

"What's wrong, Larry?"

He rubbed his face with both hands. "It's like you're not there," he said.

"What do you mean?"

"You just lie there. You don't move."

She propped her head with her elbow and looked at him. "Don't you like me?"

Hard Wheat

He took a long time to answer. "Gladys, out of this bed, you're alive. We get into this bed and you lie there like a lump. It's like you're someplace else, and I'm just doing this to your body."

"I thought you loved my body!" She was in tears.

"I do!"

"What am I supposed to do?" She pulled his face toward her. "Tell me!"

"I don't know!" He got out of bed and began to dress.

Gladys watched him through her tears.

"In the daylight," he said, "you're a person. You talk, you laugh, you order people around!" He laughed. "I know who you are when you're outside digging in your garden, or in the kitchen making breakfast. I see your eyes, and there's somebody in there!"

She turned and buried her face in the pillow, her body convulsing.

Larry finished dressing and sat down on the edge of the bed. Putting his hand on her shoulder, he said quietly, "I'm sorry, Glad. I don't know what to say."

After a while, she turned toward him and wiped her face with a corner of the sheet. "I don't know what I'm supposed to do," she said. "You never told me what you wanted me to do." She stifled a sob. "Nobody ever told me what I'm supposed to do. I thought I was doing what they wanted."

"You don't even talk," he said. "You don't tell me what's going on with you."

"I can't," she said. "It's like I'm holding my breath. I'm just feeling you inside me. I'm afraid to move!"

He sighed. "Yeah," he said. "I guess that's it."

She opened the covers to him. "Come back," she said. "I'll do what you want."

He stood and went through the door, closing it quietly behind him.

Later that week, he phoned to tell her he was on his way to the recruiting station.

Chapter Eleven - 2014

"I hope you don't have to leave right away," Heather said after she and Al had returned to the kitchen.

He looked at her for a moment before replying. "You know, don't you, that I don't have much time left?"

Her eyes filled, and she grabbed a paper towel and dabbed at them. "I'm sorry," she said, "I didn't mean to do that."

"A week ago," he said, "I barely knew you existed. Now you feel like, I don't know, a part of me."

Heather moved to him and embraced him, laying her face against his shoulder. They stood like that for a long time.

"Let's sit in the other room," she said, leading him into the living room. They sat next to each other on the sofa.

"I'm glad you're here," she said. "You've been so good for me. I can't tell you how important it is to me that you and Eliot were here. I would have totally lost it."

"You're a strong young woman," he said. "I wish I could help you somehow. I can barely take care of myself."

"Where will you go now?"

He sighed. "I came here to try to mend fences with your mother, and I was going to Butte to say goodbye to Eliot. I didn't have any plans beyond that. I don't have anybody close back in Bloomington."

"Can you stay here?" Her eyes were brimmed again.

He shrugged. "I'll end up in a hospital," he said. "I don't know how long I'll be able to stay out. The doctor gave me three to six months, but they don't know.

Hard Wheat

She put a hand on his arm. "You're my connection to Mom, the way she used to be. I'd love to have you here. I can take care of you."

"That's sweet. You don't know what you'd be in for."

"What I'm in for when you leave is to work at Hagge's every day and try to sell this old house—I can't keep it up."

"Do you know if she had a bank account?"

Heather shrugged. "I guess so. I haven't gone through her papers yet."

"Do you want me to help you do that?"

"Oh," She squeezed his arm. "Would you?"

They went into the dining room, which hadn't been used for dining in many years. In an old desk they found what seemed to be Gladys's financial records—in total chaos.

With breaks for quick meals, and a short nap for Al during the afternoon, the two of them organized the records as well as they could.

"I had no idea she had that much money," Heather said.

"Some of it may have come from the same source that paid for the minivan."

"I don't know how to get it into my name," she said.

"I haven't seen a will. If there isn't one, it will have to go through probate court. Maybe she had a deposit box at the bank. You might even have a hard time getting to that, if they find out she died."

"Oh, I don't know what to do!"

Al took her hand. "I'll stay long enough for you to get through that stuff. You said that George is a lawyer. Can you trust him?"

She looked at him with wide eyes. "Of course! He and Mabel have known me since I was born!"

"Then he can help you get all that straightened out. It might take a while. In the meantime, do you have enough money to live on?"

"Barely." She said. "If I can stay here, I can give up my room at the Jensen's."

"Heather," he said, looking at her, "I can help. I don't think anybody is going to throw you out of this house, at least until after the probate process. Probably you and Eliot will get whatever she left."

"Will you stay for a while, at least?"

"Of course." He grimaced, then smiled. "I may need to see a doctor around here. My own doc wanted me to come in next week for some tests."

She laid her head on his shoulder. He touched her face gently. They sat for a long while without speaking.

Then he said, "Why don't you ask them down at Hagge's if you can take some time off? I don't think you have had a chance to process all this yet."

She looked at him. "He doesn't have anybody else," she said.

"He can take care of his business. You need to take care of yourself first."

Heather cried quietly. "Nobody's ever taken care of me before," she said.

"Time I did." Al sighed. "I haven't had anybody to take care of in a long time," he said. "I should have taken better care of your mother."

"Nobody could live with her!"

He sat and looked out the window. "I know," he said. "It wasn't all her fault."

"I think Dad tried to make her happy. But he got uptight, and they used to fight a lot. He had kind of a mean streak in him, too."

"Ever hit her—or you?"

"No," she said. "I think he came close a couple of times." She smiled at him. "I was a brat, and I probably deserved it."

"Nobody deserves to be hit." He stood up slowly. "I got to move a little bit," he said. "My old body gets stiff if I sit too long."

Hard Wheat

"You want to take a walk while it's still light out?"

The two of them went out into the evening air. The gravel crunched under their feet. "Funny," he said, "I remember how this driveway sounds."

"You were happy here for a while?"

"Yeah. We thought we were starting out on a new life. Eliot was little and he loved the country. He'd play outside by himself for hours, digging in the dirt and making swords out of sticks. But when she came outside, he'd run over to show her something."

She watched his face as he talked.

They stopped at the end of the driveway. "I haven't collected the mail," she said, opening the mailbox, from which she pulled a large handful of mail. "Mostly junk," she said, scanning the envelopes.

Then, looking at the name on the mail she began to cry. "She'll never see these," she said, her voice catching.

Al put an arm around her. A lump in his own throat kept him from speaking. They walked slowly back up the drive to the house.

"Needs to be a light on in the house," she said. "It looks deserted."

"Ought to be a yard light, up there on the corner of the house. Wouldn't shine in the windows, but it would make the place looked lived in."

Heather smiled. "With three cars in the front yard, I guess nobody would think it was deserted."

"It's a good old house," he said, looking up at it. "We were proud of it."

"It's the only home I've ever known. Living in somebody else's house always felt weird to me, like I didn't belong, and any minute somebody was going to come in and run me out."

"You were brave to move out on your own," he said.

"No I wasn't. I was a coward. I was afraid all the time. They both yelled at me, and at each other. I hated that feeling, like any minute they were going to explode or something."

He smiled at her in the dim light of the yard. "Now, there's nobody to yell at you."

She chuckled. "Think I'll miss the fights?" Then she put her hand on her midsection. "That gives me a funny feeling here," she said.

"I hope you get used to the peace," he said.

They went back inside, and Heather turned on a lamp in the corner of the living room. "How do you feel?" she asked.

"I'm okay," he said. "I just needed a little exercise. How about a drink?"

"Okay," she said, going into the kitchen. "You like bourbon, don't you?"

"Whatever," he said. "I'll drink what you like."

In a few minutes, she returned with two glasses. "Mom used to drink wine a lot, but once I learned how to drink, all my friends drank straight liquor." She laughed. "At Hagge's it's always beer or shots—or shots and beer chaser. You learn pretty fast in that place."

He smiled and shook his head as he took the glass she offered. "Your mom and I started with beer," he said. "You remember my telling you about Moonlight Gardens in Cincinnati?"

"When your car broke down going back home."

"Yeah. They served only low-powered beer there, and you could drink gallons of it without getting drunk."

She laughed.

"But we tried," he said.

"Hard to think of my mom having fun," she said.

"She did, though. It was after we came up here, I don't know, a few years maybe, she began to get moody."

"I used to find her sitting on the back steps," she said, "smoking cigarettes and drinking coffee, looking at the wheat fields like she was expecting somebody to come walking out of the fields. When I asked her, she'd just tell me to go back inside."

"What was your dad like?" he asked.

"I told you—he was quiet, like you. Except when they got into another go-round."

"What'd they fight about?"

"He was jealous of her. Kept going on about her giving men the come-on."

"You ever see that?"

"No." She looked over at him. "She was pretty, though, when she got dressed up. Dad made her quit her job at Hagge's before I was born. She told me he couldn't stand to see her having fun."

"Not much fun around here, I guess."

"She was bored. And then she'd take it out on me or Dad—when he was around."

"He gone a lot?"

She laughed. "Yeah. He traveled around the state, fixin' machinery."

"And you were in school."

Heather picked up her glass. "Another one?"

He laughed. "You've learned to hold your liquor, haven't you?"

She smiled and picked up his glass. At the doorway, she turned and said, "I can't drink alone. I get really down on myself. But I like to drink and talk."

"You worked in a bar."

"Best place," she laughed, and disappeared into the kitchen.

They drank and talked, their words gradually coming further apart, until Al said, "I think I've run out of gas." He stood, a little unsteadily. "See you in the morning."

She sat smiling, her eyes closed. "Night."

Al was awakened by pain several times during the night. The house was dark and still. He thought of nights in the past, in this same house, lying awake wondering what to do with Gladys, who often seemed to be coming unglued.

He wanted instead to remember other, earlier times, when the night held promise for them both, their young son fast asleep in the other room, and they could entertain each other with intimate talk and touch. At certain times of the year, with the windows open and spring breezes caressing their bodies, there was a smell in the air, a good, clean country smell that Gladys loved to savor. He remembered her face glowing in the faint light, her eyes open and shining.

In the morning he awakened before Heather, and went down to make a pot of coffee. Sitting at the kitchen table, he listed the things they needed to do to get Gladys's finances in order and change her name to Heather's on the utility bills. By the time she came down, smiling at the scent of coffee, he had filled several pages in the yellow pad with notes of things to do.

"Does college still sound like fun to you?" he asked.

She just smiled more.

"We can make that happen, he said.

Chapter Twelve - 2009

He'd grown the beard again, and he had a touch of gray at his temples. "How you been?" Larry asked, grinning at her.

"You been gone a long time," said Gladys.

"You don't look any older."

"Thanks." She touched his gray, and ran her finger around his ear.

"This a good time?"

Hard Wheat

"For what?" she laughed. "If you mean Rich, he's over in Bismark for a couple of days. Heather's in school."

"Just thought I'd look you up."

"When'd you get out of the army?"

"Two years ago, actually." He looked at his feet and snickered.

"What've you been doing?"

"Got a little business going."

Gladys laughed. "That business you talked about before you re-enlisted?"

He grinned and nodded.

"Want some coffee?" She turned and went into the house, with Larry following.

Settling in the living room with the coffee table between them, they both acted shy with each other.

"Got a proposition for you," he said.

Her eyebrows lifted, and he laughed. "No, not that kind of proposition."

"So?"

You using your barn for anything?"

"Just storing lawnmowers and stuff."

He pursed his lips. "If we set up a little hothouse in there, would it be in your way? I mean, just close off one room, and put in electricity."

"Electricity? What for?" She was frowning.

"Need some lights, and a little bit of heat so it don't freeze."

"You can hook it up?"

"Yeah. May need an electrician to run the line in. And I'll pay your electric bill."

Gladys thought for a moment. "What do you want to grow?"

"You don't need to know. Just don't say anything about it to anybody."

"Rich'll want to know what's going on."

"Tell him you want to start flowers for a florist over in Fargo. I'll even share some of the profits with you, so he won't care."

"Sounds kinda risky."

"I'll handle everything."

They sat silently drinking coffee.

"How's Heather?" he asked.

She looked steadily at him. "Looks just like you."

Chapter Thirteen - 2014

Gladys felt moody and desolate. Her life was a dismal morass of old feelings. As she drove into town for groceries, only the easy glide of the van felt good to her. She'd wanted a new car for a long time, and now she had one, a good one, and it belonged only to her. It caused her a tiny bit of anxiety, however, because it represented something she couldn't quite identify, a feeling that she was doing something wrong.

Larry's "garden" in her barn was not really her responsibility. She simply rented the space to him, and she didn't even have to go back there to see it. He'd stop by every few days, and then sometimes knock on her back door on his way out, and she'd make a pot of coffee.

He even took care of depositing his rent directly into her bank account in Fargo. When the account grew, he suggested to her that she ought to buy herself a car. "Cold weather's coming, and you need dependable transportation."

So one day she went into town and chose the most expensive van she could find, trading in her old car and writing a check for the difference, giving herself a rare sense of power. Having the car, she thought, was not as incriminating as a big bank balance. For several weeks, she kept it washed and maintained. Gradually, it lost its luster, both in fact and in her feelings about it.

Her mood had a physical counterpart: a heaviness in her chest now and then. Life itself felt heavy to her. Heather had moved out, and Eliot seldom called. She missed the days when she had worked at Hagge's and bantered with the men there. She had quit because by the end of a shift her energy simply bottomed out, and she'd return home to an empty house and a near-empty bottle, to drink into oblivion in front of the television. The phone never rang.

Years before, she had looked forward to Larry's visits, at least. But after he'd gone back to the army, joining the others in her life who had abandoned her, she crossed him out of her mind. When he returned, there was a gulf between them. Their "business" relationship was just that—business.

Gladys thought with bitterness of the men in her life, all of them gone. Her feelings of abandonment brought back ancient memories, beginning with Timmy, who had launched himself into another world without so much as a look back at her, without even telling her goodbye. Her first love, torn to adolescent shreds. All her life, it seemed, she'd gone through the same feelings, only vaguely aware that somehow she must have brought them on herself.

She had known Al was about to leave when Eliot went off to college. It was as though she had to push him out, reject him before he could say the words himself—exactly the same way Rich left, years later, and even Larry. Sometimes she hated her daughter because the girl was part of that old life. And one more person in her life who had left her.

The whiskey tasted funny, and left her throat burning without the reassuring warmth that usually brought momentary satisfaction. Her chest felt squeezed, and her right arm suddenly lost its ability to support the glass. She began to perspire, a cold, clammy sweat, and she turned toward the sofa to lie down.

Donald Skiff

Cayman Liberty

NOIA, Underway

One – The Boat

Mack Jensen had retired as Chief Engineman after 25 years in the Coast Guard. He had a healthy nest egg saved up, and was content to work part-time at various marinas. He had never married.

One day he had been lolling about a yacht club near Seattle, chatting with boaters, admiring the boats, when he spotted a craft moving slowly into the jetty—an old military-looking boat, which he recognized instantly. Eighty-three feet long, painted white with a blue trim stripe running the length of the gunwale. Some kind of deck house had been built over the stern deck, extending from the wheelhouse to cover the hatch to the engine room. A faint cloud of black smoke followed the boat as it approached the public dock.

Mack walked over to the dock and watched as people appeared on deck to tie the boat up to the fuel dock.

Where the twenty-millimeter gun mount had once stood was a wading pool, with deck chairs surrounding it. Round port holes had been cut into the hull at intervals. The old radar globe had been replaced by modern antennae, along with a cluster of other navigation instruments. Large, comfortable captain chairs were mounted on the flying bridge.

A gray-haired man waited until the boat was secured to the cleats, then swung up onto the dock. The man nodded to Mack then entered the fuel station office. On deck were two women, one young and one middle-aged. They were sun-browned and bare legged.

It all reminded Mack of many years before.

Two – Liberty in George Town

Mack heard dishes crash in the galley as the cutter rolled with the continuing swells. "Can't you swing her around into that shit?" he yelled at the two crewmen trying to steer the boat by means of an oar at the stern. He ducked back into the engine room, where his fireman was struggling with bolts holding the cover on the port gearbox. It was all both of them could do to stay upright in the rolling craft.

One engine was silent; the other was running dead slow, its gearbox emitting sounds no mechanic wants to hear. "If that thing gives out, we're dead in the water," Mack said.

"I don't know what good it's going to do to open it up," complained Joe, the fireman. "We couldn't swap out any gears without pulling the shaft out."

"Only if it's the little one to the water pump. Keep at it." Mack went back up the ladder to the deck. Gus, the skipper and Chief Petty Officer, was bracing himself against the flag locker watching the two men at the oar. "What'd they say at the base?" Mack asked.

"We have to put into the nearest port. It'll be next week before they can get to us." Gus swore something under his breath.

The Coast Guard Cutter 83484, or "NOIA" (its radio call letters, painted on the top of its wheelhouse), was on routine patrol in the Caribbean scanning a 100-square-mile area for drug smugglers and other undesirables. It was 1972, and Henry Kissinger had famously declared, "Peace is at hand!" The United States Government was turning its attention from Southeast Asia to drugs.

NOIA, an old wooden boat built during World War II, its big 8-cylinder inline Sterling Viking engines having been overhauled countless times, had been returned to service after lying in mothballs for nearly twenty years. A single 20 millimeter gun stood on its foredeck pointing skyward, and a few small arms collected dust in a locker in the skipper's cabin. After six weeks on lonely patrol, they hadn't encountered any drug runners, and were on their way back to their base in Florida.

The WPBs (Wooden Patrol Boat) had picked up the slack when their newer, steel-hulled sisters, the Point-Class 82-ft cutters, were deployed to patrol the coastline of Viet Nam. Drug smuggling was "just another job" for the Coast Guard after having fought in Viet Nam, Korea and "the big one" before that, and in the occasional excitement of Prohibition before that.

"Where's that?" Mack asked the skipper.

"Grand Cayman, about a hundred miles northeast."

"A hundred miles? Christ, we'll never make that!"

"The Cape Coral is a couple of hours away," Gus said, "They'll escort us into Cayman, and if necessary tow us."

"That tub is only 95 feet long itself. It's going to tow us?"

"A tender is in Key West, and as soon as we know what we need, it'll come down and help us get repaired."

"Don't break those oars," yelled Mack at the men on the oar. "We may need them to row this thing to Grand Cayman!" The boat's rudder was all but useless given the slow speed of the cutter, so crew members had to use wooden oars to try to keep it on a proper heading toward Grand Cayman.

Gus grinned at him. "You ever hear of anybody rowing an 83-foot cutter?"

"Only across a slip in Seattle."

The Cape Coral joined them, cruising alongside as they made their way at snail's pace. Gus jumped across between the two boats when they were close enough together, to confer with the skipper of the Coral. "We might make better time if we put a towline between them, but not much," he said, "and the stress on both boats—to say nothing about our men—will be something else."

The Coral shut down two of its four diesel engines and loafed along, occasionally pulling ahead of NOIA and pausing to let the smaller craft catch up. With a crew of 15, the Coral could spare a couple of crew members to spell the oar-rudder operators.

For the next three days, the cutter made its way to George Town on Grand Cayman Island, where it tied up at a pier. The Coral tooted a farewell and went off to its regular patrol. Gus made the necessary arrangements with local officials, and the crew was given a well-earned liberty. "Be back by midnight," Gus told them. "We don't want to have to come looking for you if you're holed up in some hammock with a brown-skinned cutie."

Duty on an 83-footer was pretty relaxed for the eight crew members. Only when outsiders (that is, officers) were aboard, or when they were tied up at a regular base, did Gus insist on following formal regulations. The boat drew a small crowd of Caymanians eager to see the American sailors. Foreign ships were common in George Town, but military vessels brought a little extra excitement to the quiet port.

Mack and Joe made their way to the Seaview Hotel, where they were assured they could get good drinks. Most locals spoke a kind of pidgin English, so communicating was not difficult, once you got used to it. Guests of the hotel tended to be American or English, sometimes Danish-speaking. There was a small daytime airport, and a daily flight from Florida.

Inside the dim lounge of the hotel, they ordered European beer and sat watching the harbor through the large windows.

"We might be here for a month," said Mack. "The tender will have to come and look at the engines, and then maybe fly parts in."

"Not a bad place to be stranded," said Joe.

"Just so you stay in touch with the boat. When the tender arrives we may have to move her to another slip for repairs."

"You been here before?"

"No," said Mack. "Looks like a pretty sleepy town."

"I was here three years ago. At night the locals live it up at a couple different places. Lots of music, some girls to dance with."

Mack looked around the room. "Seems to be some tourists here," he said. "Like that sweet young thing in the sunglasses sitting over there looking out the window."

Joe grinned. "You like long hair, don't you?"

Mack stood up. "I'm gonna check that out," he said. "I'll see you back at the boat."

"Good luck." Joe took a long draw on his beer and watched Mack approach the woman, speak to her and then sit down next to her.

"Nice view," Mack said to her.

She turned and smiled at him. "I can feel the heat from the sand on my face. Feels good—I'm a little chilly in this place."

"Are you with anybody? Oh, I'm Mack, incidentally."

"Now I am," she said sweetly, "—with someone. I'm also here with my sister, but she's out shopping."

"Buy you a drink?"

"What are you drinking?"

Mack drained the beer glass. "This is Heineken's, but I'd rather have a martini."

"That sounds good to me," she said. "I'm Patty."

Mack signaled a waiter and ordered their drinks.

Patty showed him her white cane. "The sunglasses are for decoration."

Mack stammered, "I—I'm sorry. I didn't notice. You seemed to be sitting here looking out at the Caribbean."

"I understand it's very beautiful," she said.

Just then the waiter brought their drinks, and Mack took Patty's hand and guided it to the base of her glass. She picked up the glass easily, and saluted him before taking a sip. "Thank you."

They chatted comfortably as they drank, talking about the Cayman Islands and winter vacations. "Claudia and I live in New York," she said. "Where do you call home?"

"I'm in the Coast Guard, and our home base is at Cape May, New Jersey," he said, "but we've been out here on patrol for six weeks."

"Right now you're in George Town on 'liberty'—is that how you say it?"

He nodded. Patty turned her face toward him, her eyebrows lifted in question. "Oh, I'm sorry!" he said. "I forgot. Yes, I'm on liberty while our boat is in for repairs."

She smiled.

It was a little disconcerting for Mack, talking with her. Often when she spoke, she turned to face him, as though she could see him through her sunglasses. She seemed at ease, both with her sightlessness and with him. He wanted to see her eyes, partly out of curiosity, partly from wanting to see her reactions to him. When she faced the windows, he could see that her eyes were closed, as though for just that moment, and he imagined her opening them again to look at him.

To keep the conversation going, he told her about the boat and how old she was, but how graceful he thought her lines were. He blushed at that, thinking how his description could apply to this pretty young woman, as well. "We do get attached to our boats," he said, laughing.

"I would hope so," she laughed. "It's not only your home, it's your life for a time. Any woman would expect that kind of loyalty in a man."

Mack was struck by her picking up on the same theme. She was very perceptive. "Relationships are kinda important to me," he said.

During the second martini, he had relaxed into their comfortable conversation. Patty's voice gradually became softer, and she smiled more. Finally, she admitted to being "muzzy," as she called it, and suggested that they might find a more comfortable place to talk. "I understand they have rooms upstairs."

Mack didn't hesitate in making appropriate arrangements.

Three - Eyes

"Wow," he marveled an hour later, "you are so beautiful!"

"So you say," she answered.

"What does that mean?"

"I'm not really disagreeing with you, Mack. I just don't have any frame of reference."

"Oh, I'm sorry!"

"I've been blind since I was four years old. I don't remember what it means, that someone is beautiful."

He lay on the pillow looking at her. "I get great pleasure from just looking at you," he said softly. "I've seen other women's bodies, and I get more pleasure from looking at you than I have in a very long time."

She put her hands over her unseeing eyes. "That makes me cry!"

"You're a Chopin nocturne." He winced at his glib remark.

She smiled. "That flattery, I understand!" She stretched out on the bed.

He chose his words carefully, as though translating into a different language. "I'm sorry that you can't get the kind of pleasure that I can, by seeing beautiful things."

"I get a lot of pleasure like this." She rolled toward him and touched his face with her fingertips. "I get pleasure from feeling the wind blowing my hair. I get pleasure from good food. I get pleasure from smelling your skin!" She put her face close to his shoulder.

"The only disappointing thing," he said, "is that I can't see your eyes. I bet you would have beautiful eyes!"

"Are eyes beautiful, too?"

"Some are."

Little frown lines appeared. "I'm sorry. I wish I could please you."

He reached over and pulled her to him. "You do please me. I didn't mean that I'm disappointed in you. Far from it. Eyes tell me how someone is responding to me. You do that in other ways."

She smiled, and then pouted. "I need to call my sister." She felt for the phone on the nightstand.

Mack guided her hand. She lifted the handset and deftly dialed a number. "She's probably worried about me."

"Yes," she said into the phone. "I'm in room—" She turned toward him.

"Twenty-three," he said, and she repeated it.

"Yes, Claudia, I'm fine," she said, smiling at Mack. "We'll be down in a few minutes." She replaced the handset and said to him, "She gets worried about me."

"I'm not surprised. Would she—"

"Care if we're in bed?" She smiled again. "Not really." Getting out of bed, she made her way around it, brushing the edges with her fingertips. "Show me where the shower is."

He laughed. "You are incredible!" Holding her hand lightly, he guided her toward the bathroom. "Do you want me to—"

"I can bathe myself, thank you."

Her sister, waiting downstairs in the lobby, searched his face when they came out of the elevator. He smiled at her uneasily.

"I wish you'd told me where you were going," the sister said.

"Claudia," Patty said, her sunglasses hiding any emotion. "I'm all grown up, remember?"

Claudia turned to Mack. "I've spent my life taking care of her," she said pleasantly.

"And now you don't have to," Patty said.

"Not true," said Claudia. "We're a long way from home."

Patty touched her sister's face. "I know, Love."

Mack marveled at how easily the blind woman seemed to know just where to reach, to touch her face so gently. He spoke up. "Are you hungry?"

"It's early for dinner," Claudia said. "But I'd like a drink."

"Bully!" exclaimed Patty. "Of course," she added, grinning, "we've already had more than one this afternoon, haven't we?" She turned toward Mack and gave him a sweet smile that spoke just to him. "That's why we escaped."

Mack caught Claudia watching him and looked down, red faced.

"I thought I saw the two of you in the bar," Claudia said, moving off toward the restaurant. Patty collapsed the telescoping white cane she had been carrying, and took Mack's arm.

Seated, the three of them smiled at each other, Patty's smile was directed rather vaguely.

"She's incredibly self-possessed," Mack said to Claudia, who nodded without smiling.

"You speak of me as though I'm a very bright Border Collie." Patty removed her sunglasses and carefully wiped them with a tissue from her pocket. Her face appeared serene, her eyes closed as though she were sleeping.

"Why did you do that?" Mack asked.

Claudia laughed out loud. "She's making fun of us,"

A waiter came, took their order and left.

"You don't wear glasses, do you?" Patty asked Mack.

"No." he said, "but sometimes I wear sunglasses, just as you do."

"Not for the same reason."

"No."

"Do you like me better with them on—or off?" She demonstrated as she spoke.

"Patty," Claudia said, "You're teasing him!"

"You're beautiful, either way," he said. "It will take me a little while to get used to seeing your face."

"I wish I had beautiful eyes!"

"It's not that," he said. "I think all men want women to look at them, want to see how they are responding to us."

She turned toward her sister. "Is that true of women, too?"

Claudia put her hand on Patty's." Of course it is." She turned to Mack. "We've had these conversations for as long as I can remember."

"And you said I have to get used to it," responded Patty.

Claudia nodded, and Mack looked quickly at her.

"She's nodding," Patty said to Mack.

"How can you tell that?" he asked, incredulous.

"I don't know, exactly. Maybe I hear her neck bones move against each other." She laughed.

Mack turned his head toward Claudia. "Can you tell where I'm looking?" he asked Patty.

"Mack," she laughed, "I could hear the change in your voice as you turned your head. Besides, I heard your whiskers brush your collar."

"Amazing."

"No," she said, "Seeing is amazing."

"It is," Claudia said to her, "After all these years talking to you, trying to describe the world to you, trying to make you see with your mind's eye, I'm overwhelmed by the miracle of sight."

"The other day," Mack said, "I was in the dentist's chair, and here were these pretty woman's eyes, just inches from mine, but she was looking into my mouth while I was feasting on her eyes. I don't know if she even knew I was staring at her."

Claudia smiled. "She knew."

"I was surprised—ordinarily I can't focus that closely, but it was perfectly clear."

"I wish I could touch your eyes," said Patty.

He sighed. "I wish you could, too, but it would be painful for me."

"I've felt models of people's faces, but those don't feel real anyway. Why don't they make statues that feel like real skin?"

"The eyes would have to be wet, too," said Claudia.

"Like the mouth," laughed Patty seductively, and then she covered her face with her hands.

They were silent while the waiter set their drinks on the table.

"He's black," Patty said quietly after the waiter had left.

"Different scent," said Claudia, smiling at Mack.

Patty faced Mack. "You have a different scent, too."

"I'm a sailor," he said. "Maybe you smell the sea."

"You're an American, too," Claudia said. "What are you doing so far from home?"

"Sailors go all over the world," he said. "I'm on a U.S. Coast Guard boat, in George Town for engine repairs."

"I thought I saw an American ship down at the harbor," said Claudia. "It has that red sash painted on its bow."

"What do you do on the ship?" Patty asked.

"I keep the engines running."

All three of them laughed. "Don't say it," said Mack. "If I did my job, we wouldn't be here, right?"

He lifted his glass and saluted the two women. "I was just lucky. It's a very old boat, and the engines need a lot of repair to keep them going."

Patty smiled. "Would you take me for a tour of your very old boat?" she asked.

"Sure."

"It doesn't look very old," Claudia said. "Pretty and white."

"They keep her painted. Actually, she was built during World War Two, almost thirty years ago."

Patty smiled. "I like that you call the boat 'she'."

"It's just traditional. Actually, in my crew only the First Mate always refers to her as 'she'."

"But you just did."

He laughed. "I did, didn't I? I don't know why, although I have a lot of affection for her."

"And calling her feminine feels good to you?" Patty smiled.

"Yeah. I think she's pretty, too."

"And you keep her engines running." Patty said, with that same seductive laugh.

"Patty, that's rude!" Claudia said quietly.

Patty continued to smile at Mack. "I don't think so—do you, Mack?"

"Uh, this is getting embarrassing," he replied.

Claudia picked up a menu from the table. "Maybe it's time we had something to eat."

"I want Mack to read the menu to me," said Patty.

"Okay." Mack opened his menu. "They have appetizers, salads, sandwiches and entrées. What kind of food would you like?"

She held up her glass. "Something that goes with this nice white Bordeaux."

"Appetizers," he began, and read through the entire menu. Patty and Claudia smiled at him the whole time.

"Catch of the day?" Patty said.

"When the waiter comes back, we'll ask him what that is." Mack took a deep breath. Turning to Claudia, he asked, "Is she always like this?"

"Always."

"Don't you like to play?" Patty asked, smiling at him.

Mack caught the eye of the waiter, and soon their meal was ordered, along with another bottle of Bordeaux.

Just then Gus, Mack's skipper, approached their table. Mack introduced him to the women, and Patty insisted that he join them.

"Thanks, but I've eaten," Gus said, obviously impressed.

"Then have a drink with us!" Patty skillfully moved her chair a few inches to the side. She gestured toward the waiter, who hovered nearby. "Bring another chair."

"You're very gracious," said Gus, taking the seat next to Patty, and in the process knocking her cane to the floor.

Suddenly realizing that Patty was blind, he stammered, "Oh, I'm sorry!" and picked up the little cane.

She smiled at him. "Sailors are so gallant." She lifted her face toward the waiter. "Please bring another glass."

Mack turned toward Claudia. "Your sister," he said, "does not miss a thing, does she?"

Claudia replied with a wry smile. "Gets a little overbearing at times."

"Do I?" Patty pouted.

Mack and Gus exchanged glances.

"Charming," said Mack.

"Please help yourself to wine," Patty said to Gus. "That's one thing I can't do."

The four of them exchanged pleasantries while they ate. Patty played the hostess, engaging the men in conversation, while Claudia said little but monitored the others good naturedly, occasionally remarking to her sister about something such as the location of a fork or the precarious proximity of her wine glass to her plate.

Gus ordered another bottle of wine. "I'm sorry to leave such pleasant company," he said, "but I have to return to my ship. Mack here doesn't have to be back aboard until midnight." The two men exchanged glances, then Gus saluted the table. "Have a good evening."

After he had left, Claudia said, "Don't American sailors have to wear uniforms? I could take you both to be ordinary tourists."

"On a small boat," Mack said, "it gets pretty informal. In a few days our tender will be here, and we'll all pay more attention to how we're dressed."

"What's a tender?"

"A supply and repair ship. Follows the fleet around to maintain the different vessels."

"When do I get my tour?" asked Patty.

"How about the middle of the morning tomorrow?" He turned to Claudia. "Say, at ten? You'll come, too?"

"I'd love to."

"It will involve going up and down ladders," he said. "You okay with that?"

Patty smiled at him. "You mean I shouldn't wear a skirt."

"The crew would love it."

Four – The Tour

As the two women, smartly dressed in white slacks, pastel blouses, and large floppy hats, stepped aboard, they had the full attention of the crew. Mack admired how Patty was able to manage the low step across the gunwale almost as easily as her sister. Both responded charmingly to the proffered hands of the sailors to navigate around the boat. One man always descended a ladder first, gently holding an elbow but ready to catch the full weight of a woman in case she slipped. The tour was as much a treat for the crew as it was for the sisters.

Afterward, Mack and the bos'n escorted the women ashore and up to the hotel.

"We'd love to treat you to lunch," Claudia said to them.

The bos'n looked at Mack, who nodded. "Thank you."

They settled in the air-conditioned dining room overlooking the bay. "Pretty hot in the sun," observed Mack, wiping his brow with a handkerchief. He noticed little beads of perspiration on Patty's forehead when she took off her hat, and almost had the courage to wipe them off.

"You ladies are from New York?" asked Rolo, the bos'n.

"Yes," said Patty, "and you sound as though you're from the islands down here."

"Puerto Rico," he said, smiling. "My family moved to New York when I was a youngster."

"Your accent is so musical!"

Rolo's shy smile looked as though it were a permanent part of his face. He kept glancing at Patty.

Mack noticed that Claudia was watching everything, noticing who was speaking to whom, who was reacting. *Big sister,* he thought, *but nice.*

As the meal proceeded, he was aware of Claudia watching him closely—but not in a big sister way. It made him feel shy—unusual for him. Yesterday, he had been a man of the world, even if slightly embarrassed by knowing that she knew what her sister and he had been doing in the room.

If she judged him, it didn't show in the way she interacted with him. On the contrary.

When the lunch ended, the two men took their leave. "We have work to do," Rolo said, grinning.

"I hope we'll get to see you again before you leave," laughed Patty, aware of the peculiar use of the word *see*.

"I hope so, too," replied Mack.

Five – Claudia

After the Coast Guard tender arrived in George Town, the NOIA crew was kept busy around the clock repairing the engines and preparing the boat for the trip back to Cape May.

On their final evening in port, Mack went up to the hotel for dinner, hoping to run into Patty. They hadn't been together since the day he took her and Claudia on the tour of the boat.

Claudia was seated in the dining room when he arrived, so he went to greet her. "I'd been hoping to see you and Patty," he said.

Claudia smiled. "My sister got herself badly sunburned yesterday. She won't come down for dinner—would you join me?"

"Thank you," he said. "I'm sorry she isn't feeling well."

"I tried to tell her she was overdoing it on the beach."

"Thank you for the tour of your boat," she said. "I've never been in a ship's engine room."

"Patty seemed to enjoy it, too, but my crew mates wondered how she could get anything out of it."

"Believe me, she was enthralled with the sounds and the smells, and excited by just the sense of being in such a place."

Over a glass of wine, they exchanged polite conversation. Then Mack said, "You said the other day that you've spent your whole life taking care of Patty."

"Our mother assigned me that job when I was six years old," she said. "I've felt like I've never had a life of my own. Even when we were in school, we had the same friends and went to the same places."

"She seems so self-sufficient," Mack said.

"She likes to think she is. Then I have to rescue her."

"Helen Keller had a long-time companion, didn't she?"

"Anne Sullivan." Claudia sighed. "I don't want to be her!"

"Well, from what I've seen, if you are responsible for how well she has adjusted to being blind, I'd say you have done a wonderful job."

"People tell me that, but they don't know what it has cost me!"

Mack saw this attractive young woman in a new light. When he had seen them together, they appeared to genuinely like each other and share their experiences so easily. "What would you really like to do with your life?" he asked.

She looked down at her hands. "Oh, it's not like we're joined at the hip," she said, "although it used to feel like that. She spent three years in a blind school, and I saw her only on weekends." Claudia looked up at Mack and smiled. "It was like I got out of prison! For three whole years!"

"Is there any way you can make other arrangements for her so you can live your own life?"

Tears formed in her eyes. "I'm responsible for her." She looked down. "Our parents made sure we would always have enough money. Our mom and dad are gone, now, and there's nobody else. Bottom line—there's nobody else!"

"Wow," he said softly.

She put a hand on his arm. "I'm sorry. I didn't mean to unload all this on you. Let's have dinner—and a drink!"

During dinner, they agreed to avoid the subject of Patty as much as they could, but Mack kept thinking about the young woman whom he had had in his bed, who had seemed competent and well-adjusted. Was she so dependent upon her sister, or had Claudia developed a frame of mind that could not allow Patty real independence?

"You didn't tell me what you would really like to do with your life," he said, "separate from Patty."

"I love art," she said. "I'd love to learn to paint. I'd love to learn to play music. I'd love to learn how to write poetry." She sipped her drink. "I've actually written a little poetry. I took classes when Patty was in blind school."

"You have a creative soul."

Claudia smiled at him. "Do you always flatter women you're with?" When Mack looked surprised, she said, "Patty told me that you said she was a Chopin nocturne." She laughed. "It was exactly the right thing to say to her at that moment."

Mack's face colored.

"She tells me everything," Claudia said. There was a playful look in her eyes.

"I thought we weren't going to talk about Patty."

"Okay," she said, "let's talk about you, then. Do you write poetry?"

He laughed. "No, I'm a mechanic. I do like music, but I've never learned to play anything."

She leaned her chin on her hand. "What music? Besides Chopin."

"Most of the Romantics," he said. "Last night I was listening to Respighi's Pines of Rome, and thinking how much I like that, even though it's been years since I'd listened to it."

"For me," she said, "it's Sibelius. His moody horns. I feel it, sometimes almost despondent, and then, like, *defiant*."

Mack grinned. "The final chords in his fifth symphony, where he lets you hang there, holding your breath waiting for the end."

She laughed. "He knows he's got you."

The two of them sat in silence, gazing into each other's eyes for a long time, feeling a link that went deep into them both.

Finally, Mack finished his glass of wine and said, "We're sailing tomorrow morning."

Her eyes brimmed with tears. She fumbled for a tissue in her purse. "Now you tell me," she said hoarsely without looking at him.

"When are you going back home?" he asked.

Still avoiding his eyes, she said, "I don't know. We'd thought about Cancun. New York is so dismal this time of year."

"I have some leave coming. After we get back to Cape May, I could …"

"Sailors!" It was almost an expletive.

Mack sighed. "I'm sorry," he said. "I just didn't think to say anything."

She pushed her half-eaten plate of food away. Suddenly looking at him, she said, "You won't get to say good bye to Patty."

He shook his head.

"She'll be crushed!"

"I'm sorry." He gazed at her eyes, feeling as though he had struck her, wanting to touch her, not daring.

After a silence, he asked, "Can I go up to see her?"

She shook her head. "She's miserable enough." Then she looked at him. "Yes. Go see her. I want to be there. I want to see *you* when you tell her." Her eyes flashed.

The heat in her words stunned him. He signaled the waiter for the check. They sat waiting, without speaking. Mack sighed deeply, trying to dissipate the tightness he felt in his chest.

On their way to the room, Claudia stopped at the desk to use a phone. "Patty, are you dressed? Put on a robe or something. Mack and I are coming up."

In the room, Patty was sitting stiffly in a chair, avoiding contact with the back. She smiled. "I fell asleep in the sun," she said.

"Patty," Mack began, then cleared his throat. "I needed to see you before I left. We got our orders to sail first thing in the morning."

Without her sunglasses, Patty's face showed first shock, then dismay. She touched her lips with her fingertips.

"I'm sorry," he said. "Claudia and I were having dinner. I wish you'd been there."

She slumped, touching the back of the chair, then quickly sat upright again. All the light had gone from her face. Her voice was wooden. "I guess I should have expected it. You're a sailor, after all, ashore on liberty." She gingerly picked at the robe on her shoulders. "I missed out."

"No, I missed out," he said, glancing at Claudia, who stood beside him stone-faced.

"I enjoyed you," Patty said. A tear leaked from beneath one closed eye.

"I didn't know I'd feel like this," Mack said.

"How do you feel?" Her face had changed. She was challenging him.

"I don't want to leave. I don't want to leave you." With that, he turned to look at Claudia.

She looked back at him steadily, accusingly, without saying anything.

"I told Claudia," he said, "I've got some leave coming, when we get back to Cape May. I'd like to see you again."

"We don't know where we are going from here," said Claudia vaguely. "Back home in the spring, I guess."

Mack went to the desk and wrote on a pad of paper. "Here's my mailing address," he said.

Neither woman replied.

"Can I write you?" Mack stood uncomfortably beside the desk, the slip of paper in his hand. After a moment he laid it on the rough-hewn surface.

Claudia finally went over to him. Taking the pen, she wrote on the pad, tore off the page and handed it to him.

Mack turned toward the door. Nobody said anything. As he touched the knob, however, Patty stood up, crossed the room and reached for him. He started to embrace her, but stopped, his hands a few inches from her back. Instead, he touched her face gently. "I hope you get over your sunburn and have a wonderful vacation," he said. "I'll miss you—both of you!"

He went out the door. Looking back just before closing it, he saw the two women still standing, their faces showing no emotion, not seeing each other or him.

Six – Journey Home

Mack stood leaning on the flag locker, looking over the stern of NOIA at a receding George Town. A small cloud of steam and smoke billowed up behind the cutter, partially obscuring its wake.

"Hold 'er heading at three twenty," he heard Gus tell the seaman at the helm. Then Gus called down to Mack: "How do they sound?" gesturing toward the newly repaired Viking engines.

"Like new," Mack answered, although his mind was elsewhere. The sun was rising over Grand Cayman, a kind of beacon keeping his mind on two women he couldn't stop thinking about. They were to him like Janus, the god of beginnings and endings, the past and the future—or transition. The easy physicality of Patty, bright and forthright, and the soul-deep feeling of Claudia. He'd been quick and deliberate with Patty, and delighted at her ready response to him. Claudia took him by surprise. And he'd had to leave, abruptly, roughly—cruelly, he felt.

They weren't the first women he'd played with in ports along the coastlines he'd traveled since enlisting in the Coast Guard ten years ago. After Julie had broken off their relationship in Ohio, they weren't even the first he'd fallen for—always disastrously. Most of the girls (early on, they tended to be young and silly) and the women that he had bedded, since Julie, had accepted the temporariness of their encounters. A sailor, met in a bar, sharing a drink or two, maybe dinner, usually a night in a hotel, wasn't a good prospect for a long-term relationship. Mack had been comfortable with his life. One or two had flattened him emotionally when he suggested something beyond a mutually pleasant hookup.

Mack took refuge in music. He'd felt the pull of serious music ever since as a boy he had been given a recording of a Ravel's ballet music *Daphnis et Chloe* by an aunt, and had worn out the record on his old phonograph. Out at sea these days, he spent hours on his bunk, isolated from the rest of the crew by his headphones while they played poker in its many variations. Suddenly, Claudia had reminded him that there were other people in the world who felt like he did in his depths. It wasn't just music; Patty, as he had told her, had felt like a Chopin nocturne, soft and warm. Claudia had felt like the Sibelius she liked so much, sometimes somber but complex and deep. Not Sibelius's romantic *Finlandia* but mysterious, pulling at his gut, leaving him breathless and yearning. With her, for that brief moment, he felt things he didn't know were in him.

He remembered looking at Patty, stretched out languorously on the bed, so completely unselfconscious, maybe because she couldn't see herself or him. Nakedness didn't seem to exist for her. Then he thought of Claudia's eyes, locked on his, something profound passing between them.

Joe, his fireman, emerged from the engine room hatch. "Purring like some really big cats," Joe said. "Those buckets suck gasoline like a big straw in a tall rum drink."

"When we get around Punta de San Antonio, we'll cut her back to nine hundred for the rest of the way to Key West," Mack said.

"I'm goin' down for coffee," Joe said. "Want a cup?"

"Thanks. Yeah."

When Joe disappeared into the wheelhouse, Gus came down the ladder from the bridge. "You had a couple of fine specimens there, Mack." He smiled broadly.

"I was nervous about the blind one," said Mack, "going up and down the ladders."

"What could she hope to get out of going into those little spaces where she couldn't see a thing?"

"She got more than you'd think," Mack said, taking a proffered mug of coffee from Joe, who had managed to bring two full mugs up the ladder from the galley one-handed. "Thanks."

Joe grinned at Mack. "Interesting threesome."

Mack didn't reply, letting a smile tell the others what they wanted to hear.

Joe turned to Gus. "Will we be in Cancun before evening, do you think?"

"That's only a fuel stop," Gus said. "You'll have to be satisfied with passing close by one of those humongous cruise ships and waving at the girls."

Mack went up to the bridge, where Cliff, the seaman, leaned on the binnacle and rested his hand easily on the wheel. "How's she handling?" Mack asked.

"Had a little trouble at first keeping them synched, but now they're right together."

Mack touched the throttles, easing them back the smallest amount. "Keep them just under twelve hundred," he said.

Big clouds lay ahead, the remnants of the latest system to come through from the Atlantic. No dramatic weather this time of year. Cancun would be full of cruise ships, though. If they were lucky, they could be gassed up and underway in a couple of hours. Forty more hours to Key West. Then two days to home.

Mack went down to his bunk and found a cassette of Sibelius. Inserting it into his recorder, he lay down and put on his headphones.

Donald Skiff

Seven – The Past

"Damn it!" Mack wiped his bloody hand on a shop towel and rolled out from under the car.

"What did you do?" Julie reached for his hand. "You really banged it. Let's go clean it up and put a bandage on it."

Mack protested that it was too little a wound to bother with, but he enjoyed the attention. He was soon back under the car.

She hung around a lot while he worked on cars, but it was obvious that she'd rather they were out someplace else, doing something together. She did admire his facility with mechanical things, however. It was just that she wanted him to do more with his life than work in his uncle's garage. She herself intended to go to college in the fall.

Mack felt at home with a wrench in his hand. Uncle Paul had encouraged him and taught him a lot about car repair. "You could come into this place with me in a couple of years," Paul had said.

Mack had been out of high school a year before Paul had hired him. Mack was uncertain about his future— college had never entered his mind. He figured that the draft would get him sooner or later, and any future beyond that was problematic. Julie kept reminding him that college would keep him out of Viet Nam for a few years, but he continued to procrastinate. Finally, before she left for college that fall, she told Mack that she didn't want to continue their relationship. "It will be too hard to keep up with the distance between us," she said.

Mack was devastated. He had had no inkling that Julie was dissatisfied with their relationship. Before she left, he pleaded with her, even promising to enroll in classes. Julie had made up her mind.

A week after she left, Mack enlisted in the Coast Guard, and was sent to Cape May, New Jersey, for boot camp. He and Julie corresponded occasionally for a while, but made no plans to get together.

In 1962, the U.S. Coast Guard was not involved in Viet Nam. So when Mack finally decided to enlist, he chose the Coast Guard, partly to lessen his chances of being sent into combat, and partly because it seemed a more admirable service. Three years later, when the military instituted patrols along the Viet Nam coast, twenty-six of the Coast Guard's 82-foot patrol boats were deployed, followed by a number of Swift Boats (PCF), all of which saw extensive duty in Viet Nam.

Mack was fortunate to avoid being sent to Viet Nam, instead being assigned to U.S. coastal patrols, his latest duty aboard an old 83-ft wooden patrol boat plying the Caribbean, looking for drug smugglers. He had advanced to First Class Petty Officer as Chief Engineer. When his initial enlistment was nearing its end, he signed up for another hitch. He thought that perhaps he would be a career sailor.

Eight – Cape May

After returning from its Caribbean patrol, NOIA put into drydock for extensive inspection and repairs. Mack remained assigned to the boat to oversee mechanical repairs, along with Gus, the skipper. The rest of the crew were reassigned to other duty. Mack felt grateful that he again escaped from duty in Viet Nam. He also managed to escape cold weather patrols. NOIA was small enough to be enclosed for repairs in a building during the winter. It was not warm, but it was out of the worst of the winter weather.

When mild weather returned, he knew that his shore duty would soon come to an end. On an impulse, he pulled out the slip of paper with Claudia's New York phone number on it, and left a message on her phone.

The next day, she responded. "Good to hear from you," she said, without much emotion.

"Are you back in New York to stay?"

"We'll be here for a couple of months, and then we're going to Norway for a cruise."

"I'm in New Jersey," he said. "Could I see you?"

"Wait," she said, then muted the phone. In a few moments, she returned and said, "Patty and I have tickets to the Philharmonic Friday evening. We could get you a ticket if you'd like."

"I'd love it," he said. "What are they playing?"

"Shostakovich. Don't remember which one."

"Tell me how to reach you," he said.

She gave him directions and they agreed on a time. After the call, Mack felt slightly disappointed. Claudia had sounded merely friendly, as though she were talking to a distant friend.

That's what we are, I guess, he told himself. He had thought about both women often since they last saw each other in Grand Cayman, but had not made any attempt to reach them, even after he had arrived in Cape May last fall. Without verbalizing it, he had hoped that they—especially Claudia—would have similar warm feelings for him. *I don't do very well with relationships,* he thought. *I haven't even called Julie.*

Sailors get interrupted. Out to sea, they have only their duties and their thoughts (and Mack, his music). When they go ashore, they want company. They've had enough of their crew mates. The local bar is a magnet for loneliness. Ports of the world are filled with bars and clubs catering to sailors. Women, with varying agendas, are drawn to these same haunts.

Mack arranged with Gus to take a long weekend liberty so he could go up to New York City.

Gus knew about Claudia because Mack had often spoken of their time in Grand Cayman and how struck he was with that quiet woman who seemed to have such depths. "I'm expecting our orders next week," he told Mack. "We could be shipping out by the first. Just have to collect a new crew."

NOIA was back in the water, sitting quietly in her slip, getting her paint touched up, the engines tested daily, a week-long shakedown cruise finished. Like a horse, patiently waiting for her riders after a long winter in her stall.

Mack and Gus had been living ashore in the barracks, tending to the boat as needed. Mack looked at her sometimes from the top of the gangway to the dock, admiring her lines. While boats and ships bound for the Far East were uniformly gray, most of the Coast Guard cutters were painted the traditional white with red viceroy-sash-like diagonal stripes near the bow. *Classy,* he thought, *and proud.* He wondered how the crews on Viet Nam patrols thought about their boats.

For him, wanting to avoid going to the Far East was less about avoiding combat than it was about why he had chosen the Coast Guard to begin with: Most of the duty along the coasts of the United States was helping people. Air-sea rescue seemed an admirable thing to do. He'd participated in many more humanitarian efforts than trying to catch narcotics runners. Crews on NOIA, like those on most of their sister vessels, had plucked people out of the Caribbean off the coast of Florida, people attempting to reach the United States from Cuba, Haiti and other islands.

Mack wondered if their next assignment would be close enough to New York that he could see Claudia and Patty.

Nine – New York

When Mack was buzzed through the apartment house door, he climbed the stairs with some apprehension. He wasn't sure what kind of reception he would get. As he remembered their phone conversation, Claudia had seemed distant, even though she had invited him to the concert with them.

Patty answered his knock on the door with a wide smile. She wore dark tinted glasses, not sunglasses, and he could see her closed eyelids behind the lenses. But her smile was warm as she extended her hand toward him. Leading him into the living room, she called to Claudia, "Here's our long-lost sailor!"

Both women wore startlingly short skirts. Her sister stood and took his hand. "Good to see you again, Mack."

"I didn't know when you'd be back in New York," he said.

"You could have called," Claudia said.

Mack looked down, feeling chastened. Then he looked up at them and smiled. "I'm not very good at maintaining relationships."

"We thought you'd forgotten us," said Patty, pouting.

Claudia looked at him without speaking.

"I'm sorry," he said. "I hadn't forgotten you. I felt bad leaving you on such short notice, and I guess I was afraid you wouldn't want to see me again."

Patty sat on the sofa and patted the seat next to her. "Come sit with me."

Mack sat down, but looked over at Claudia. "Did you want to see me again?"

Claudia nodded slightly without replying.

"She did," said Patty.

After an extended silence, Mack said, "This is a little uncomfortable."

"Why?" asked Patty.

He smiled at her, then remembering her sightlessness, turned toward Claudia. "I like you both," he said, "very much. And I'm not sure how to handle that."

"Please," said Claudia, "we're not a package." She gazed at him steadily.

"Okay." He looked at Patty. "You two are so different," he said, "and not just because Claudia can see."

"Tell me what that means," said Patty.

He laughed awkwardly. "You are so open and direct, and you're incredibly sensuous. Your sister is quiet and ..."

"Deep," said Patty, smiling.

Claudia stood up. "Would you like a glass of wine?" She started toward the kitchen.

"Thank you," he said.

"I like that about her, too," said Patty, searching for his hand with hers.

Mack sighed. "I don't know either of you very well," he said softly.

Claudia returned with a wine bottle and three glasses. "I have to admit," she said, "I get jealous, sometimes, because Patty is so easy with people." She smiled at Mack and poured the wine.

Mack picked up one glass and started to hand it to Patty.

"No," Patty said, "just show me where it is. I have to know where to put it down again."

"Wow," he said, replacing the glass. "You are amazing." He took her hand and guided it to the wine glass. "How did you know I was going to hand it to you?"

"How your body moved," she said simply, lifting the glass carefully to her lips.

He looked at Claudia, who smiled and nodded.

Sipping his wine, Mack leaned back on the sofa. "So, what are we going to hear tonight?"

"Shostakovich's Fifth," said Claudia.

"I don't know it very well," he said. "I remember there's a slow, sad movement in it."

"Makes me cry," said Patty.

He looked at Claudia, who nodded again.

"Do you both like the same music?"

"Some," said Patty. "I don't like to work so hard."

Claudia laughed. "Twentieth Century music."

"Lots of Twentieth Century music is easy to listen to," said Mack. "Rachmaninoff, Howard Hansen, Ferde Grofe."

"She has a hard time with Stravinsky and Bartok," Claudia said.

"I guess I do, too," said Mack. "Music's a gut thing for me, so I usually go for the Romantics."

"What do you like in popular music?" asked Patty.

"I've been caught up in the folk music, in the counter-culture," he said. "But I haven't heard many of the current groups."

"Our parents forbad us to play any rock and roll in the house," Claudia said. "Our father was a violinist—played for a while in a community orchestra in Rochester, where we lived years ago."

"I'm hungry," said Patty, finishing her glass of wine and expertly replacing it on the coffee table.

The conversation ended with talk about where to eat dinner and how much time they had before the concert that evening.

During the Largo movement of the Shostakovich symphony, Mack noticed that Patty did have tears streaming down her cheek.

After the concert, Mack was invited to sleep on the sofa, but was told that the women had to leave by noon to attend a gathering of friends. As they sat drinking cognac, they talked about the concert. Mack watched both women as they talked, marveling at how different they were and yet how attracted he was to each one.

Later, he lay in the dark wondering if he might be invited into a bed, but anxious about how it might complicate the situation. Waking briefly as dawn was seeping through the curtains, he felt relieved that he had been allowed to sleep alone.

In the morning, Claudia woke him to say that the bathroom was available for his use and breakfast would be ready in half an hour. She smiled warmly at him and asked if he had slept well.

"A comfortable sofa," he said, noticing that she was watching him, a slight smile on her face.

When he emerged from the bathroom for breakfast, Patty was already seated at the table, drinking orange juice. "Good morning, Mack," she said. "Come sit by me."

It was as if they were old friends, easy with one another, comfortable in the knowledge that their friendship would continue indefinitely.

On the ride home, Mack wondered if he had been expected to go further, seeking something more than friendship. Most of his female relationships, particularly since he had been in the service, were primarily physical. Friendships, if they developed at all, tended to be superficial. Affection was expressed mostly as something pleasant experienced between them. Occasionally, undercurrents of reserve made such relationships difficult.

Sailors teased each other about their "black books" of women in various ports. Mack had few names of women in his address book, and his doubts about himself seldom led him to try to reconnect with those he'd spent time with on earlier visits.

So he didn't call Claudia and Patty for a while after returning to his boat. He decided to wait until he heard where NOIA was to be sent next.

Eventually, they were directed to report to the Coast Guard Station in New London, Connecticut. Officers at District Headquarters told Gus, however, that duty in New London would likely be short, as the newer boats would soon be returning from Viet Nam. Their old wooden boat was to be decommissioned as soon as it could be replaced.

Ten – Connecticut

Mack recognized Patty's voice on the phone when he called to tell the women of his move to New London. "Claudia's got a luncheon date," she said. "She needs to get out by herself more often."

"I gathered that," he said. "That means you're home alone?"

"Poor me!" she laughed. "I can get my own lunch."

"Anyway, we're going to New London the middle of next week. Can I see you the weekend of the twenty-third?"

"I'd like that," she said. "I don't think we have any plans, but I'll have to check with Claudia."

"Can you show me around New York?"

"That would be fun. Of course, it will look different to you than it does to me." She laughed.

Mack enjoyed how Patty seemed so good natured about her sightlessness. He wondered how it really was for her. They'd never had a serious talk about it. "Patty," he said, "Would it be possible for you and me to have some time alone?"

"What are you thinking?" she asked slowly, a laugh in her voice.

"I'd just like to be with just you for a while. I'd like to have some alone time with Claudia, too. I really want to get to know both of you better, but it's hard for me having you together."

"You don't want to make love to both of us?" Now her voice was playful.

"Uh, well," he began. "You are so *out there*, aren't you, Patty? You're putting me on the spot." He chuckled, but he was uncomfortable.

"I'm sorry, Mack!" she said. "That was rude, wasn't it?"

"I'm not used to someone being so frank."

"The times they are a-changing."

He laughed. "They sure seem to be changing in Washington."

The line was quiet. Then Patty said, "I'm worried about our country."

"Me, too," he said. "The President is my boss, but I don't feel good about him right now."

Her voice changed. "But we can still have a day in the Big Apple, can't we?"

"I can get into New York on Friday, the twenty-third," he said.

She was her gay self again. "Then let's do something, even if Claudia has other plans! You come down Friday—what time can you get here?"

"Evening. I'm not sure how long it takes to get there from New London."

"A couple of hours by train."

"So we can have dinner."

"Yes!" she said. "I know a great little place just a block from us."

Mack felt easier when he hung up.

The trip north on the NOIA was an easy three-day cruise, with two stops to refuel. As they moved slowly up the East River, the crew all stood on deck to gaze at Manhattan. Johnny, Mack's new fireman, was exuberant about visiting the city after they got settled into their station.

Standing with Mack on the flying bridge next to the seaman at the helm, Johnny watched the skyline. "I have to see Greenwich Village," he said. "That's the center of the universe!"

"You ever been to New York?" asked Mack.

"Man, I ain't ever been east of the Appalachian Mountains, except for Cape May."

"Where you from?"

"Saint Louis," the young man answered. "I joined the Coast Guard to see the ocean! All they have back home is the Green Banana, a big old sternwheeler."

"Green Banana?"

"Actually, the Coast Guard Cutter Greenbrier," Johnny said. "We just called her that because she's shaped like a banana." He gestured to illustrate the curve of the hull.

"I think I remember her," Mack said. "When I was a kid, we watched a Coast Guard paddlewheel boat tie up in Cincinnati."

"Different world," Gus said, joining them on the flying bridge. "River boats are for Tom Sawyer."

"Water's deeper here," said the helmsman. Gus turned to look. "That's Execution Rocks right over there. Just past that, set the helm to forty-two degrees."

Soon they were in the open water of Long Island Sound, headed for New London. Sailing along the coastline, they all watched the scenery go by, the small port towns and the huge mansions on cliffs overlooking the Sound.

The sun was low over the hills as they sailed close by the New London Ledge Light and into the mouth of the Thames River.

"That's Powder Island," said Gus, "and Fort Trumble beyond. Head for that long dock over there. That's the Eagle. We'll tie up across from her."

Mack felt a tug of pride as they passed the Coast Guard three-masted barque. "She's almost three hundred feet long," he told Johnny.

"Who gets to sail on her?"

"They have a permanent crew of about eighty, and they take about a hundred fifty cadets at a time out for sea-going classes."

"Officer Candidates," put in Gus.

"You mean from the Coast Guard Academy?" Johnny was impressed.

NOIA rounded the end of the dock. Mack put his hand on Johnny's shoulder. "Go below," he said. "Watch that starboard throttle—it sticks sometimes."

The rest of the crew became busy fending the boat off the dock until lines were secured and the engines shut down. Mack went down into the engine room and helped Johnny tidy up. The lights suddenly brightened, indicating that they were now on shore power. Mack felt a familiar disappointment. He loved the throb of those big engines, and in port it was almost as though *he* were shut down along with them.

"Funny," he laughed to Johnny, "Shutting those down is like my mom telling me it's bed time."

Johnny looked at him, wondering if he were joking. "No shit?"

"Engines are my world," Mack said. "What made you choose the engine room?"

Johnny shrugged. "That was the school they recommended me for."

"You into cars at home?"

"My dad was. He was always working on some old junker in the garage. I got to like the smell of oil."

"Okay, sign the engine log and let's go find a beer someplace."

The two men wandered off base and found most of the rest of the crew in a nearby bar, where sailor talk went on to late in the evening. Mack was also thinking about a couple of young women in New York City.

Eleven – New York

"Yes?" came Patty's voice through the intercom.

"Hi, it's Mack," he said, close to the instrument.

"Come on up!" The entry door buzzed.

Patty opened the apartment door just as Mack knocked on it. Without glasses, she presented him with a great smile and offered her face for him to kiss. "Are you used to me like this yet?"

He chuckled. "This is how you look, and I love it."

"Claudia's here, but she's getting ready to go out. Let's have a drink before we go, okay?" She walked confidently around furniture and into the kitchen, with Mack following.

Patty gestured toward a cluster of liquor bottles on the table. "What would you like? We have wine in the fridge." She leaned against the counter, facing him, smiling.

"I'd enjoy some of that vodka, with a bit of lime, if you have it."

"Of course," she said, opening the refrigerator and extracting a fresh lime. "If you'll slice it, I'll get us some ice."

"I was expecting you to show me how you can use a knife," he laughed, taking the lime from her hand.

"I haven't cut myself in almost a week," she joked, filling two glasses with ice from the freezer.

They returned to the living room with their drinks. "Claudia!" Patty called, "Time for a drink?"

Just then Claudia appeared, wearing a black sheath dress that was slit to her thigh. "Just barely," she said. "What are you drinking? Hello, Mack."

"You look great," he said sincerely.

Claudia held out her hand to him. "You can't kiss me—I just put makeup on."

"Straight vodka," Patty answered, "with a twist."

"Oh, my!" Claudia turned and went into the kitchen. "I think I'll have wine."

"Mack thought I'd show off by slicing the lime," said Patty.

Claudia came back into the living room. "I wouldn't be surprised. Where are you eating?"

Just then the doorbell rang. Claudia, wine glass in hand, went to the intercom and pressed the access button. "I want you to meet a friend of mine," she said over her shoulder to Mack.

After a moment, a light tap on the door announced the visitor, and she opened to an elegantly dressed young man with carefully groomed hair down to his shoulders.

"Yves," she said, "This is Mack, our sailor friend I've told you about. He never seems to wear his uniform, though."

Mack and Yves shook hands, and the young man went to Patty and kissed her lightly on the lips.

"Claudia won't let you kiss her until after dinner," Patty laughed. "Took her most of an hour to put on her face. What do you think of that outfit?"

Yves studied Claudia for a moment. "Gorgeous."

"Would you like a drink?" Claudia asked him, smiling broadly.

"That dress feels as good as it looks," said Patty. "Mack, feel it!"

Mack backed away, flustered.

"White wine," Yves said, turning toward the kitchen. "I can get it." Mack noticed a very slight European accent.

Claudia looked at Mack. "Yves runs a gallery."

"I'll take you there tomorrow," Patty said. Turning toward Claudia, she said, "Love, would you put lipstick on me, please?"

Claudia took her hand and led her into the bathroom. There, with the two men watching, she deftly applied a soft pink lipstick to her sister. "You need eye makeup, too," she said.

"I'll be wearing glasses."

Back in the living room, Patty said to Mack, "They're going to a fancy art show. We're going to a neighborhood restaurant—not where I'd wear a gown like that."

For the first time, Mack noticed the aqua pants suit that Patty was wearing. "I like what you're wearing," he

119

said, feeling as though he'd made a faux pas by not commenting before.

She laughed. "I used to let Claudia pick out my clothes, but I get more objective opinions from the sales people."

"And some of them I've had to take back because they looked so ghastly on you." Claudia sipped her wine, and turned to Yves. "Do we need to leave?"

"Lots of time," he answered.

Patty found Mack's hand and pulled him toward the sofa. "Let's sit for a moment," she said. "I don't want to spill this drink."

Yves took a seat across from the sofa. "Claudia says you're in the Coast Guard."

"Yes, we've just moved to New London."

"That's where the Coast Guard Academy is, isn't it?"

"We're docked where the big sailing ship is—the Eagle."

Yves put down his empty glass. "I understand that used to be a German training ship."

Mack laughed. "The spoils of war. We took it at the end of the Second World War."

"I'm surprised it wasn't a casualty of the war."

Mack and Yves were making polite conversation, not especially interested in each other. In fact, Mack was a little jealous. He'd have wanted to escort Claudia in that black dress. But he turned toward Patty.

"The Eagle is a large sailing ship," he said. "Very beautiful."

"Larger than your boat?"

"Much larger. We have a crew of eight. The Eagle has a permanent crew of eighty."

"Takes a lot of sailors to handle the sails," added Yves.

She shook her head. "I can't imagine."

"I've heard that there is a model of her at the Academy," Mack said. "Maybe they'd let you touch it."

Yves stood up and carried his glass to the kitchen.

"Ready?" asked Claudia.

The two of them waved and went out the door, leaving Mack and Patty on the sofa. She sighed.

"What's that for?" he asked.

"I don't know Yves very well. Gay men are mysterious."

"I'm glad you said that. I was jealous of him."

She laughed. "He's just a friend. Lots of gays among our friends here, men and women."

Mack was silent for a while, taking a couple of sips from his drink."

"Talk to me, Mack," she said, "what are you thinking?"

"Getting a glimpse of your social life makes me realize how simple mine is."

"A sailor with a girl in every port." She was smiling at him.

He looked down. "I don't have a girl in every port. I feel like a stranger wherever I go."

"You don't feel strange to me. Yves feels strange. You have felt comfortable to me ever since we met in George Town."

"At first," he began, then stopped.

"At first you thought I was just another loose woman." She reached over and kissed his cheek. "Now you'll have to wipe that lipstick off."

Mack laughed. "No, not just another loose woman," he said. "There was something—something *delicate* about you. Even though you were very forward."

She laughed. "Forward? That's different from loose?"

"Straight. Honest. Most women I meet in my world like to play games."

"The sex game."

"Yeah. Like, 'We're not really doing this, but if you're nice to me ...'"

"But that's like 1950!"

"You didn't dangle it in front of me."

Patty touched his cheek. "The times they are a-changing."

"You were like fresh air."

"I thought you'd make a good friend. Friends fuck." Her voice was serious.

He laughed. "I thought that was just in San Francisco."

There was laughter in her voice. "So I'm a flower child?"

"Is that how you think of yourself?"

It was her turn to be silent. Then she said, "I grew up thinking of myself as less than everybody else, because I couldn't see. There was a world I could never be a part of."

"But you're so open to everybody!"

"What else can I do? I can't give you what I see. I can only give you what I feel. Can seeing be any better way to share myself than to touch you?" She reached out a hand and touched his arm.

"To most people I know," he said, taking a sip of his drink, "sex is something very private, something you guard."

She giggled. "The first time I was kissed I was astounded. I'd never felt anything like it. Our parents never kissed us."

"Wow."

"And now there's The Pill," she said simply.

Their silence now was a comfortable thing; both of them lost in memory and reverie. Mack was thinking about how different his world was—his Midwestern world, his world of the sea, his world of seeing. He'd always thought of it as the only real world. Patty was aware of her different world that lacked seeing. But that wasn't missed unless someone pointed it out to her. She wasn't aware that Mack's Midwestern sailor's world was different from what she experienced.

"Let's go eat, shall we?" she said, rising and handing Mack her white cane.

A short walk along a busy sidewalk ended in a small, unpretentious restaurant. Inside, a middle-aged, rather paunchy man came up to them smiling. He took Patty's hand. "Hi, Beautiful!"

"This is my friend Mack," she answered. "He's a Coast Guardsman, on liberty to take me around the city."

The man led them to a table in the far corner. There were few other patrons.

"Smells wonderful," said Mack.

"Doesn't it? Their food is delicious, 'From the old country,' as Michael puts it."

As the waiter graciously seated them, he said, "For you, Beautiful, I have a new—for us it's new—Austrian red wine, a *Grüner Veltliner*, that I think you'll love. Not too astringent. Just how you like."

"Thank you, Michael," Patty said.

When the waiter disappeared into the kitchen, Patty leaned close to Mack. "That's Michael Douglas."

"That's his name?"

"The actor. You can't mistake that voice."

"But," stammered Mack, "Michael Douglas is a young fellow, Kirk Douglas's son."

She smiled at him. "You can't mistake that voice. Claudia watches his television program all the time."

Mack looked toward the kitchen. "His voice is very similar." Flustered, he thought it better to drop the subject.

When "Michael" returned with the wine, he said, "This is on the house, Beautiful."

She spoke in a stage whisper. "I've told Mack that you are the Michael Douglas who is on television."

"What can I say, beautiful lady, I'm an actor. I can be whoever you want."

She turned to Mack, smiling. When Mack looked up, the waiter was also smiling at him.

"Tell me what you think of the wine," Michael said, pouring some into Patty's glass.

"Delicious!" she replied. "I can't pronounce it, but you'll remember the next time we come in, won't you?"

"Without question." He poured into both glasses.

After a suitable time, the waiter returned again and took their food order. By the time they left the restaurant, both Patty and Mack were feeling relaxed and affectionate. Mack was surprised how steadily Patty walked, holding his arm and navigating with ease the uneven sidewalks and curbs.

"We drank that whole bottle of wine!" Mack said.

"It was very soft, wasn't it?"

Later in Patty's living room, they continued their conversation over cognac. "Claudia will be coming in late, if I'm not mistaken," Patty said. "That gallery crowd goes on and on."

Mack grinned. "I've been wanting to get you alone."

They kissed.

"My bed is more comfortable than this sofa," she said softly.

In the morning, Mack was surprised to hear someone moving around the apartment. Patty still slept next to him, and he hadn't heard Claudia come in during the night.

There were voices. "Do you have a bit of brandy?"

"In that cupboard."

"Thank you."

Patty stirred, turned her face toward Mack and smiled. "I smell coffee," she said sleepily.

"Others are up," Mack whispered.

"Claudia always gets up early." She kissed him passionately, but when his hand wandered over her body, she stopped him. "I need to pee," she said, getting out of bed.

Mack laid back and sighed with contentment.

A few moments later, Patty reappeared in a robe. "You can get into the bathroom now," she said. "There are towels in the closet there."

Mack quickly showered and returned to the bedroom to dress. Patty had gone into the kitchen. "You're making eggs!" he heard her say.

In a few minutes, he found the kitchen bustling. Yves was standing to one side, drinking coffee. Claudia was at the range, and Patty, still in her robe, was setting the table. "Good morning!" Claudia greeted him.

Mack and Yves nodded to one another.

"Help yourself to coffee," Patty said to him. "Yves has doused his with cognac." She pointed to the bottle.

After Claudia, with a flourish, served scrambled eggs and set a dish of bacon on the table, they all sat and ate.

"The show was spectacular," said Claudia. "Yves has a real knack for hospitality."

"Do you paint?" Mack asked Yves.

"Oh, no. I gave that up a long time ago when I discovered how many superb painters there are in New York."

"He has done some very nice work, though," said Claudia. "How was your dinner—with Michael Douglas?"

Mack grinned, and Patty nonchalantly said, "He brought out a new Austrian red. Really smooth."

"It's a nice place," said Mack. "They treated us like royalty."

"That waiter loves Patty," laughed Claudia. "We eat there a lot."

When they had finished eating, Yves finished his coffee and stood up. His hair was slightly awry. "Thank you for breakfast. I must be off," he said, nodding again to Mack and kissing both women.

"Your gallery is probably a mess," said Claudia.

"The price you pay."

After he had left, the others sat over another cup of coffee. "He slept on the couch," Claudia explained.

Patty laughed. "Too bad! I bet he'd be a gentle lover."

Mack smiled but said nothing.

"But," Patty continued, "I see you wanted to make a point."

Claudia looked at Mack with a slight smile.

After a moment, Patty said, "Mack and I are going to explore."

"Take a cab to the Village." Claudia turned to Mack. "That area is becoming a real gathering place for hippies."

"Hard to get into the clubs at night," Patty added.

"I've heard," Mack answered. "My fireman is dying to visit there." He laughed. "He's from Saint Louis."

"You have a fireman on your boat?"

"Technically, he's an engineman. His military rating is Fireman First Class. The title came from the old days when ships were coal-fired. A fireman kept the fires going."

"You must bring him in," said Patty. "We'll take you there—won't we?" She turned toward Claudia.

"Love to."

Twelve – New York

Patty and Mack had seen the city—in their distinct ways. Patty knew where all the tourist sites were, and gave Mack detailed instructions for getting around.

At the top of the Empire State building, they stood in the chilly breeze. Mack admitted to feeling a little uneasy with the height.

"I don't have any sense of height," Patty said. "I can feel the building sway, though." She grasped his sleeve. "Come over here so you can see the World Trade Towers."

They looked up at the two nearly completed towers. "They will be the tallest buildings in the world," she said, then laughed. "Some people describe them as looking like the boxes that this building and the Chrysler Building came in."

"Impressive," he responded. "I've been up in the Arch in Saint Louis, and I thought *that* was high. This is something else!"

"Had enough height?"

He nodded, then said, "Yes."

Back at street level, they took a cab to Patty's neighborhood and had lunch in a Jewish deli before returning to her apartment. Claudia had left a message on their Ansaphone that she would return before dinnertime.

Mack laughed. "Neat gadget. Guess you can't very well leave each other notes on the fridge, can you?"

They sat on the sofa and drank and talked. Patty kicked off her shoes and complained about sore feet.

"We'll take you to a different place for dinner," she said after a while. "Do you want to take a nap before she gets home?"

Mack smiled. "Is that an invitation?"

"Silly man. Do you need to be invited?"

He stood and took her hand, leading her into the bedroom.

They were asleep when Claudia came home. Mack began to get out of bed quickly, but Patty stopped him. She kissed him on the cheek and pulled the covers up to their chins, smiling widely.

Claudia looked in at them. "You look comfortable," she said.

"Very, answered Patty. "How was your day?"

"Not as good as yours, I gather."

"We needed a nap after all that walking."

"No doubt." Claudia turned and went to the kitchen. "I need a drink."

As the two got up and dressed, Mack felt guilty, but recognized other feelings as well. Delightful as Patty was to be with, he still felt strongly toward Claudia. He was apprehensive that she might withdraw from him if she felt his relationship with Patty becoming exclusive. He tried to let the feelings go. The women seemed comfortable with the situation.

"The twin towers are nearly done," Patty said after they had gathered in the living room.

"Will they have an observation deck?" Mack asked.

Claudia shrugged. "Don't know."

"Uh," began Mack, looking at Claudia, "I'm feeling a little uncomfortable."

Both women faced him silently. Patty smiled slightly.

"Does it bother you to find us in bed?" He could feel his face growing hot.

"Thank you, Mack," she answered. "But no. Am I just a little jealous? Maybe."

He looked at Patty, who was still smiling. "We've been through this before," she said.

He continued to watch Claudia. "But I haven't. I just don't want us to be uncomfortable."

"You're sweet," she said, smiling at him.

"You are two amazing women. I've never met anybody like you."

"We're typical New Yorkers," Patty said. "We know a lot of people, but we don't have many friends—not close friends."

"When we met you in George Town," put in Claudia, "there was something about you that both of us felt good with." She touched his arm and looked into his face. "A connection."

"I felt that, too."

Patty laughed. "We don't meet many sailors!"

"It takes me a while to get to know people," he said. "I've spent a lot of time in bars trying to get to know somebody, but there's like this—" He hesitated. "this *wall* they put up, that they're hiding behind. You weren't like that."

"Must be a lonely life, a sailor's life."

"Guys complain a lot, most of 'em get married, and then it's worse for them when they're away from their wives."

"Not the way we picture sailors," Patty said.

"Maybe the Coast Guard's different from the navy," Mack said. "And with the war, a lot of guys are away from people they love."

"I hate the war!" Claudia said. "I don't understand what we are over there for."

"At least Nixon did one good thing," added Patty, "he went to China."

"Don't let's talk about politics," Claudia pleaded. "I'm sorry I brought it up."

Mack grinned. "Comes up a lot."

"Tell me about your home," said Patty. "You are from the Midwest, right?"

He nodded, then said, "Yes. A little town near Cincinnati." Laughing, he added, "I keep forgetting you can't see when I nod."

"What's the little town?"

"Milford."

"What was your life like in Milford?" Patty was facing him with an intense look on her face.

"Like all the other guys there," he said "I wanted out. I wanted to see what the world looked like. I thought about getting involved in the civil rights thing, but I didn't have the guts, I guess. So I worked in my uncle's garage."

"You have a girl?" asked Claudia.

"Yeah, and she kept after me to go to college, but I didn't know what I wanted to study for."

"So you joined the Coast Guard?"

He shrugged. "I thought I'd get drafted anyway."

"What happened to your girl?"

"She went to college, and we sort of split up."

Claudia smiled at him. "So here are you, a garage mechanic, and you join the Coast Guard to avoid the draft. Where'd you get interested in music?"

"I don't know," he said. "Somebody gave me an album of Ravel when I was a kid, and it sort of touched something up here." He tapped his head.

"I'm getting myself a glass of wine," Patty said. "Can I get you anything?"

Mack got up immediately and followed her into the kitchen. "Let me help," he said.

She took a bottle from the fridge and then turned to face him. "Claudia was asking you about music," she said. "You walked out on her."

"Oh, uh" he stammered. "I wanted to help you."

"There are some things I can't do. This is not one of them."

"Sorry," he mumbled. Feeling chagrinned, he returned to the living room.

Claudia sat with a glass in her hand, looking at him.

"Sorry," he said. "I was rude."

She faked a pout. "I made you uncomfortable with my questions."

"No," he said, then hesitated. "Maybe. I thought Patty was going into the other room to get away from the conversation."

Just then Patty reappeared, skillfully carrying two glasses of wine. She handed one to Mack. "Thank you," he said.

Setting his glass on the coffee table, Mack appeared flustered. He opened his hands. "Sometimes I don't know how to act."

"Come here," said Patty, "sit between us."

He remained standing. "That's the problem," he said. "I can't seem to be with you both at the same time."

"You don't see us fighting over you, do you?" asked Claudia.

"No. You're both so graceful," he said. "I feel like a country boy, out of his depth."

Patty laughed. "You're not a country boy to me!"

"You feel pulled between us?" asked Claudia.

He nodded, then caught himself and answered aloud, "Yes."

Patty's forehead wrinkled. "Mack, I'm sorry. It wasn't my place to correct you. Claudia can take care of herself."

"I didn't feel abandoned," said Claudia. "Mack answered my question." She looked at Patty. "Love, you're taking care of me again."

Patty grinned. "You do that to me all the time."

"That's what I mean," said Mack. "There's always something going on between you two that I'm not following."

"Okay," she said, "let's start over. You were talking about your interest in music, and I interrupted you by going out of the room. I'd like to hear more."

He took a moment to respond. "Nobody in my family listened to classical music very much, but it got to me for some reason. Most guys I knew," and he grinned, "were listening to rock and roll, Elvis and all those singers. I was discovering Tchaikovsky."

"Your girl have anything to do with that?"

Mack blushed and looked down. "Yeah, probably." They all laughed. "She wanted me to have more class."

He was beginning to relax. The three of them chatted for a while about music, and then prepared to go to dinner.

On the train home, Mack thought back over the weekend and how uncomfortable he had become trying to pay attention to both women at the same time. *I should be able to just be myself,* he thought. *Relax and enjoy their company, the way they do.*

Thirteen – New London

It was early when Mack stumbled sleepily out of his bunk aboard NOIA and made his way to the galley. Johnny, his fireman, was sitting drinking coffee.

"Hey, Chief," the young man greeted him.

Mack poured himself a cup of coffee and sat down at the table. "I got home really late. Walked from the train station."

"You visiting those gals in New York?" Johnny grinned broadly.

Mack nodded. "They said they'd show us around in Greenwich Village sometime."

"Good. I'm ready anytime." Johnny got up and disappeared into the crew's quarters, reappearing a moment later carrying a guitar. "I'm gonna learn to play this thing," he said.

"You just bought that?"

"Yeah. Got it in a shop uptown. They give lessons there, too." He beamed, stroking the smooth surfaces of the guitar and plucking the strings.

"You the next Bob Dylan?"

Johnny smiled. "No," he said, "I just want to make music."

"Well, good luck." He took a sip of coffee. "Meanwhile, we need to tear down the generator while we're in dock. It needs bearings."

Later in the engine room, both men were sweating as they replaced the bearings. "Easy job when you got the right parts and the right tools," instructed Mack.

He liked the young man. There was a bit of ambition in him, but also a sensitivity to what was going on among the crew. His work was competent for the limited experience he had, and he readily took suggestions. "Good man," Mack told Gus later.

They were standing on deck; Gus was smoking one of his thin cigars. "You going to have that generator back together today?"

"Sure. He's buttoning it up already. Have it ready to run in an hour."

"He bought a guitar?" Gus was frowning. "We're not in for a lot of rock and roll, are we?"

"I don't think so," replied Mack. "It's an acoustic guitar. More like what they play folk music with."

"No amplifier?"

"No amplifier."

The phone rang below. "I thought it was too quiet," said Gus, heading for the ladder.

In a few minutes he reappeared. "Where's the crew?"

"Bunch of them ashore in the canteen."

"We've got a fishing boat aground off Block Island. Find Buck."

In a few minutes, the bos'n and the rest of the crew rushed aboard. Mack went below to the engine room. "Got 'er together?" he asked Johnny.

"Almost. Needs oil."

"We're shoving off in ten minutes. We don't have time to test it. Start the engines."

Back on deck, Mack joined Gus on the flying bridge. "We don't have a generator yet," he said. "Johnny has to put oil in it."

"We'll run on batteries until then."

They watched the stern for the familiar billows of black smoke as the engines started. The deck crew stood by at the lines, waiting for the signal to cast off.

Gus was on the ship-to-shore telephone. "Roger," he said. "Underway in one minute." He turned to the bos'n. "Cast off." Then to the seaman at the helm, "Slow astern. Ease to starboard."

The cutter backed slowly, still tethered by the spring line, its bow moving away from the dock. Then, "Ahead, slow. Cast off the spring line."

Once clear of the pier, the cutter roared out into the river channel and headed for open water. Mack inhaled the cool air. He loved the excitement of being underway at full speed. While the old boat could pull only eighteen knots (most big passenger ships could outrun her), she looked and felt like what she was: a ship on a mission.

Mack leaned down into the engine room hatch to see Johnny busy with the generator engine.

Johnny looked up. "Where we headed?"

"Fishing boat went aground on Block Island. Tide's coming in, so we ought to be able to pull 'er off if she doesn't have a hole in 'er." Mack withdrew his head and climbed down the ladder.

The two of them worked at reassembling the engine.

Guided by radio contact with the fishing boat captain, they found the boat on the beach sheltered by a high cliff. The captain assured them that his boat was undamaged, but that he hadn't been able to pull off the sandy beach by himself.

NOIA eased up close to the stern of the fishing boat, and the deck crew threw a line between them. Once the line was secured at both ends, the cutter slowly moved away from the beach. The line lifted out of the water and grew taut, then slack again as the fishing boat floated free of the beach.

"Make sure his engine works," said Gus. The bos'n spoke with the captain of the other boat, then nodded to Gus, who added, "Okay, tell him to let go of the line."

As NOIA turned back toward the mouth of the Thames River, the fishing boat headed northeast along the coast. The Connecticut hills loomed darkly over the first glimmerings of shore lights.

"How could he run into Block Island?" Mack asked Gus. "In broad daylight, how could he miss a goddamn island? Must be a hundred feet high!"

"Said they were eating lunch."

Mack ducked down into the engine room. The light was dim, the only lights powered by the batteries, and Johnny had rigged a flashlight to a stanchion to finish his job on the generator. He looked up and crossed his fingers. Touching the starter, he fiddled with the throttle. The little engine coughed and groaned, struggling to turn against the resistance of the new bearings.

The shaking caused a socket wrench, which Johnny had laid temporarily on top of the main electrical panel, to fall down into the circuitry. A flash and a loud report—as startling as that from a large gun—left the engine room in darkness except for the little flashlight. The generator engine stopped.

Mack and Johnny looked at each other, momentarily unable to process what had happened. The air was filled with the smoke of molten metal.

Gus's voice came from the hatch, "What the hell was that?"

"Short circuit," answered Mack.

"We've lost all electrical power," shouted Gus.

The two main engines continued to run, with throttle control maintained by the arrangement of cables from the bridge. Mack grabbed the flashlight and peered behind the panel.

"Melted the whole mess!" he called. "The wrench shorted out the main bus bar!"

"Oh, shit!" moaned Johnny.

"Why did you leave that wrench up there?" accused Mack, backing out of the confines of the machinery.

Johnny hung his head, humiliated.

Gus came down the ladder. "What's it look like?"

"The main bus bar is melted through. I don't know how we're going to fix it." Mack, holding the flashlight in his mouth, began removing covers from the electrical panel.

"We don't have any communication," said Gus. "Can't call for help. The engines should run as long as the gas holds out. I told Jerry to run slow but not so slow that the engines cough. We've got three people with flashlights to keep other ships from running into us."

"Can we can make it back to base?" asked Johnny.

Mack continued his work, muttering through the flashlight in his mouth.

"How'd this happen?" Gus asked Johnny.

"A wrench fell down behind the panel."

"Jesus!"

"I'm sorry!"

"You get topside and tell the bos'n to give you a lantern so you can see what you're doing. You guys have to get us back up, pronto!"

Just as Johnny disappeared up the ladder to the deck, both engines suddenly went quiet.

Mack took the flashlight out of his mouth. "Those new electric fuel pumps! We should have kept the old ones."

"We're dead in the water!" Gus's voice carried his despair. He rushed up the ladder.

Buck and the helmsman stood on the flying bridge, looking down at him, helpless. Johnny emerged from the crew's quarters carrying an electric lantern.

"Get your ass down there and fix it!" Gus yelled furiously, climbing up to the flying bridge.

"No other vessels within sight range of us," said the helmsman.

"Keep the guys signaling toward anything that moves," said Buck, and the helmsman left.

"Can they fix it?" asked Buck.

Gus shrugged. "Mack'll think of something."

"We've got locator beacons in the life rafts."

"Won't help if nobody is looking for us."

"Tomorrow sometime, they'll miss us."

Gus looked around in the darkness. Shore lights were visible in nearly every direction. "How far are we from shore?"

"Ten miles or so."

"That old Coast Guard Station still there on Fishers Island?"

"No," said Buck. "That was decommissioned ten or fifteen years ago. Just an automatic light now."

"Let's get a fix on it and on something on Block Island, in case we can get electric power back up and can call District."

Meanwhile, Johnny held the lantern and flashlight while Mack probed the damaged electrical panel.

"This is a fucking mess!" said Mack. "We have to get our lighting system back first, so we can call for assistance."

The boat rocked gently. "Tide's coming in," said Johnny.

"Been coming in. We must have drifted out from the lee of Block Island, and the swells are hitting us from the Atlantic." Mack pulled a hot piece of metal out of the wreckage of the panel, and dropped it quickly on the decking. "There's your wrench," he said.

"How can I help?"

"Take the flashlight and go up and ask Gus to get you the blueprints of this panel."

In the wheelhouse, Gus and Buck were pouring over nautical charts. Buck sighted over the binnacle to get the direction of a distant light while Gus called out the reading on the instrument.

"Okay, we should be about here," Buck said, pointing to the chart. He made notes of time, latitude and longitude.

Johnny told Gus what Mack had asked for. After rummaging by flashlight through filing cabinets, Gus sent him back down with the blueprints.

"You could get busted for this," Mack told him as he peered at the documents.

Johnny didn't say anything.

"It was a stupid thing to do!" Mack sighed, and his voice became a little softer. "We may get pulled out of New London now."

"I'm sorry."

"Shit, so am I." One part of Mack was thinking about the task before him, but another part was thinking about Patty and Claudia. He could very well get reassigned to a station a thousand miles away. "They got a shit load of Swift Boats and 82-footers on their way back from 'Nam, and need someplace to station them. This old tub might cost more to fix than it's worth."

"We have to go somewhere to fix it?"

Mack laughed. "The Electric Boat Company, right across the river from us. They built these boats."

"I thought they built submarines."

"Yeah, but during the last war they built a lot of other things." He reached a hand out from behind the panel and wiggled his fingers. "Hand me a big screwdriver."

In a few minutes he emerged, carrying a piece of apparatus. "See? This is burned in two." Rummaging through a box of parts, Mack found a heavy piece of cabling. "Get me two cable clamps from there."

A half-hour later, he switched the main power on. The battery-powered lights came on. Johnny heaved a loud sigh of relief. Mack nodded at him. "Now, if those batteries hold out, we can get home. Watch that ammeter, and come and get me if it goes over twenty."

Mack climbed the ladder to the deck. Gus, Buck and the helmsman cheered from the flying bridge. Over their heads, the running lights again showed that power was restored. "Ready to start the mains?" Mack asked.

Gus waved affirmatively to him. Below again, Mack told Johnny to make sure the fuel pumps were full, then start the engines. The starter motors labored, but in a moment both engines were filling the engine room with their reassuring racket.

Mack and Johnny grinned at each other. "Watch that ammeter," yelled Mack. "I don't want to risk starting the generator until we're in our berth."

Mack shook his head as he went back up on deck, joining Gus and Buck. Gus was on the ship-to-shore telephone, reporting the incident to District Headquarters. When he hung up, he asked Mack, "Can we make it back home on those batteries?"

Mack nodded. "Long as the cook doesn't plug in the coffee pot," he said, laughing.

The bos'n handed the rescue report to Gus, who scanned it quickly then signed it. "Let 'em know at District that we completed our mission," the skipper said, heading down the ladder for a cup of cold coffee.

Fourteen – Greenwich Village

Mack and Johnny settled into their seats just as the train began to move. Johnny pulled a newspaper out of his jacket pocket. "Village Voice," he said, opening the paper. "Look—here's all the music clubs."

"The girls'll guide us to the best places."

"It's like all the big groups are breaking up." Johnny frowned, leafing through the newspaper. "Peter, Paul and Mary, Simon and Garfunkel ..."

"The Beatles. The Mamas and the Papas."

"Yeah. Wonder why that happens."

"Show business," said Mack. "Everybody gets their own ideas about what they want to do."

Johnny was quiet, reading the newspaper.

Mack looked at him. "You want to get into all that?"

"You mean, play professionally?" Johnny grinned. "It'll never happen. I just want to play my guitar."

"Stay in the Coast Guard?"

The young man looked down thoughtfully. "I don't know," he said finally.

"You got four years to think about it."

"Three and a half." Johnny looked up at him. "You in it for good?"

"It's a good life."

"I don't want to go to 'Nam."

"You won't. It's over there." Then Mack added, "For us, anyway." He hoped that was true.

For most of the trip south, they stared out the window at the passing scenery. Mack thought about Claudia and Patty; Johnny thought of coffee houses in Greenwich Village filled with the heady odor of pot smoke.

Mack realized that this trip was going to be expensive for him. He would obviously pick up the cost of whatever and wherever they went, including for Johnny, who likely had no idea of how much an evening in Greenwich Village would cost; he was young, he was from the Midwest, and he hadn't been in the Coast Guard long enough to accumulate any savings. Mack had been in that situation himself, ten years before.

Claudia and Patty were not living in rent-controlled quarters, so they probably had more money than he. As "liberated" as they seemed, they were undoubtedly accustomed to having their escorts pay the expenses of nights on the town. Claudia had made a faint effort to refuse the cost of the symphony ticket that Mack had thrust into her hand but she finally accepted it.

Still, Mack watched his expenses. He'd grown up in a home where change was counted at the grocery store. Knowing he'd never get rich in the service didn't bother him. Some of his service friends seemed to have a lot more money than he had, some of them driving late-model cars and renting expensive hotel rooms for their one-night stands. But he was usually satisfied with what assets he had.

When they arrived at the apartment, they were buzzed up immediately and, as before, Patty greeted them at the door wearing a tie-dyed peasant blouse and full skirt. She hugged and kissed both men. Claudia was slightly more reserved, both in dress and behavior, offering her cheek and her hand.

Johnny was impressed. Mack smiled at Claudia when the younger man stammered a greeting and seemed not to know what to do with his hands. She winked back at him. He recognized music by the Lettermen playing softly on the stereo.

"Come sit by me," said Patty, reaching for Johnny and taking his hand. "You're only the second sailor I've known!"

"What do you want to drink?" Claudia started for the kitchen, then paused and looked at the others. "Vodka and lime for you, Mack?"

Mack nodded, and Johnny started to say something and stopped.

Patty put a hand on Johnny's arm. "Drinking age in New York is eighteen—you *are* eighteen, aren't you?"

Johnny blushed, and Claudia chided her sister. "Don't be rude, Love," she said. "Johnny, you can have anything you want, unless your superior officer has an objection."

Mack laughed. "I think if he's old enough to die for his country he's old enough to drink."

"Do you have beer?" Johnny asked.

"Johnny," Mack said, "as far as I know, you're old enough. If you're not, don't tell me, okay?" He followed Claudia into the kitchen, feeling a very small tug in his gut thinking of Patty and Johnny sitting together on the sofa.

Claudia smiled at him, saying nothing.

"I'm not used to being responsible for someone else," Mack said.

"He's a nice chap."

"He just bought a guitar. This trip to the Village is a big thing for him."

She set out glasses and put ice in them. Pointing to a cabinet, she said "Vodka's in there. We only have Heineken's beer."

Mack went to the doorway. "You drink Heineken's?"

Johnny turned and looked at him. "Beer?"

He laughed. "Yes."

"Sure."

Moving toward the refrigerator, he caught Claudia observing him, a slight smile on her face.

Mack blushed. "Am I that obvious?"

Her expression changed. "Be careful, Mack," she said softly. "Patty is a free spirit."

He took a deep breath. Grinning, he picked up two drinks and went into the living room. Bob Dylan was singing on the stereo.

"Johnny plays the guitar!" Patty exclaimed.

"Can't really play yet," mumbled Johnny.

Claudia joined them with the other drinks. "I think we should toast the United States Coast Guard."

The four of them raised their glasses.

"May you protect our shores," Patty said, "and stay away from Southeast Asia!"

The atmosphere was relaxed and jovial. The women seemed at ease and enjoying the company, and Johnny was obviously enchanted with them. They each had another drink before going out for dinner and a tour of the Village. In the cab, Mack sat in the front seat, leaving Johnny squeezed delightfully between the two women.

None of them wanted to waste time in a fancy restaurant, intent upon visiting as many music venues as possible. They ate quickly in a homey-looking place, pouring over a map that Claudia produced from her purse. All the clubs were crowded with people. Patty clung to Johnny's arm the whole evening. He seemed to bask in the attention.

Many of the coffee houses didn't serve alcohol, but enough did that the party quickly became very relaxed. Mack stopped drinking when he began to realize that he was the only one feeling the need for some kind of restraint. Being more sober than the others left him conscious of his own unease watching Patty and Johnny interact. He wasn't enjoying the music as much as the others.

By midnight, the others agreed with him that they should call it a night and go back to the apartment. At one point in the cab trip, he turned just in time to see Patty and Johnny kissing. Claudia was lying back with her eyes closed. Jealousy flooded his body. At the end of the ride, he helped the others out of the cab and paid the driver, feeling resentment and anger.

Upstairs, they all flopped down on the furniture, exhausted and drunk. All except Mack. He offered to make coffee, but no one else was interested. Instead, Patty asked for "just a thimble of Cognac."

As he poured the drink for her in the kitchen, Mack tried to regain his composure. Claudia came out and touched his arm. "Are you okay?" she asked.

He mumbled something about "a long evening."

"I'm sorry, Mack."

He turned to look at her.

"She's not domesticated."

He managed a wry smile.

"Don't blame her. She's still that girl we both love." She took the glass of liquor from the counter. "I'll take it in. You sit here and breathe for a minute. She held his eye. "Okay?"

Feeling chided, on top of his jealousy, Mack drew a glass of water and sat down. He knew he needed to control his feelings, or the rest of the weekend was going to be ruined.

Claudia came back into the kitchen. "Talk to me, Mack," she said quietly, taking the other chair.

"I feel like a teen aged kid."

"We all have that in us."

"I know I don't own her," he said, distractedly moving the glass around on the table.

"It's just her being Patty."

He put a hand on hers. "You don't have to tell me."

"I'm sorry. I can see that you're hurt, and I want to make it better."

Close to tears, he closed his eyes. Some quiet music began in the other room. He sighed. "Thank you, Claudia."

She took his hand in both of hers. "I get jealous of her, too. Sometimes I can't stand her behavior. She's just so charming, men eat her up."

He managed a smile. "Yeah, I know."

"We can sit out here and talk, and not watch them."

They were quiet for a few minutes. The romantic music from the living room intensified the conflict in him.

Then he sighed deeply, and looked at Claudia, who was watching him closely. "You are something else," he said.

She smiled and cocked her head. "Tell me."

"I don't pay enough attention to you." He squeezed her hand.

She looked down at her other hand, lying in her lap. "I don't want your pity."

"That wasn't pity."

She looked up at him, her face serious. "And I don't want to be second choice."

His agitation was softening. "Ever since that first time you and I had dinner together in George Town, I've thought about you. You're not second choice."

"What am I, Mack?"

"There's something about you that touches me here." He gestured toward his chest. "I want to know you better."

Her eyes glistened, but she said nothing.

They sat in silence for a long time. Finally, Claudia said, "I think the children are asleep."

He snorted in amusement.

"Let me look." She got up and peered into the living room. Turning to him again, she said softly, "Like babies."

They smiled at each other.

Claudia reached a hand toward him silently, and led him into her bedroom.

Mack woke to a sound, and at first didn't know where he was. Lying in bed, he watched a light spot high on the wall, a reflection from sunlight on something in the room

No one was in the bed with him. The sound of water running came from the bathroom,. He remembered last night, without the desperate feeling he'd had then in the pit of his stomach.

Part of him wanted to confront the situation, to face the others and demand—at least—clarification. But the impetus wasn't there. It was as though he were remembering a movie, calmly trying to analyze what had happened and what it meant for the future. He didn't feel anything, and wondered why.

He remembered entering Claudia's bed, and feeling her arms holding him closely, and wiping a tear from her cheek. They hadn't made love, but simply lay entwined until sleep erased everything. He wondered without emotion where Patty and Johnny were at that moment. There were no other sounds in the apartment. He waited.

Claudia emerged from the bathroom wearing a robe. She smiled at him. Kneeling on the bed beside him, she said softly, "The others are still asleep. I'll make coffee for us." Then she left, trailing a soft scent.

Mack went into the bathroom—a familiar place, but somehow different from his earlier experiences of it. He knew where the towels were kept, and how to get the right temperature from the shower. He had entered it before from Patty's room.

Under the hot spray, he remembered Claudia's words, "She's still that girl we both love."

No, he thought, *she's not. She's a stranger now. I don't know how to think about her.*

Anger—the anger he'd felt last night—wasn't there. He felt strangely detached from that whole experience. Even Claudia, who had been so warm and comforting, so understanding, felt now like someone else, not a stranger like Patty but less familiar to him.

He dressed and went into the kitchen, deliberately avoiding looking into the living room where he had last seen Patty and Johnny lying together on the sofa. They wouldn't likely still be there anyway, he decided, but he didn't want to see.

Claudia smiled warmly and kissed him quickly. "I'm fixing waffles," she said, "and we can go ahead and eat, since they're best right out of the griddle. There's coffee." She pointed at the pot that was filling the room with its rich aroma.

He sat with his cup, watching her work. Neither spoke. When the sweet scent of the waffle reached its peak, she expertly extracted it, laid it on his plate and cut it in two, taking half to her own plate. Warm maple syrup came from the large Amana Radarange.

The two sat opposite each other at the table, smiling together, eating silently. Mack shook his head slowly, still holding her eyes.

"Tell me," she said softly.

"Sibelius." When she cocked her head in question, he said, "That dinner we had together, just the two of us."

"And then you told me you were leaving." She was still smiling. "I'm teasing, Mack."

He laughed. "You were really mad."

"Anger covered up the hurt."

"Still mad?" He caught himself. "Still hurt?"

"At you? No. You came back, didn't you?"

"Thank you for last night."

She speared a bite of waffle and reached it across the table toward his open mouth.

Chewing slowly, he said, "You feed me here," and pointed to his heart.

When they heard sounds coming from the bathroom, Claudia stood and moved to the waffle iron. "Better have another before they get here. Patty is a glutton for waffles."

They were eating their second waffle when the other two entered together, smiling sheepishly. Johnny's hair, short as it was, showed he had just gotten out of bed.

"I smell waffles!" exclaimed Patty, going directly to the griddle. She turned her head quickly toward the others and smiled.

"Another one will be done in a minute," said Claudia. "Johnny, help yourself to coffee. Cream's on the table."

Neither Mack nor Johnny had spoken.

"Mmm," said Patty. "I love your waffles." She took two cups from the cupboard and poured coffee for herself and Johnny.

Johnny, obviously ill at ease, took a cup from her and sat at the table. Mack avoided looking at him.

As waffles came out of the griddle, the four of them sat and ate. Patty smiled sweetly at Mack. "We heard some great music last night," she said.

"We did," he agreed. He couldn't help but return her smile.

"Too bad James Taylor was sold out," Claudia added. "He's one of my favorites."

"Joan Baez was down there last week," said Patty between mouthfuls.

"Johnny, who's your favorite?" Claudia asked.
"Bob Dylan."
"Wish he'd been playing last night."
"He's out on tour, isn't he?" asked Mack.

The two men were at least speaking. Mack decided that his previous night's difficulties would best be discussed after he and Johnny were on their way back to New London. He wasn't sure how much Johnny knew about his relationship with Patty, and he could give him the benefit of the doubt. Besides, he knew how seductive Patty could be.

The conversation remained about music and the night's festivities, and eventually the atmosphere softened. Patty acted as though what happened was of little importance. Mack and Claudia exchanged occasional glances.

Settled in their seats on the train, Mack and Johnny continued to talk about Greenwich Village. "Thank you," Johnny said, "that was a great evening."

Mack was no longer angry. He felt a tinge of something not quite identified when Patty's name came up.

"That blind girl is the sexiest gal I have ever met," Johnny said.

"She did take a liking to you."

"I wasn't sure what to do, when we got back to their apartment, but it looked like you and Claudia kinda hooked up together, so I figured it was okay."

"Like that Simon and Garfunkel song goes, "'Girl does what she wants to do, and I know I'm fakin' it.'" Mack half-sang the lyric from the song.

Johnny laughed. "Don't she."

They were quiet for a while, and Mack relaxed more. He guessed that Johnny didn't have any idea how tense

Mack was the evening before. "I think I'm in love with both of them."

Johnny laughed. "I won't ask."

The conversation went back to music and The Village.

Fifteen – Train to New York

"You have a week off?" asked Patty when Mack called from New London.

"Our boat is officially out of service," he said, "but we can't get her into the shipyard for them to repair the electrical system for a week. So I took some leave. The crew doesn't have much to do. I left Johnny in charge of the engine room."

"What are you going to do?"

"I don't know. Maybe go back home for a few days."

"Why don't you come down and stay with us?"

"Could you put up with me for a week?"

"Silly! Of course. You can come and go as you want. We have a few things planned that you probably wouldn't be interested in, but you can shift for yourself—and we'd love to have your company!"

It was tempting. He had considered going down to New York for a day or so, and was hoping he could see her and Claudia. But he still had some uncomfortable feelings from the Greenwich Village incident. "I don't know," he said.

"Do come!"

"Can I talk with Claudia first?"

He heard her cover the mouthpiece, and then Claudia came on the line. "Mack, I would love to have you here for more than one evening."

Claudia's voice was warm and almost intimate. Mack's reservation melted. "Okay, for a few days, anyway."

On the train to New York, he took stock of his feelings. Patty seemed different, somehow, inside his head. He could admit to himself that she didn't belong to him; she was an independent person with the right to choose whom she went to bed with. To him she now felt a little bit like all the one-night stands he'd known since joining the Coast Guard. No, he decided, there was more to their relationship than that. She was open and honest like no woman he'd ever known before. Truly, a *flower child*, like the girls he'd read about in San Francisco, freely giving of their bodies and their affection, never demanding anything in return other than respect and the kind of caring that comes from intimacy.

Until now, he himself hadn't been that generous. He wondered if he could be.

It's not that Patty was insensitive to other people. Her perceptiveness was amazing to him, considering that she was blind. In her inebriation the night of their Village adventure, she didn't appear to know how hurt he had been. Indeed, part of his distress had been from recognizing the enthusiasm that she'd expressed with Johnny—exactly as she had been with him that first day in Grand Cayman.

He felt old, thinking about Patty and Johnny together. Old and traditional. The Hippies were a different sort. Even though Patty had not abandoned all her cultural privileges and gone hitch-hiking to California, accepting the dole from the Diggers and other benefactors, she could let go of her inhibitions (if she had any to begin with) and be vulnerable—and available.

Claudia, of course, was the responsible one. She had to be; she'd had to be for most of her life, watching over her sister, worrying, he supposed, like a mother would. Patty's spirit could be free only because Claudia's was not.

And that, he thought, might be what he was attracted to in the older woman. He could trust her, somehow, in a way that eluded him with Patty. She was the deep one—her intensity came out of those depths, an emotional familiarity with suffering.

He laughed at the thought of Claudia being "the older woman." *She's only a few years older than Patty, and still years younger than I am!*

He remembered Julie, his first love, patiently waiting for him to grow up and take charge of his life, then finally letting go. She had wanted him to realize his potential, whatever that was, but she knew her own path and thought that he should know his own.

Claudia seemed not to have any of that imperative, even with her blind sister. For so many years she had stifled her own desires in her sensed responsibility for Patty's welfare. Like the owner of a pet animal, not expecting conformity to her own values but paying attention to the needs of a fellow creature. Perhaps, he wondered, Patty had become Claudia's alter ego, the person she was inside, the perpetual child.

As he mulled through these thoughts, he recognized that all those characteristics were inside him, as well, both Patty's and Claudia's. As chief engineer on his boat, he had responsibility not only for the equipment in his care but for Johnny and the other young aspirants to the job. He had gone in this professional direction because he loved engines and machinery. He could tend them and repair them and feel satisfaction when they performed as they were designed to do. It was harder with his firemen; humans were less predictable, and he felt less competent as a supervisor. One can't have dirty fingernails in dealing with people. One has to be an example. Even in training an animal, one has to act confidently and surely.

Mack felt embarrassed thinking about his breaking down in the kitchen after the Village tour. He'd been helpless in the face of his own impulses. Only Claudia saw it; only Claudia had the presence to help him. She'd had years of experience.

He felt a sudden desire for Claudia.

Sixteen – New York, Again

Unexpectedly, it was Claudia's voice that answered the intercom. She immediately buzzed him through, and met him at the open door to their apartment. She kissed him and held him tightly for a moment.

Patty was out somewhere, she said, "probably shopping." Mack and Claudia settled at once on the sofa with white wine. "I don't often get you to myself," she laughed, and kissed him again.

"I want to take you two out for dinner," he said, "but I think you know all the good places and so you have to choose where we go."

"Actually," Claudia chuckled, "Patty is shopping for groceries—we want to eat in tonight." She waved a hand in a gesture of frustration. "Restaurants are so noisy!"

He smiled. "You always feed me so well."

Her eyebrow went up. "I remember you using those words the last time you were here."

"Slightly different circumstances, but the meaning is the same."

"Mack, that's a two-way thing. With you, I feel cared for—I feel *known*." She grinned at him over her drink. "Even when you are engrossed in Patty."

"I told Johnny on the train going home that I think I'm in love with both of you."

Claudia, her eyes serious, gazed steadily at him across the top of the glass that she held with both hands. Then she murmured, "I guess I'll take what I can get."

He took the glass from her hands and set it on the table. Then he pulled her to him and kissed her lingeringly.

The clung to each other for a long time, until they heard Patty's key opening the door.

"Oh, my goodness!" Patty exclaimed, standing with her cane in one hand and a large bag of groceries. "Have you two finally discovered sex?"

Mack felt embarrassed. Claudia laughed. "You don't know what we're doing!"

"Oh, yes I do. I can smell sex."

"Bull-oni. You're good, but you're guessing wrong."

Patty moved into the kitchen and put the bag of groceries on the table. Turning toward them, she laughed. "Actually, I could hear you coming apart."

"Coming apart?" Claudia asked.

"You know what I mean. I could hear you moving. And your scent, Claudia—it gives you away."

Mack looked at Claudia, who had a slight smile on her face. "She can pick me out of a crowd," she said softly.

A little relieved, Mack smiled. "Could you tell it was me?"

"Of course. Claudia, would you be a sweetie and fix me a martini? I'm exhausted!"

They all went to the kitchen, and soon returned with drinks. Patty set her glass on the coffee table and extended a hand toward Mack. "Come sit by me."

Claudia nudged his arm in Patty's direction. Then she sat opposite them. "Mack, I planned to make a simple risotto, mushrooms and sausage and other stuff. Okay?

"She makes a great risotto," Patty said, squeezing Mack's hand. "All I can do is warm up leftovers."

"You two make a good team." He glanced at Claudia as a flicker of annoyance crossed her face, and he regretted his remark. "Can I help?" he offered.

Claudia smiled. "Let's have our drinks first."

"Everything in our freezer is labeled," Patty said, squeezing his hand again. When he looked at her, she said, "You saw our braille machine, didn't you?"

"No."

"Oh, I have to demonstrate it for you!" She stood up and held out her hand to him.

"Come on, Love!" Claudia said, her voice carrying a tinge of irritation. "There's time for that later!"

Her sister sat back down, chastened.

They sipped their drinks in silence. Claudia and Mack exchanged understanding glances.

Finally, Patty asked, "Your boat is in drydock?"

He nodded. "Yes—or it will be as soon as there's space for it."

The subdued conversation continued for a few minutes, until Claudia drained her glass and stood up. "Want to make a salad?" she asked Mack.

"Sure."

Over dinner and wine, they all relaxed. Mack watched the women, marveling at their seemingly easy accommodation to their circumstances.

"I don't think of myself as blind," Patty said, "except when someone reminds me, or when I can't do something like put on makeup." She turned toward Claudia. "My ever-patient sister watches over me, and I'm afraid I've gotten too used to it. I should learn to be more independent."

"I see you as really independent," said Mack, chuckling. "I'm amazed at how much you can do!"

Claudia smiled wryly. "At times she tries to do too much, and I have to bail her out."

"Sometimes we go to weekend retreats, where people try to overcome their resistance to living fully." Patty laughed. "That sounds pretentious, doesn't it?"

"I don't know what it means."

Claudia spoke up. "A couple of years ago we were at Esalen Institute, out in Big Sur—" When Mack looked puzzled, she added, "in California? They teach you to explore your deeper self, to be a more authentic human being. It's a big hippie thing."

Mack shook his head. "Uh, what is a more *authentic* human being?"

"More trusting, for one thing," said Patty. She laughed again, and the lilt in her voice reminded Mack how much he enjoyed her. "Like—one of the exercises is for two people to walk together, with one of them blindfolded, trusting the other person to guide them and protect them. Soon they're running arm-in-arm along those curving paths!"

"Patty, that's easy for you," put in Claudia. "You've been trusting people all your life."

"I wanted to be the trust guide sometime, but they wouldn't let me."

"Well, lots of people there were inspired by you."

Mack grinned. "Were you two hippies?"

Claudia laughed. "We didn't have the nerve. We're pretty traditional."

"Not from where I'm standing."

"I think Patty would be right at home in the Haight-Ashbury in San Francisco," Claudia said. "I get scared for her sometimes."

Patty smiled. "We went to see the musical *Hair* just before it closed here last year. I got really turned on. It was so exciting! I kept wishing I could be up on the stage with them just to be part of that!"

Claudia laughed again. "Actually, at the end of the show they invited the audience to come up on the stage and meet the cast—the 'Tribe', they called them—but I was afraid for Patty. It was too crowded."

"I don't understand nudity," said Patty. "I do, but I don't. I don't remember ever seeing anything, although Claudia says I lost my sight when I was three or four. It's a mystery to me. What's it like, to *see* another person?"

Claudia smiled at Mack. "She's been asking me that same question all our lives."

"Mack," said Patty, "How would you describe it?" Her face was serious.

Mack fumbled for a way to answer. "I don't know. I've seen you *sense* things that I couldn't understand, either."

"She hears a lot more than other people do," said Claudia.

Mack was feeling the liquor, and he struggled to speak clearly. "When I touch you, I can *feel* what you look like."

Tears ran from Patty's closed eyes. She didn't say anything, and Mack felt her sadness. He touched her cheek, gently wiping a tear away with his thumb. Patty grabbed his hand and held it to her face. He glanced at Claudia, who looked as though she, too, might cry.

"I'm sorry," he said. "My hands are pretty rough from working on machinery."

"I love the way they feel on my face."

The three of them sat silently for a long moment. Then Patty spoke, so softly Mack had to strain to hear. "In the land of the blind, the one-eyed man is king. Someone said that a long time ago."

"Erasmus," said Claudia.

"In the land of the—" began Mack. "In the land of the visible, you are the queen."

Patty laughed, and then her expression changed. She shook her head.

"Love," said Claudia, "he means that you have a lot more sensitivity without your sight than the rest of us do with it."

Patty sighed deeply. "I think I can see the sunlight, but the doctors say that it's just the warmth that I feel on my eyelids."

The conversation was subdued, with long silences. Then Claudia said, "Why don't we go into the other room? These chairs are not very comfortable."

As they rose, Patty put a hand on Claudia's arm. "Would you two do something for me?" The plaintive sound of her voice nearly broke Mack's heart.

"Of course, Love." Claudia looked at Mack.

"I feel," she began hesitantly, "like one of the big things I miss without sight is what people look like. Mack said once that he missed seeing my eyes so that he could tell how I was responding to him. Well, that goes both ways—I know from how people talk that bodies are all different, and people get a lot out of seeing that difference. I can tell, of course, that that's true, because I've touched different people." She made a little gesture of frustration, and almost whispered, "Could I touch you both? I mean together. Could we take off our clothes so I can feel us? All of us?"

Mack looked at Claudia, who nodded. Then he said, "Sure, Patty. I'd like that." Inside, however, he felt apprehensive.

Patty smiled. "I know, I've touched you both. But I want to see what the differences are. Is that weird?"

"No, Love." Claudia took her sister's hand and led her to the bedroom. Mack followed, uncertainly.

In the next hour, Mack experienced overwhelming tenderness toward both women. While sexual excitement was part of it, he avoided those impulses and allowed hands to touch and caress his body, and reciprocated in kind. Patty seemed to go into a different state as she touched the bodies of the other two, seeming to explore deeply enough to try to capture the sight that she had never had. He noticed that her touch was not like that of others who had touched him. She didn't go directly to his erogenous areas, but scanned his body as she would a statue.

At one point, she said simply, "Like braille."

Claudia's touch was different. Mack glanced at her as she ran her fingers over his body. Her face carried an intensity that he had never seen.

Then suddenly, Claudia got out of bed and went into the bathroom.

"Come back!" Patty cried. She held Mack to her with both arms. "Don't leave!" she said softly.

"I'm here."

They lay together quietly, feeling each other's warmth. Then Patty whispered, "I want you. Do you want me?"

He embraced her tightly. "Yes, but I don't think it would be fair to Claudia right now."

"Later," she promised.

In a little while, Claudia came back to the bed. Guiltily, Mack rolled away to hide his erection from her.

"I'm sorry," said Claudia softly, sitting on the side of the bed. "It's too much for me."

"Tell me, Love," said Patty.

Claudia smiled. "Mack knows—don't you, Mack?"

"Remember the time I told you that I get uneasy being with both of you at the same time?"

"Yes," answered Patty.

"Is it like that?" he asked Claudia.

"I feel left out—I don't mean deliberately."

Patty sighed. "But an orgy sounds like such fun!"

Claudia stood up and began dressing. "Maybe some day."

Mack felt relieved. Patty seemed disappointed. "All right, Love," she said. They all dressed and returned to the living room.

"Who wants something to drink?" asked Claudia, moving into the kitchen. Mack followed her.

She moved close to him and whispered, "I don't want to share you that way."

Mack kissed her gently on the cheek. "No."

"I was ready to scream."

"I'm sorry."

"No! I just couldn't take any more, being that close to you without making love to you."

Even though they were whispering, when they returned to the living room with drinks, Patty's face told them that she had heard everything.

They sat in silence for a while, then Patty said, "I don't own you, Mack."

"I know," he said. "I don't own you, either, just because we've made love. But it's such a personal thing for me. Last week I was so jealous I couldn't stand it. But I got over it." He shrugged and laughed in a self-deprecating way.

Patty smiled. "Thank you—both of you—for indulging me. It wasn't a sexual thing—not at first, anyway—I just wanted to try to imagine what it's like to *see*."

"We know that, Patty," Claudia said. "I hope you got what you were looking for."

Patty reached a hand across the coffee table, and Claudia met it with her own.

When she sat back on the sofa, Patty said, "The differences between your bodies are more than I expected, though. I knew—but I didn't know."

Claudia and Mack both laughed. "The differences, Love, are crucial," answered Claudia.

Patty joined in the laughter. Then she began to cry. "Sometimes," she managed between sobs, "I feel like I'm locked in a room, and everybody else is out there—" She gestured broadly. "—and I can't be with them."

She wiped her cheeks with a hand. "Our little *touch fest*—" and she giggled, "was wonderful. And yet it just emphasized that wall around me!"

Mack handed her a tissue. "Patty," he said, "you taught me a lot in there. You teach me all the time, things that I didn't know I didn't know."

As he spoke, Mack was aware of other feelings that he couldn't say at that moment: He had become keenly aroused by Patty while lying with her on the bed, and although he had assured her that it wouldn't be fair to Claudia to act on it, his desire for her was even now clouding his judgment. It was difficult for him to pay attention to what she was going through at the moment, as much as he cared for her. His thoughts kept going back to the feel of her body next to his.

He glanced at Claudia, and wondered if she could detect what he was feeling. If he had been alone with either one of them, he knew he wouldn't be able to resist moving on his feelings.

Claudia stood up and went around the coffee table to the sofa. "Move over. I want to sit next to Patty." She gestured to indicate that she wanted to sit on the other side of her sister.

The two women embraced, holding each other for a long time. Mack, feeling relieved from the responsibility for Patty's distress, slumped back. Shame swallowed his desire. After a moment, he went into the bathroom to give the others some privacy. He wished that he could return to his boat.

As his hormonal urges quieted, he thought about the power of those feelings. In the past he'd lost some dear friendships because of them. In their grip, he sometimes felt helpless to control them.

Once, while standing watch on board a Coast Guard ship with an older man in the middle of the night, they'd engaged in a rare conversation about sex. The old seaman was near retirement, and Mack admired his quiet acceptance of ageing.

"One of the things I don't miss," the old fellow had admitted, "is that physical urgency, the way those feelings controlled me when I was young."

At the time, Mack didn't understand. He thought of sex as he thought of a rich dessert, something one yearned for and delighted in whenever it was available. Its attraction was a mystery to him but he never avoided the feelings. Still, there was something raw about it, something not respectable. Being rejected by a woman was devastating because he felt accused of being some kind of shameful brute.

It was rare, in his experience, to encounter a woman as openly and as cheerfully sexual as Patty. Even the prostitutes that he'd met seemed to treat sex with a seriousness that he found off-putting. Patty treated it as play—a tender, innocent kind of play.

It seemed to him that to Claudia sex was indeed serious, a deep and important engagement between two people. She seemed to accept Patty's playfulness as she might accept that of a beloved puppy. Amusing, but ...

Feeling thoroughly subdued, he returned to the living room, to find Claudia and Patty quietly sitting together, holding hands. They both turned toward him as he entered.

Claudia's voice was low. "Are you okay, Mack?"

"Yeah," he answered. He sat across the coffee table from them.

"You don't sound okay," said Patty.

"It's been a pretty intense evening. Brought up some old stuff for me."

"Want to talk about it?"

He shook his head. "Some other time."

Claudia pointed to his glass and smiled at him. "You've barely touched your drink."

"Sometimes alcohol isn't the best thing for me."

Patty sat upright. "You know what I'd like?"

Mack and Claudia looked quickly at her, expecting some more intensity.

She grinned. "Ice cream! I want some of that French Silk ice cream that's in the freezer!"

Claudia laughed, and Mack stood up. "I'll get it."

As he went into the kitchen, Claudia called to him, "The scoop is in the right-hand drawer."

Dishing out ice cream eased the tension Mack felt. He smiled to himself.

"Put just a dab of chocolate syrup on mine," Patty called.

"Not on mine," said Claudia.

When he returned to the living room with the desserts, everyone was smiling again.

Comfortable conversation filled the rest of the evening, until Patty began to yawn. They arranged the sofa for Mack, and all retired, Mack was relieved that the tension was gone, and soon fell asleep.

He awoke in the darkness some time later to find soft lips pressed against his. He recognized Claudia's scent, and recalled Patty's remark about that as she stood in the doorway with the bag of groceries in her arms.

Silently, Claudia took his hand and led him into her bedroom, where they made love for the first time. For Mack, it was a perfect experience. The sweetness of their joining fulfilled his fantasies about this deep and serious woman, and afterward they lay entwined for a long time, until he sensed that she had fallen asleep.

Mack gently disengaged from her and returned to the sofa, where he also drifted off.

The next day, nothing was spoken about the evening before, although Mack and Claudia exchanged occasional looks. Patty was in good spirits, and the three of them went out to brunch at a favorite neighborhood restaurant.

The weather was mild in New York City, and the scent of flowers spilled from the lamppost planters. After eating, they joined hands and strolled to Central Park along with hundreds of others celebrating spring.

Patty turned her face to the sun like a flower, smiling and breathing deeply. Mack, conscious of the two small, soft hands grasping his, mimicked Patty's gesture. Claudia squeezed his hand.

The next few days were blissful for Mack. He and the sisters hung around their apartment, went for walks, sat and listened to music—Patty got out their album of the Broadway Cast performing the music from *Hair*—and they had long discussions of the changes that seemed to be happening in the culture.

"It's the children," Patty exclaimed, "they're our hope in the world! It really is the Age of Aquarius, and only the young people see it!"

"I don't know," said Mack. "It's one thing for young girls to stuff flowers into soldiers' rifles, but it's a lot harder to negotiate between governments. President Nixon has at least gotten North Viet Nam to agree to an end to the fighting."

"It's the moral cost that gets to me," said Claudia. "Politicians can't be trusted anymore. Our military leaders keep saying they're winning, but still our soldiers are coming home in body bags."

"They caught those burglars in the Watergate building, spying on the Democrats!" Patty's face was getting red. "I don't trust Nixon!"

Mack took a deep breath. "I don't know how to make the world a better place. Those songs we just heard feel true to me, but I don't know what I can do about it all. I can't even control my own little world."

"You're right," said Claudia, smiling at Mack. "There's so much that's wrong in the world, so much hatred and hurt. But I have to feel that love is the answer, somehow. I just don't know how to make it happen."

Patty put her hand on Claudia. "You do make it happen, Love. You make me love you!"

Mack laughed. "You two sure have enough love to remind me how I want to be."

Patty went to the stereo and extracted an album from the cabinet. Showing it to Claudia, she asked, "Is this it?"

Claudia smiled. "Yes. Play that."

The track "What the World Needs Now is Love/Abraham, Martin and John" came from the speakers. Patty handed the record jacket to Mack.

"I think I've heard this," said Mack, when the track ended and Patty lifted the needle. "I don't know who Tom Clay is."

"It gets to me," said Patty, "Just like the songs in *Hair*."

"He's a D.J. in Los Angeles," added Claudia. He just made the song from what he heard on the air."

Patty switched off the stereo, and the three of them sat in silence for a while.

"Mack is leaving tomorrow," Claudia said finally. "Can we think about something else?"

Of course we can, Love," answered Patty. "We've been saving that wonderful bottle of Austrian wine Michael Douglas gave us for a special occasion. Let's celebrate Mack Jensen!"

After dinner and several nightcaps, they retired to their respective beds.

During the night, Mack was again awakened. This time it was Patty, but the result was the same.

Until the next morning.

Emerging from his shower, Mack could tell that things were not right. Claudia was in the kitchen preparing breakfast, but she was not singing. She offered only her cheek to his morning kiss.

Patty breezed in as usual, then stopped at the kitchen door. "What's wrong?" she asked, reaching out her hand. Claudia was busy at the stove, and Mack thought better about taking Patty's hand in that moment. She let it drop, and stood quietly.

Mack silently prepared the coffee pot, feeling as though his life was suddenly changed. Shame gripped his midsection.

No one spoke through the entire meal. Finally, Mack couldn't stand the tension any longer. "I'm sorry, Claudia," he murmured. She simply looked at him, her eyes rimmed with red.

"Neither of us owns him," Patty said.

"I know." Claudia's words barely came out in a hoarse whisper.

A longer silence followed. Mack stood and poured coffee, then sat down again.

Claudia looked from one to the other, then said to Mack, "I can't share you, not like that."

He looked down at his coffee cup. "I know that."

"Love—" began Patty.

"Don't call me that!" Claudia voice rose. "You're not my love, not at this moment!"

"I didn't think you would care that much," said Patty. "I didn't mind when you two, the other night, when you made love in the night."

"I'm not like you!" Claudia almost screamed it.

Mack turned to Patty. "You knew about that? You didn't say anything." He was aware that his breakfast was not digesting very well.

"Of course I knew it. I *wanted* you to do it! I wouldn't have mentioned it unless you had, but I felt good about it."

Mack suddenly wanted to cry. He got up from his chair and retreated to the bathroom. Just as he reached it, nausea overcame him. He managed to close the door before kneeling at the toilet.

Faintly, he heard the words, "I HATE YOU!" coming from the kitchen. He thought about dying.

A long time later, he found the two women, still silent, sitting at the kitchen table. He touched them both gently on a shoulder, then sat down.

As they sat there, Mack thought about what the old sailor had told him, that midnight watch on the buoy tender, "One of the things I don't miss," the old fellow had admitted, "the way those feelings controlled me when I was young." Mack now knew what he meant.

After a while, Patty began to sing, very softly, "What the world needs now, is love, sweet love ..."

Mack glanced at Claudia. The corner of her mouth twitched.

Patty was smiling.

It was still long minutes before they began to talk again. Mack repeated his apology to Claudia.

She looked directly at him. "I thought you were different."

He laid his head down on his arms. There was nothing more to say.

"You know he loves you," Patty said gently to her sister. "More than me."

Mack raised his head and faced Patty. "No," he said. "I love both of you, but differently. I don't know what to do with that."

"It's not fair," Patty said to Claudia. "It's not his fault."

"I know," Claudia answered. "I just can't deal with it."

Patty spread her hands, palms up, on the table. "All right." She sighed. "He's yours."

A part of Mack was relieved. He couldn't have proposed that himself, because he didn't want to hurt Patty. But he was becoming clear that his relationship with Claudia was the more important one to him.

He wasn't sure why that was. Patty was like fresh air in his life, playful, spontaneous, *innocent*—that gave him simple joy in the physical part of himself that he'd never experienced before. He loved her for that.

Claudia meant something different to him. Sex was secondary. But just looking at her, just thinking about her, filled his heart like no woman had ever done. He could not bear to have her withdraw from him.

Claudia looked steadily at her sister. "I don't hate you, Patty," she said quietly. "I'd as easily hate myself—maybe I do."

"Don't!" cried Patty. She began to cry.

Mack took a deep breath. He reached his hands out, one toward each woman. In a moment both responded in kind. Then they grasped each other's free hand. He was conscious of stretching his arms uncomfortably across the table, but held their hands tightly. He started to speak, then stopped, his words catching in his throat.

Finally, he said, "I've said before that I'm in love with both of you. Since I've gotten to know you more, I'm even more in love."

Patty was smiling, her cheeks tear-stained. Claudia's face still held her expression of desolation.

"A big part of why I love you is the beautiful relationship that you have with each other." He nodded to Claudia. "I know it's not always easy for you."

She squeezed his hand.

"I don't want to jeopardize that relationship. It means everything to me. I'd give up sex altogether to protect it."

Nobody spoke for a long time.

Gradually they released each other. Mack's shoulder hurt from stretching his arm. Patty found a tissue and wiped her face. Claudia seemed to relax.

Mack was afraid he'd gone too far, that his words had come across as superficial and childish. He believed what he had said, but he was now wondering how the other two took it. "Maybe I should leave." He stood.

In a small voice, Patty pleaded, "Don't leave. Not like this."

"I don't want us to end it like this," Claudia said, her voice hoarse with emotion.

Patty stood and searched for Mack's hand. "Come into the other room where we can touch each other."

Mack looked at Claudia, then as she stood up he allowed himself to be led into the living room.

Patty wordlessly arranged them into a tight circle on the carpet, touching each other. She sat Buddha-like, her legs crossed, her face serene. Softly, she said, "Let's not say anything for a while."

As Mack sat there, his knees touching those of the two women, he became aware of a different side of Patty. She was not simply the grown girl, the flower child that he had perceived; she was taking on responsibility—responsibility that he felt he should assume. He'd been paralyzed by his shame.

Claudia, he understood. She had been feeling just the way he had felt the previous week, wracked by jealousy. He looked over at her.

"I'm sorry," she said softly, holding his gaze.

"You have nothing to apologize for," he answered. Turning to Patty, he said, "You don't either. I was a kid in a candy store."

Patty chuckled, but Claudia's face remained serious. She looked from Mack to Patty. "I've spoiled things for us, haven't I?"

"You have a right to your feelings, Love." Patty reached for Claudia's hand. They leaned toward each other, their heads touching gently.

A long time later, Patty said, "I have to eat something. My stomach is growling like a lion."

Mack looked at his watch. "It's one-thirty."

Slowly, the three of them rose from the floor, flexing stiff leg muscles. Mack took Patty's hand to help her to her feet. She squeezed his hand and smiled silently.

"I'll warm up the risotto from the other night," Claudia said, going into the kitchen.

They all moved slowly, as though under water. Mack went back to the bathroom and rinsed his mouth of the acid taste that still reminded him of that morning.

Seated again at the table, they ate quietly. A profound silence held them, each one trying to make sense of what had happened. Their world was different.

His week had begun on such a high note. He found it hard to remember the previous few days. He knew he had been happy—it had been a delicious time. He'd felt cared for and pampered by two beautiful women he'd grown to love. They'd laughed and kissed and teased each other. There hadn't been any love making, except those two times, but sex had made the air tingle, a promise like an approaching holiday.

But now, a leaden weight dragged at him. He tried to swallow a lump that kept creeping into his throat. The rest of the evening floated on like an ebb tide, pushing detritus up on the beach to clutter the atmosphere.

"Mack sighed. "I don't know what to say."

"I don't either," said Claudia.

"Just being still together is healing," said Patty.

At some point they went to their separate beds, physically and emotionally drained. Before retiring, Mack packed his sea bag.

Long before dawn, he wrote on a piece of paper and left it on the kitchen table, and slipped quietly out the door.

The note simply read, "Please forgive me."

Seventeen – New London

Stepping onto the platform, Mack felt disoriented. He'd been sleeping most of the way from New York, and his eyes were still clouded. He had taken the early train so he could log in on the boat before eight.

New York City had seemed strange when he had left in the dark; Penn Station was almost deserted. Few people leave the city at five in the morning, although the arriving trains dumped them out like cattle.

New London was foggy when he arrived just after dawn. It reminded him of the old London he'd read about, with horse-drawn carriages clattering along cobblestone streets in the fog. Here, the train platform was eerie, the lamps surrounded by bright balls of cotton-light that didn't even reach the ground. The air matched his mood.

He picked up his sea bag and slung it over his shoulder. He didn't see a cab, so he started walking down the street toward the base. An old pickup truck stopped alongside and a voice called, "Hey, sailor, want a lift?"

Mack poked his head into the window. "You going near the Coast Guard Station?"

"I'll drop you at the gate," the man said.

Mack threw his sea bag into the back and got into the truck. "Thanks."

Driving along the empty road, the man said, "I hear you're just back from 'Nam."

"No, just coming back from leave. My boat's been here since May."

They didn't say anything more until they reached the gate. Mack thanked the man again and extracted his bulky sea bag. He signed in at the guard house with a barely audible greeting to the guard and started down the hill toward NOIA.

But it wasn't there. In its place sat a gloomy-looking boat in battleship gray, its outlines obscured by the fog. Only the mast-head light was visible. Even the Eagle, tied up on the other side of the dock, had an ominous look to her in the morning grayness.

Mack stopped, confused. He'd been away a week, and hadn't heard anything about NOIA, simply assuming it would be in its usual berth. It was likely across the river with the submarines at the Electric Boat Company.

Not wanting to trudge back up the hill to the guard house with his heavy bag, he continued down to the mysterious boat and climbed aboard. There was a light visible through the hatch. Dropping his sea bag on the deck, he went below.

"Mornin'," said a young sailor sitting at the table with a cup of coffee and a magazine before him.

"I was expecting *my* boat to be here."

"You from the eighty-three footer?"

"Yeah."

The sailor reached his hand over the table. "Lon Gibson," he said. "Welcome to the Lieutenant Greenburg eighty-two-three-twenty-two. Grab some joe." He gestured toward the coffee pot on the stove.

"Mack Jensen. How long you been here?"

"Three days. Up from Cape May to hold your place, maybe here for permanent duty." He laughed. "They don't tell us nothin'."

Mack poured a cup of coffee and sat down. "I've been on leave while the boat is being repaired. Guess she's still across the river."

"Still foggy out?"

"Yeah."

"I hear your engine room blew up."

"No, only the main electric panel."

"Old boat."

"She's a fine ship," Mack said, aware that he sounded defensive. "Just a little accident when we were overhauling the generator." He looked around. "All wood, inside and out." He knocked on the steel bulkhead.

"What's her speed?"

"Eighteen knots."

"We needed a lot more'n that over in 'Nam."

"I don't doubt it." Mack finished his cup of coffee and stood up. "I got to go over and log in."

"Good luck."

"Yeah."

In the cab carrying him to Groton, Mack thought about the future of NOIA. *Depressing,* he thought. *She's a fine ship. Too good to end up as somebody's old yacht or fishing boat.*

The guard at Electric Boat Company checked his ID and the boat's roster and waved him through. Finding NOIA was easy—the only white thing in the whole shipyard. She was tied up in a slip, waiting, he felt, just for him. He hoped the panel repairs had all been made.

Nobody was aboard. Mack went below and threw his sea bag on his bunk. He was relieved to see a guitar lying on Jimmy's bunk. He made a pot of coffee.

"Ahoy," called a voice from the deck. "Anybody aboard?"

Mack went up the ladder to see a young sailor, his sea bag perched on his shoulder, at the gangway.

"The guard told me everybody was on liberty,"

"I guess so. I just came aboard."

The two men introduced themselves, and sat down in the galley with cups of coffee.

Claude Dansforth, the newcomer, was a seaman just out of boot camp. This was his first duty. Soon, Mack was giving him the history of NOIA and stories of each of the other crewmen.

"They told me this is to be a temporary assignment," Claude said.

Mack sighed. "There's a Point-Class steel boat over at our dock, just in from Viet Nam. We may be surplused when we get out of here."

He felt angry—about the fate of his boat, about the casualty of his relationships. He should have done better. The kid sitting across from him, fresh-faced and eager for adventure, was probably just out of high school. He had no idea how disappointing life would be.

Soon the rest of the crew arrived aboard. Gus shook his hand. "They're sending us back to Cape May. She's being decommissioned."

"Shit," said Mack.

"I'm going to take my thirty-day leave and go lay on a beach somewhere." Gus threw his hat on his bunk.

"Any word about the rest of us?"

Gus lowered his voice. "I'm not supposed to tell you this. I think you're going to Thirteenth District—Seattle. Or maybe Alaska."

Mack's mood darkened even more. "When do we shove off?"

"Oh-eight-hundred hours. Tomorrow."

Eighteen – At Sea

Mack sat on the forward deck leaning against the wheelhouse, feeling the throb of the engines against his spine, squinting in spite of his sunglasses, trying to write on the pad in his lap. He looked up to see the Statue of Liberty passing a mile to starboard.

Gus had told the helmsman to "open her up as soon as we're in open water," and NOIA was plowing into the sun, head high, on her last trip down the coast toward Cape May. Mack could hear the water parting, giving way to the white hull that had claimed her place on the sea for thirty years. He hadn't often seen her underway from outside, usually being aboard tending the big engines, but he could imagine the sight, and always felt proud to be a part of her.

He was trying to write the letter to Claudia and Patty, explaining the cryptic message he left on their answering machine before it had cut him off.

Their outgoing message, recorded by Patty, had said simply that they were off to see the fjords, and "please leave us a message" so they could respond as soon as they returned. Mack didn't remember when that was.

He wrote that the Coast Guard was sending them back to New Jersey, probably to be decommissioned, and he didn't know where his next duty would be. Promising to write again as soon as he knew, he apologized again for the sad way things had gone, and hoped that they could see each other again. He signed it "with love to both of you" but he pictured Claudia's sad face the way he remembered her, sitting on the floor looking at him.

It all felt inadequate. Writing was hard for him. The letter would be mailed from one of their fuel stops down the coast.

The bow began lifting on the swells as they met the sea coming in from the Atlantic. The sky was cloudless, the sun hot on his face. He folded the letter and put it into the envelope. A tug of regret in his midsection made him sigh as he got to his feet and followed the handrail aft, toward his engine room.

Nineteen – Oregon, Two Weeks Later

Mack made the decision to stop for the hitch-hiker even before he saw that it was a girl. She was sitting on her huge backpack at the side of U.S. 101 in Western Oregon, holding a square of cardboard that said only "SF" in black letters.

Pulled to the side of the road, he watched her in his rear-view mirror, hurrying toward him with the pack slung over one shoulder. Reaching across to open the window when she appeared beside him, he said, "Throw your pack in the back."

She knew the drill, and in a moment she was sitting next to him, grinning broadly. "Thanks."

Mack was shocked at how young she was. Long, blond hair pulled back with some kind of ribbon, red and white plaid jacket, blue jeans and heavy boots. "You're going all the way to San Francisco?" he asked.

"Yeah. Got a sister there."

He wasn't sure how to talk to this young woman. He'd heard about kids gravitating toward San Francisco as though it were some kind of California Shangri-La. Everybody knew about places like the Haight-Ashbury District, where young people collected, seemingly free from the normal constraints of society, experimenting with life, rejecting the expectations of their parents.

He'd also read some of the horror stories, of drug overdoses, predators and things just gone wrong. These were the kids, he'd read, of middle-class families who had never learned how to take care of themselves. They simply followed the lure of freedom and adventure that sometimes obscured the risks of being anonymous in a big city.

He had mixed feelings about the term "counter-culture." He'd never been a rebel, particularly, and made a point of treating others with respect. But lately he'd been feeling as though something were seriously wrong in the country. The Viet Nam War was a part of it. Unlike the Second World War, and even the Korean "Police Action," it didn't seem that "we" and "they" were so clearly identified with right and wrong. Too many people were suffering for a vague kind of cause. Watergate was in the news almost every day.

He could sympathize with those who chose to "drop out" and try to make their own kinds of lives, following leaders such as Stephen Gaskin, the former English professor who led a caravan of hundreds of people from San Francisco to Tennessee, where they formed a commune known as The Farm dedicated to peace and social services. People were looking for different ways of living.

He wondered what he himself was doing. With thirty days leave from the Coast Guard, he'd bought this Volkswagen bus in Seattle and launched himself down U.S. 101 along the Pacific Coast, only vaguely conscious of where he was going. The bus was his camper, his home, with just about everything he owned stowed in the back. His temporary superior at the base in Seattle had suggested he take his leave while waiting for a permanent assignment somewhere in the Thirteenth Coast Guard District, which included Washington and Oregon.

"Taking a vacation from school?" he asked.

"Yeah," she said. As he kept his eyes on the road, he could see that she was watching him. "That where you're going?"

"Not sure. I'm on leave, and I just decided to head south."

"Military?"

"Coast Guard."

"Been to 'Naam?"

"No."

"Good."

They rode in silence for a long while. Mack wanted to know all about her, wanted to ask her personal questions, but he was half afraid of what she might reveal. A girl, hitch-hiking alone along the highway, maybe running away from home. Maybe running from the law. She seemed in good spirits, but said little. He was glad to have company.

"Oh," she said suddenly, "Stop for him!"

Another hitch-hiker was standing at the side of the highway, his backpack at his feet. He didn't even have his thumb out, but he was obviously waiting just as the girl had been. Mack pulled over and took him in, the three of them a little crowded on the bench seat.

The two knew each other, exchanging greetings like old friends. "I saw you get a ride back in Washington," she said to him.

"That old pickup truck was on its last legs."

"You also going to San Francisco?" Mack asked him.

"I guess so. Haven't decided yet."

"I haven't either. I've got thirty days, just seeing the countryside."

The three of them chatted a little, but the youngsters talked between themselves as companions on a journey that seemed completely open-ended. Mack felt old, and remembered a hippie slogan he'd read someplace, "Don't trust anybody over thirty." There was something appealing, if irrational, about their chosen life. The world had gotten out of control; even he could tell. All the old rules didn't apply anymore. The kids were willing to let it all go and just follow their hearts, trusting (as Patty always had) that safety was real and the world would provide for them somehow.

Thinking of Patty, Mack drifted back into his own thoughts while his two passengers talked a language he barely understood. He hadn't heard from Patty and Claudia since he had left Connecticut, except for the cryptic message they had left on their answering machine about "seeing the fjords." He didn't know if mail addressed to him in New London would find its way to him Out West. He thought that he'd call them when he got back to Seattle.

The Oregon coastline was spectacular. The summer weather varied from sunny to foggy to rainy. Several times he stopped at overlooks to drink in the view, although the young people seemed more interested in continuing on the road. When they stopped to eat in Crescent City, California, the others insisted on paying for their own food. *At least,* he thought, *they have some money.* In the Redwoods Park south of Crescent City, Mack said he was ready to stop for the night. He wanted to enjoy the views and the smells of the forest and relax from the tension of driving. His passengers, however, said that they wanted to continue on. At the park entrance, they left him and took separate stations along the highway, where they would be more likely to be picked up by motorists. "A lot of people don't have room for two people and their packs," the girl said. As he caught a last glimpse of them in his mirror, Mack felt apprehensive.

Later, sitting on a log overlooking the Pacific Ocean, he wondered how he had never managed to make that life connection that most people seem to have. Loneliness shared his sleeping bag with him that night.

Twenty – San Francisco

He spent the next night in a truck stop somewhere north of the city. When he emerged from the rest room early the next day, he saw a familiar figure perched on her backpack just beyond the truck stop exit. Approaching her on foot, he grinned. "We seem to be going the same direction."

She smiled back. "I got held up back there somewhere."

"Want a lift into the city?" He gestured toward his Volkswagen.

"Sure."

They walked over to his bus, tossed her pack in the back, and drove south. He glanced at her, thinking that she didn't look as young as she had earlier. High school, anyway. She had a slight sunburn on her forehead. "I'm Mack," he said.

"Teresa—Terry."

"You got a little sun yesterday."

"Yeah." She turned and smiled at him, but didn't offer any explanation.

The Golden Gate Bridge was swallowed by fog as they approached, but midway across the sun came out and the legendary city spread out before them. Port cities were nothing new to him, but the beauty of this one caused the hair to stand up on the back of his neck. The radio in his bus was playing some classical music.

Immediately on the other side of the bridge, he lost the highway somehow, and found himself driving on neighborhood streets near the waterfront. He stopped and pulled out a map of California. Detail was sparse in the little San Francisco inset. "Do you know where you're going?" he asked. "I'm lost, but I'm in no hurry to get anywhere."

Terry pulled a slip of paper from her pocket. "Haight and Central."

He looked around the neighborhood they were in. An odd, circular structure caught his eye, and he turned toward it. Across a park and a reflecting pond stood a group of buildings that reminded him of classical Athens.

"Mind if we stop for a minute?"

She shrugged.

He stopped at the curb and got out of the bus. The morning air was warm. "I haven't had breakfast," he said to her. "Want a sandwich?"

She shook her head.

Making himself a sandwich from his cooler, he sat on a park bench and took in the sight, enchanted. Terry stayed in the bus. He could hear the music from his radio, playing a piece he'd never heard before—dramatic, slow music that exactly fit the mood he was experiencing sitting before the structure reflected in the pond. A seagull swooped down and landed at the edge of the water. The moment was magical. He couldn't move from the spot until the music ended. The announcer's rich baritone told him that the piece was something from Thomas Tallis—Mack couldn't quite make out the rest of it.

The spell dissolved, and he got back into the Volkswagen and turned off the radio.

Driving through clean, sunlit neighborhoods, he kept remembering the themes from that music. It was not the San Francisco he was expecting—hordes of young people on crowded streets and old buildings like he'd seen in Greenwich Village.

He worked his way down to the waterfront, which looked more the way he expected. There were parks everywhere, and many boats and small ships at the docks. He didn't see any large vessels, however. Soon he was in the shade of another huge bridge—the Bay Bridge, he guessed—and then he turned away from the waterfront and through the main business section of the city. Surprised at the lack of heavy traffic and pedestrians, he said, "Looks deserted."

"Sunday."

"Oh, that's right."

Following Market Street toward a pair of high hills within the city, he spotted a sign pointing to Golden Gate Park, a place he'd read about.

"There's Central," Terry said, and he turned into it.

Unlike the downtown business district, this neighborhood was crowded. Like much he'd seen of San Francisco, homes and businesses were painted bright, gay colors. People stood on sidewalks wearing tie-dyed clothing and colorful head scarfs. Musicians sat on curbs playing guitars, saxophones—anything that would produce sound. *This* reminded him of Greenwich Village.

They followed Central Avenue until Terry exclaimed, "There's Haight Street!" She put her hand on the door handle, obviously excited.

Mack pulled to the curb. "I thought Haight and Ashbury was where everybody is," he said, smiling.

"That's around here somewhere. Thanks for the ride, Mack." She turned, kissed him quickly on the cheek, and went out to the bustling sidewalk, dragging her pack behind her.

He wanted to stay there for a minute to make sure Terry was where she wanted to be, but just that quickly she had struck up a conversation with others on the sidewalk, so he pulled away.

Following the signs to Golden Gate Park, he drove slowly through a magical city, filled with young people. The smell of marijuana permeated the air.

At the entrance to the park, the atmosphere changed. Suddenly, he felt connected with the natural beauty of curving roads and bicycle paths and trees everywhere. There were still people, strolling, sitting in groups on the lawns, throwing Frisbees and balls to each other. But the mood seemed less—*urgent* was the word that came to him. It was a Sunday in the park.

He found a place to park and turned his radio back on. Radio station KKHI continued to feed him classical music. After sitting in the bus soaking up the atmosphere for a few minutes, he took his sleeping bag from the back seat and spread it out on the lawn. He left the radio on and the door open.

He was awakened by voices. Looking around him he saw a circle of people surrounding him, sitting quietly, legs crossed. A pipe was being handed around.

"Man," said one, "you looked so peaceful, we all wanted to soak up your vibes."

Mack looked toward his Volkswagen. The door was still open, and KKHI was still playing music. After a moment of apprehension, he decided that he was in no danger. Three of his visitors were women—or girls—and everyone appeared to be stoned.

"You got a great hippie wagon."

"Uh, I guess I fell asleep."

"Like a baby." The one who was talking had a scraggly beard, and his knees protruded through worn jeans. He was barefoot.

Mack sat up, and someone offered him the pipe. He shook his head. "I have to drive."

"They call me Dragon."

A girl laughed. "*Magic* Dragon."

Mack smiled. "As in *Puff?*"

Dragon smiled. "Lookin' for a pad?"

Mack shook his head. "I'm just passing through. I'm on vacation. Wanted to see this place."

Dragon gestured vaguely behind him. "It's goin' down. Used to be a groovy place."

"Why's that?"

"Smack. It's got the people goin'."

"You live around here?"

"Got a head shop down on Hayes. Thinkin' about blowin' this town, though."

"Where would you go?" Mack was curious about this man who, behind his hippie persona, seemed to be educated. He also seemed less stoned than the others.

"My family's down in Carmel. If I can talk my old man out of a couple acres, we could all go down there and have a real life." He gestured to include the group around them.

"Thought I'd hang around here for a couple days," Mack said, "n' then head back to Seattle."

"That home?"

Mack explained his circumstances to them.

"Coast Guard?" someone asked.

"Been to Naam?"

"No. Caribbean, mostly. East Coast."

Dragon puffed on the pipe. "I was in Cuba one time—while you could still go there."

Mack gathered his sleeping bag and threw it into the bus.

"Need a place to crash?" Dragon asked. "Can't park overnight anyplace here."

Mack looked at him, perplexed.

"I got a parking spot behind my shop. You can crash in my place."

"Show me where it is." Mack got out his map.

Dragon pointed to a spot. "Driveway, right next to the shop. Pull in there and come find me."

For some reason Mack felt he could trust this fellow. He looked at him for a moment, then shook his hand. "Thanks."

He drove on along the park drive, leaving the group still sitting in a rough circle on the grass.

Driving more or less at random through the city, Mack felt a strange euphoria. He found his way to the top of Twin Peaks and back down, even eventually making his way down the peculiar Lombard Street. It was indeed a magical city.

His intent was to go north again, across the Golden Gate Bridge before stopping for the night. But as the sun dropped below the hills, he wanted to experience San Francisco one more day. He followed his map to Hayes Street, and pulled into the narrow driveway between the buildings. A small group of people were standing at the far end of the drive, and when they saw his bus they waved him in.

"Dragon said I could park here," he said to one of them.

"Yeah, I know. Put it in there," the man said. Mack thought he recognized him from the circle in the park.

Inside the shop, he found Dragon sitting in a beanbag chair, puffing on a pipe. "Hey, Man!" Dragon said, laboriously getting to his feet. "Cecil, show the man where to throw his bag."

The air was thick with marijuana smoke. Cecil took Mack to a small room on the second floor and pointed to a spot of bare floor. "You can sleep there," he said. "Be sure to lock your bus."

Mack spent the rest of the evening listening to the conversations in the crowded building. Everyone was informal, offering him tokes on their smokes and bites from mysterious sandwiches. Eventually, he curled up on his sleeping bag and tried to sleep.

He was awakened at some point in the night. Somewhere in the neighborhood music was being played very loudly, a Beatles song, "If I Needed Someone," and he could hear every word. *This was a mistake,* he thought. He should have found a place on the road someplace and parked for the night.

Something made him open his eyes. A young woman was sitting next to him in the dim light, cross-legged on the floor, watching him. "If I needed someone," she said, her voice husky with smoke. You need someone, Mack?"

He propped his head on an elbow to see her better, and recognized that she had been in the circle on the grass in the park. He grinned. "It's pretty loud."

"You need someone?" she repeated.

He'd always been careful about sex with strangers; he knew too many sailors who had spent miserable days with venereal diseases. Almost automatically, he said, "Not sex, just company."

She unfolded her long legs and lay down next to him. "Me, too."

"You know my name." He liked her smell, except for the pungent marijuana.

"You told us," she said, "in the park."

He stretched an arm out so she could rest her head on his shoulder. There was little light in the room coming through the window; too dark to see the color of her eyes.

"You need someone?" she asked again, looking up into his face.

"You keep asking that. You need someone?"

"That's the song."

Mack realized that she was pretty high. He pulled her close to him for a moment, then relaxed his arm so he could see her face. "Your song."

She smiled. "Everybody's song. We all need someone."

"The song's about timing—the guy doesn't need someone right then, but he's interested."

"Sing it to me," she murmered, moving closer to him.

"I can't sing. He's just saying, 'carve your number on my wall, and I'll find you maybe later."

"Pretty heartless."

Mack thought about Claudia. "That's my life," he said, and rolled onto his back.

The woman put her head on his chest. "Why didn't you call her?"

He took a deep breath, and let it out slowly. "You know a lot about me."

She reached up and kissed him, then returned to his chest. "I can tell." After a long moment, she said, "Call her."

"Yeah."

He must have dozed off, for when he awoke again, she was gone. The loud neighborhood sounds had softened. Lying awake, he wondered about the woman who had come to him in the dark. He almost decided that he had simply dreamed about her, but his clothes still carried her scent.

When daylight began to show through the window, he could see others asleep in the room, some on bare mattresses, one man curled up on the floor, his head on his backpack. Mack hadn't been aware of anyone else in the room—except her.

He quietly rolled up his sleeping bag and went down the stairs. The head shop was dark except for the light coming through the storefront windows.

Outside, the air was cool. Mack walked around his bus, estimating the maneuvering he would have to do to get it back on the street. He could hear sounds of the city, but the Volkswagen engine seemed very loud in comparison, echoing from the walls around the driveway.

He was hungry, and his body felt gritty—he had slept in his clothes, and the woman's scent haunted him. Out on the streets of the Haight-Ashbury district, he found his way back to Market Street, where he knew he could make it back to the Golden Gate.

He was no longer curious about this beautiful city that now seemed haunted by something that he felt inside himself—lost. Terry, the hitchhiker he had brought into the city, seemed swallowed up in it almost instantly. He had awakened twice to find people staring at him, now he felt, like ghosts or zombies, expecting something from him. People, like him, disconnected and drifting.

"If I needed someone," the ghost woman had said to him last night, "you need someone, Mack?" The words of the song kept running through his head:

If I needed someone to love
You're the one that I'd be thinking of
If I needed someone
...

He pulled to the curb and sobbed into his arms on the big steering wheel.

Twenty-One – Washington

By the time he was approaching the Columbia River Bridge at Astoria, Mack was beginning to wonder why he had suddenly abandoned his "vacation." He thought back to the trip up 101 along the spectacular Oregon coastline and realized that he hadn't really seen much of it. He just wanted to belong somewhere. When he came to the junction where 101 headed toward the coast again, he took Route 107 instead, over the mountains toward Olympia, back toward Seattle. He wasn't sure what he would do for the rest of his thirty-day leave, but

191

at least he had a connection to something there—the Coast Guard.

But then as he neared Olympia, he encountered the other end of the U.S. 101 loop around the Olympic Peninsula. His map showed that the scenic highway circled the entire peninsula. On an impulse, he turned north.

Stopping for the evening in a small campground, Mack found a pay phone. He dialed the New York number of Claudia and Patty, wanting to hear a familiar voice. Instead, their answering machine repeated the message he had heard two weeks before. Patty's voice, so gaily announcing that they were "off to see the fjords" reminded him even more intensely how lonely he was.

The next morning he continued north, following the shore of an inlet from Puget Sound, with the sun reflecting off the water and through the trees. He felt better. He was used to being alone, after all, spending days at a time underway on the boat, listening to his music, tending to his engines. With the mountains rising immediately to his left, and the narrow strip of water to his right, he thought of fjords. This area was so different from the East Coast, wild and green. He could imagine cruising up this fjord aboard the NOIA. He just needed to be back in his element.

Then the little VW engine sputtered and died. Mack pulled to the side of the road. At least, here was a situation he was very experienced with, a mechanical problem.

Right after he had bought the Volkswagen bus, he had found a book store that carried lots of support books and magazines for these vehicles. They were popular with the young people who seemed to favor the Beetle. He chose the one that had the most interesting illustrations; its title was *How to Keep Your Volkswagen Alive: A Manual of Step-by-Step Procedures for the Compleat Idiot.*

He'd been a mechanic long enough to be confident in his ability to diagnose and repair any engine, particularly one as small and simple as this little air-cooled VW. He didn't consider himself a "Complete Idiot," but he also knew he could save himself time by referring to instruction manuals, should the occasion arise. And now the occasion had arisen.

Under the hood—actually a flat door on the rear of the bus—he studied the engine for a few moments, and then opened the repair manual.

Just then a vehicle pulled up behind him. The familiar sound of the engine made him smile. It was a bug—a Volkswagen Beetle.

"Got a problem?" came a voice.

Mack turned to see a young man dressed in farmer's overalls, and shirtless. "She just died," he answered.

"Probably the coil." The man reached a hand in the engine compartment. "Yep. Hotter'n hell."

Ten minutes later they were in the Beetle, headed for a nearby auto repair shop that the man knew about where they could buy a part, and within an hour Mack was on his way again heading north on U.S 101. For him, it was a lesson in humility. At first glance, he had thought the young man rather uncouth and of doubtful competence. *Hayseed*, a term of derision from his childhood in the Midwest, was the word that came to him. The fact that he had driven up in a Volkswagen himself persuaded Mack to let him have access to the engine. It was, after all, a new vehicle to him. And the fellow, exuding confidence, had not only pinpointed the problem almost at a glance, he knew what to do about it. Mack never told him of his own professional qualifications, and afterward was grateful that he had not. It was the kind of situation that young men encounter frequently: a competitiveness regarding knowledge of cars. Working in his uncle's auto shop years ago, Mack had learned to wait before challenging others, and the habit had stood him in good stead over the years. He avoided confrontations and gained knowledge in the process. There would always be someone who knew more than he did.

The man had not accepted any payment for his services, saying with a smile, "We got to take care of each other." When Mack turned the key and the bus engine started immediately, the stranger drove off with a wave.

As he drove, Mack thought about how young people seemed these days. There was a kind of community spirit that he had not encountered in his years in the military. Overseas, young men were fighting and dying every day, and from what he had heard, few believed in what they were doing. Back here in the States, there seemed to be developing a culture—"counter culture," they called it—in which people connected with each other. The words, *The kindness of strangers* came to him. Where had he first heard that expression? Perhaps also from his Midwest childhood, probably in Sunday School.

Dragon, back in San Francisco, had offered Mack a place to sleep and a spot to park his bus, all without knowing anything about him or asking anything from him. Terry, the hitchhiker, seemed to know that culture and trust it. Even the woman who had joined him on the floor above Dragon's head shop had said, "We all need someone."

And this farm boy, encountering him on the side of the road, had simply offered his help, without any expectations.

Maybe the world was changing, after all.

At some point—Mack wasn't sure where he was, only on 101 heading north—he came to an intersection. He knew from his map that the highway eventually circled back to the Pacific Coast, but a sign at the intersection pointed to a town he had never heard of: Port Townsend. He turned toward it without a second thought.

Another body of water lay on his left now, and he realized that he had left the fjord some miles back. It was still very rural, with small farms and isolated homes among the trees. In a little while the forests gave way to flatter land, and there were more farms and occasional businesses along the road. Then there was water ahead, he guessed Puget Sound itself. The road skirted along the shore line into Port Townsend, a small town at the end of a peninsula. He saw a ferry approaching its dock.

In the middle of a small marina sat a white boat, larger and cleaner than the typical small fishing boats around it. The red sash angling down from the deck to the waterline identified it as a Coast Guard vessel.

It wasn't a wooden boat, like the NOIA, but about the same size. Mack was instantly curious. He pulled into the parking lot next to the marina. After a couple of weeks away from his domain, he felt something like homesickness. Here was where he felt he belonged.

Approaching the white vessel at the end of the dock, he noticed a figure on deck, splicing the end of a rope. "Ahoy," he called.

The sailor looked over at him and gestured for him to come aboard.

Once he had identified himself and explained his circumstance, Mack was treated to a tour of the boat. "The crew is out to lunch," the sailor told him. "Our cook is on leave, and nobody else wants to cook."

He described the boat as a Point-Class vessel, similar to the one that had replaced NOIA in New London, but it had never been to Viet Nam. "They've had cutters here like forever," he said. "We get called out all the time to rescue old fishing boats and capsized sailboats."

When Mack asked about drug-runners, he grinned. "There are rumors," he said mysteriously. "We haven't caught any since I been here."

The engine room was unfamiliar to Mack. The twin diesel engines were much smaller than the big gasoline buckets on NOIA, "not so good for towing," the sailor said, "but she'll do twenty-four knots in smooth water."

"Good duty here?" Mack asked, interested in this vessel and this location.

"Yeah. Pretty cushy. A couple of the crew are married and have apartments in town. Used to be an army base here, Fort Worden, but it closed down and now it's a juvenile detention center." He laughed. "They said a sailor used to have to be careful around town at night, with all the soldiers."

"Got a chief engineman?"

"Gerry's just a First Class, but he's working on Chief."

Mack realized as he asked the question that he'd need additional training to qualify for diesel engines. "I don't know where they're going to send me when I get back off leave," he said. "I'd hate to get shore duty."

He suddenly felt discouraged again, and soon took leave from the boat. Back in his bus, he explored the town for a while, and went into a dark bar to get a drink and something to eat. He liked the atmosphere in the place: tie-dyed fabrics hung all over from the ceiling, lending the room a mysterious, counter-culture feeling. Among the six or seven tables in the room, a single couple sat with beers. The man signaled to Mack to join them.

"We're here for the music later," he said. "You new in town?"

Mack nodded and sat down with them. "I'm hungry, mainly. Like the atmosphere here. Good food?"

The woman shrugged and grinned. "It's okay. There's a group playing here tonight that we like."

"Getting a head start on it," added the man, lifting his bottle. "Charlie Mann." He stuck out his hand.

"Mack Jensen."

"This here's Sadie." He cocked his head and looked at Mack. " Jensen—you Swedish? Lots of Swedes around here."

"Don't know," said Mack.

Someone from the back room came to the table, and beer was ordered all around. Mack was glad to have someone to talk to. When the beer arrived, he ordered a cheeseburger.

A while later, Charlie called to someone behind the counter. "What happened to the group? Weren't they supposed to start?"

The waiter came to the table. "Amos got fried this morning," he said. "They won't be here tonight."

Charlie turned to Mack. "Amos is their lead guitar." To the waiter, he asked, "Can you put a record on? Too damned quiet!"

"Okay." The man disappeared into the back room. Soon Mack recognized the beginning track from the new Pink Floyd album *Dark Side of the Moon* starting, as a lot of their music did, with some weird sound effects that included a heartbeat. The music was very loud.

By the middle of the album, all three were bouncing to the beat and quaffing their beer. Sadie got up and danced by herself, her head lolling around.

"Amos's group plays all country," Charlie shouted to Mack. "I like rock better anyway."

Mack nodded. He was thinking of how tame the folk sounds he heard in San Francisco seemed, compared with Pink Floyd. Especially the Beatles song, "If I needed Someone" that had kept him awake while his ghost woman lay with her head on his chest. Hard rock overpowered your thoughts instead of reminding you of your loneliness.

"Church music!" shouted Charlie. "Pink Floyd is like church music!"

It didn't make any sense to Mack right then, but later he was to remember the remark and wonder about it. In that dark bar, he moved with the music, feeling it in his gut. He liked the way the chords fit together and didn't challenge him to understand.

Toward the end of the album he caught some lyrics, *"There's someone in my head and it's not me."* That fit the way he'd been feeling lately, as though he didn't know who he was anymore.

By the time the three of them stumbled out onto the street, Mack was ready to curl up and sleep. He knew that that he'd better not try to drive, so when he got to his bus that he'd parked on a side street, he simply locked the doors and climbed into his sleeping bag.

The next day he headed back south, crossing over Hood Canal to Kitsap Peninsula and down to Bremerton. Just missing the ferry to Seattle, he drove all the way to Tacoma, across the suspension bridge and up Interstate 5 to The City.

Back at the base, he found an empty bunk and settled in. Since he was still on leave for another week and a half, he had no duties except to stand bunk inspections. He spent his days either going into town or reading in the library. He checked the post office every day for mail.

One day he was rewarded by a postcard from Claudia. The card, written two weeks earlier, had been forwarded several times.

"We were so sad to hear that you were taken away from us again," she wrote. "We are seeing Norway, but the weather hasn't been good over here. Ready to return home, but can't for another ten days. Patty sends love. XXOO Claudia."

That was enough to get him to try to phone them again. Driving down from Port Townsend, he'd been thinking of her continually, missing her sweet smile.

"Mack!" Patty cried when he'd made the connection. He heard her turn away from the phone. "It's Mack!"

He told them where he was and that he still didn't know where he'd be assigned. Patty and Claudia took turns at the phone, gushing over him. They all promised to stay in touch.

When Mack hung up, he wondered, *What is it about them that I can't forget them? It's like they're both inside me somehow, like parts of me. Patty's the part that wants to play, and Claudia's the part that wants to sit and listen to Chopin and get drunk with her, and feel her...*

He sighed, and went immediately to Personnel, where the officer in charge was shuffling papers at his

desk. He told the officer about visiting the boat in Port Townsend and realized that he wanted to get sea duty again, not be stuck on some island somewhere.
"Well," the officer told him, "you have this one problem. Most of the boats are diesel, and you're only rated for gasoline engines."
"How can I get a diesel rating?"
The officer leaned back in his chair. "There's only one diesel school on the West Coast, and that's at the navy base in San Diego. Maybe we could get you in there."

Twenty-Two – California

Patty and Claudia were delighted when he called to tell them that he was in San Diego. "I'll be here for six weeks," he said.
"We'll come see you!"
"I don't know anything about the city. But the bay is really special. I've never seen so many warships in one place."
Claudia was silent for a moment. Then, "I want to see you, not warships."
Of course. She would. She and Patty had both expressed their horror about the war in Southeast Asia. Mack agreed, and yet he felt pride when he looked out over the San Diego harbor. These were somehow *his* ships. Without having been aboard any of them, he knew them, inside and out. He could smell the oil in the engine rooms, could imagine tapping a gauge with his fingertip before recording what it said, feel the pulse of the screws clawing the water under him.

All those feelings surfaced in him and then died away as he sat in the non-com rec hall and watched the television sets broadcasting the fall of Saigon. He wondered what those kids in San Francisco were feeling as they, too, watched civilians trying to climb the fences into the American Embassy, and the helicopters taking off from inside the fence with Americans fleeing for their lives. He wanted to be on one of those hundreds of boats offshore, rescuing people from the terrible war gone terribly wrong.

Others in the room sat silently watching, unbelieving that the United States had lost something more precious than ever before in history, more than Pearl Harbor, more than abandoning the Philippines, or Wake Island, or Seoul. He watched a young petty officer sitting near him lean over to tie his shoe so that others would not see the tears on his face.

That mixture of feelings, of pride suddenly submerged under guilt; the gut-pulse of engines that he understood overwhelmed by knowing that he should have been there, doing his part and yet wrenched by the certainty that it was all, somehow, wrong.

He could have been there, offshore saving people like the amateur sailors at Dunkirk had done thirty years before. This was no heroic rescue, this was throwing up hands in defeat, abandoning a war that should never have been fought.

The sailors in the cafeteria were quiet that evening. A few remained in front of the television rather than eating dinner.

Mack remembered an old movie as John Wayne, the skipper of a PT boat in the Philippines early in World War Two, on orders to leave their base before it was overrun by the Japanese, leaving one old American civilian who refused to go, sitting on the steps of his repair shop, a shotgun across his knees, with music from a harmonica softly playing "Red River Valley." Even though Mack had seen the movie long after the war had been won, he was clutched by the sadness of loss, of simple humanity facing the end like those South Vietnamese peering through the fence at hope suddenly gone.

The class in diesel mechanics gave him something positive to think about. He had no trouble with the course; he simply had to translate what he had long known about engines from gasoline power to diesel power. He liked the sound of diesels, as someone had described "like an old Chevrolet with noisy tappets." There was a solidity to the sound, of metal meeting metal, that a gasoline engine didn't have. Like the reassuring clicks of a bolt-action rifle being cocked, a dependable mechanism that gave the world meaning.

Something totally different from music. Music could tear the heart open.

He met Claudia and Patty at the airport. Watching Patty, with her sunglasses and little white cane that never touched the ground, her hand lightly on the arm of her sister, he felt something in his throat. Both women were smiling at him as they approached.

"First time I've seen you in your uniform!" cried Claudia. "Love, he's dressed up just for us."

"Actually," Mack said, hugging each of them in turn, "I have to wear this here. It's a navy town, and they want everybody to know it."

"But you're not in the navy."

"All the more reason. The Shore Patrols watch me closely. I don't dare step out of line."

Patty was exploring his face and his clothing with her fingertips. "We are staying at the Holiday Inn Chula Vista. Is that near your school?"

"Not far. I borrowed a car so I can take you there, if I don't get lost." Mack laughed. "It's a very busy city."

As he dodged uncertainly through traffic, he felt exhilarated, almost giddy. "You smell good!"

Patty laughed.

Claudia fingered his white hat, which he had tossed onto the dashboard when they got into the car. "Cute little hat!"

"I hate 'em," he said. "No place to put them."

"And your little-boy sailor collar!" she laughed.

"At least we have regular zip-up pants now. After two hundred years of fourteen buttons to undo."

All three laughed frequently as they made their way to the hotel. Claudia checked them in, and Mack escorted Patty, pushing their luggage cart up to their room.

Inside, they hugged and kissed. Mack felt euphoric. "Did you get anything to eat on the plane?"

"They fed us well. Complimentary wine and all," said Patty, removing her sunglasses.

"It was a long flight," Claudia commented, sitting down and slipping off her shoes.

"At least we could fly first-class," said Patty. "Claudia said the regular passengers were crammed together in the back, like on the subway."

"What airplane did you fly in?"

"DC-Ten." Patty touched Claudia's shoulder. "Is that right?"

"I think so. It's huge! They have two aisles!"

"It was like the big double-deck plane we flew to Oslo in," added Patty.

Mack flopped down in a chair and grinned at the women. "I'm glad to see you again. I've missed you!"

Patty made her way to him and sat down on his lap. "I've missed you, too. We thought we'd never see you again!" Tears drifted down her cheeks.

Claudia went to the bed and lay down on one side. "Come lie between us," she said softly. "I want to touch you!"

As the three of them lay quietly together, Mack felt at peace for the first time in months. The crisis of the last time he saw them in New York seemed very long ago. They talked generally about the cruise in Norway and about his trip down U.S. 101 to San Francisco and back. At some point he realized that Patty had fallen asleep, her head on his arm.

He looked over at Claudia. "I think she's had a full day," he whispered.

"We both have." She smiled and closed her eyes. "This is how I pictured us."

A few minutes later all three of them were asleep.

When he awoke, Patty was not beside him. He could hear water running in the bathroom. Claudia was still asleep on his arm. He lay there, not wanting to disturb her, until Patty came out of the bathroom, feeling her way carefully back to the bed.

"Hi," he whispered. She sat on the edge of the bed and touched his face without saying anything, running her fingers through his hair. He touched her cheek.

Claudia lifted her head from his arm. "Your arm must be hurting."

He withdrew it and stretched both arms over his head. "Worth it."

"When do you have to be back?" Patty asked.

"I have to return the car, but then I can come back. I'm on liberty until Monday morning."

"How far is it?"

"A short bus ride. I can be back in time to take you two ladies to dinner."

"Let's have a drink first," said Claudia, moving to the minibar.

"Not me," he replied. "If I'm driving, I don't want even a hint of alcohol on my breath. Shore Patrol would love a chance to toss a Coastie in the brig."

"Okay, when you come back. We can freshen up while you're gone.

Driving back to the base, Mack thought about how relaxed everything felt. Ever since he had left New York in the early morning, a knot had lain in his gut reminding him of his transgression. Now it was gone, but he wasn't sure yet if it was all over. Claudia had seemed truly glad to see him.

They had a lot of talking to do.

The women were waiting for him in the lobby when he returned. "I couldn't stand being in that hotel room any longer," Claudia said.

"Well, there's a nice quiet bar where we can sit and talk." Mack loved to look at them, both so different from each other, although both were wearing sunglasses.

Their conversation over drinks ran to the mundane, each one getting accustomed once again to their being together. Mack asked again about their cruise in Norway, and they asked about his trip down the West Coast in his "hippie wagon."

Claudia's face became serious.

"What's going on?" asked Mack.

She pursed her lips, hesitating. "I've been thinking a lot about us," she said finally.

"So have I."
Patty sat silently.
"We both love you," Claudia went on, "but I've decided that you and I shouldn't have sex anymore."
Mack waited, stunned.
"I can't deal with it," she said. Putting a hand on his, she sighed deeply. "It's too important to me, and I hated the feeling I had, the jealousy. Patty has told me over and over that she will not go to bed with you, but she's too important to me to have that between us. She's the most important person in my life—she always has been."
Mack looked over at Patty, who sat stone-faced. He wished he could see her eyes to tell what she was feeling. "Patty," he began.
Tears streamed down Patty's face. "It's her decision," she said hoarsely.
Mack squeezed Claudia's hand. "Claudia, I know I hurt you."
"It's not that," Claudia replied. "I value you as a friend." She looked over at Patty. "We came all the way across the country just to see you. You're a good man, Mack. I don't want to feel those things about you." Her eyes, on him again, glistened.
"O-kay," Mack said slowly. Suddenly, the euphoria of an hour ago was gone. The knot was back in his gut.
They were silent for a long time. Then Mack sighed again. "In the room upstairs, you said you wanted to touch me. You kissed me."
"Yes. I love you and I'm attracted to you. But I don't own you—I don't *want* to own you! You're a sailor, and you're gone to sea, and you have a right to your life. You should get married, Mack."

"Would you marry me, Claudia?" The words came out of him without thought, even without his being prepared for them.

She touched his face with the tips of her fingers and tilted her head. "Sweet Mack. But no."

Patty searched for his hand on the table.

Mack's face screwed up with intensity. "I didn't know I was going to say that. I meant it, but I haven't thought about anything like that." Something crossed his mind, something awful that he pushed away at once. *Maybe Patty ...*

Patty removed her sunglasses and wiped her cheeks with a tissue. "It's not fair," she said softly.

Mack sagged like a deflating balloon.

"Mack," Claudia began, "can you live with that? Am I important enough to you that you can accept that and still be my friend—" and her voice caught—"*our friend?*"

Mack's heavy sigh quavered. "Yes," he said. "I guess I don't have a choice, do I? Of course I want to keep you both in my life. I've always said it was difficult for me to love you both. I've felt pulled sometimes."

"Excuse me," Patty said, "my timing is terrible, but I have to pee." She began to stand up.

"I'll take you." Claudia rose immediately and escorted her sister to the rest room.

Mack sat, his arms dangling at his side. He picked up his drink and put it back down without tasting it. *We should be seeing the town,* he thought, *having a good time. How long will it be before I see them again? They flew all the way across the country to see me! I can live without sex—whatever it takes!*

And then, anger gripped him. *She could have told me in a letter! Or on the phone! Now I have to look at her and want her and know that she doesn't want me. What do I do with that?*

Everything had lost its luster. His career, his music, his ambition. Even this weekend, that he had been looking forward to so much.

I thought she loved me!

He thought of escape, of leaving a note and walking away, as he had done before. They could manage to get back to the airport and back to New York by themselves. They were seasoned travelers, and they were used to being just the two of them. They didn't need anybody else.

The women had been gone a long time. Mack stood up and paced around, wanting this moment to be over, wanting to go back to his barracks and suck his thumb. He looked at the three glasses on the table, half finished. A trace of lipstick marked Patty's glass.

Maybe Patty could take back her promise. If Claudia didn't want him, Beautiful Patty still might. *No. It will never be the same. Even if Patty and I could have our playful sex, Claudia would always be between us.*

He couldn't live with that. He needed to move on. He thought of the woman who had put her head on his chest in the dark room in San Francisco. He thought of several other women he had liked, some he thought he had loved, who might still ... "Shit," he said aloud.

"Sorry it was so long," Claudia said at his elbow. "We needed to work on things." She looked up at him and smiled wanly. "Patty took it worse than you did."

Patty wordlessly found her chair and sat down. She had her sunglasses on again, but Mack could tell she had been crying.

He helped Claudia sit before taking his own chair. He watched her face, and she met his eyes.

"I'm sorry, Mack. On the flight over—I didn't even tell Patty—I realized I had to draw a line between us."

She took a deep breath. "I want to protect our friendship!"

He sighed. "Kinda takes the fun out of the weekend." Then he caught himself and put his hand up. "I didn't mean that the way it sounded."

She took his hand and pressed it against her cheek. "I know what you mean. I didn't want it to come out this way either." She looked around in the almost deserted bar. "I thought we could talk about it."

"I've never felt that sex was the most important part of our relationship," he said. "I always wanted to go deeper with you."

"I've wanted that, too. You always could see me, Mack, somehow, in a way other people don't."

A long silence.

"I'm not very deep," Patty said almost in a whisper.

Mack stood up and took her hand, pulling her to her feet. They stood there embraced for a long time. She laid her head on his shoulder. Then they sat back down.

After another long silence, Mack spread his hands out on the table. "Now what?" His voice sounded dead even to him.

"I don't know," said Claudia. She looked from Mack to Patty. "I've pretty much ruined our visit, haven't I?" Her face was drawn with desolation. "I'm sorry!"

"Claudia, I said that sex isn't that big a thing, not compared with all the things we have had, all the happiness you've brought me."

"But it's the center point of it all," she said. "It always is. It's the way people really connect with each other. We say, let's just be friends, but it leaves a hole in us."

Patty spoke softly. "Friends fuck. They do."

"Not always, Love," Claudia said to her. "We have friends that we'd never go to bed with."

Cayman Liberty

"But they aren't—" She stopped, then in a small voice, "They aren't Mack."

Mack turned to Claudia. "You say you still want us to be friends, but then you say sex is the center point. Are you saying you don't want to see me anymore?"

"No!"

"You mean you want to see me, and touch me and kiss me, but never make love to me—and that's okay?"

"It has to be."

He shook his head. "I don't know if I can do that. I said I could, but now it feels like it makes a farce out of the whole thing—out of *us*."

"No. No." She wilted. " I don't know. I just know that I don't want to feel jealous of you—especially with Patty!"

"It's me, isn't it, Claudia?" Patty said, her voice flat. "You can't stand my loving Mack. You've always been jealous of me!"

Claudia covered her face with her hands and sobbed. The other two sat silently and watched her. Then as she began rummaging through her purse, Mack handed her his handkerchief.

Finally she began to speak. "I was so excited to be coming here to see you. But the more I thought about it, the more anxious I got. All those hours in the airplane, I kept thinking that we'd be right back where we were when you left. I couldn't stand to share that part of us, even with Patty—whom I so dearly love—*especially with Patty.*"

"But why, Claudia?" Patty cried. "We've always shared. We've even shared a man before, at Esalen." She stopped and turned toward Mack. "I'm sorry, Mack. That was a long time ago, long before you."

"But," Claudia broke in, "that was, as you call it, fucking friends. He wasn't that important to either one of us." She turned to Mack. "You don't want to hear all of this, Mack."

He sighed. "We're adults, aren't we? When we first met, that wasn't the beginning of our lives, none of us. I wouldn't ask you about your previous relationships, and I wouldn't offer any explanations about mine, unless they were relevant to us." As he spoke, he felt helpless to express what he was feeling. Nothing was coming out right. Nothing he was saying made any sense to him. It was all just words, when he needed to howl in pain.

Now what? He needed to think. "I have to have some time," he said finally. "I don't want to hurt either of you with all this going on inside me. I need to go back to the base." He stood up. "I'll call you tomorrow."

As he walked out, he felt drunk with despair. Nothing was any good anymore.

Twenty-Three – San Diego Harbor

Mack sat on a fire hose locker at the harbor, looking out at the warships tied up. Ships of pride for him for so many years, now in his mind were tinged with shame and tragedy. Just a few days ago, he had looked at them as somehow his ships. They had represented the power of an ideal, something beyond his little world of Coast Guard cutters and buoy tenders and light houses.

All these new feelings were twisted up with his despair about Claudia. Something had come between them, that wasn't just about sex. His memory of that first evening in the George Town hotel when they first really connected on a deep level, deeper than he had ever felt before with anyone, now that memory seemed laden with irony. She was unexpected in his life, and suddenly it was changed.

He was used to being alone, to separate an important part of himself from others, and to protect that part by withholding it, even in the delights of intimacy—or, what he had identified before as intimacy. He had built a persona with his hands, mastering the intricacies of engines that were his connection to the world. Hidden behind that public face was a vulnerability, soothed by music, guarded against the world. Claudia had revealed that part of him, made him feel it long before he could name it.

Patty had not touched it. Ever the flower child, the perfect playmate, she was blind to something Claudia had exposed. True, she loved him, and she loved her sister enough to sacrifice her own pleasure for her. She knew on some level the sacrifices Claudia had made all their lives so that a blind girl could meet the world with confidence and grace. But she could not see how deeply her sister had given.

Claudia was no saint; she had simply been taught to take responsibility for another the way a mother learns to protect a child. Hidden from the world there was another soul, despairing of ever seeing the light of day.

Somehow these two tender souls recognized each other over a dinner. Just for a moment, they felt a kinship. But the reality of everyday living, differently as it affected each of them, was a chasm separating them.

Claudia could not escape her bonds of responsibility; Mack could not escape the armor that he had built around him. She had to push him away to protect herself; he had to interpret that as rejection of the vulnerable soul he had to protect. They tried to tell each other, to cry out. Inside, perhaps, both knew anyway.

The sun had long since disappeared behind Silver Strand across the bay. Mack made his way back to his barracks, and found a phone message tacked to his door: *Returning to New York. Love, C.*

He wasn't surprised. He didn't know what he would have done or said if he'd been there for her call.

Getting a bag of pretzels from a vending machine, he went to his room and tried to read about diesel engines, finally giving up and going to bed. He didn't even hear his roommate come in late that night.

Twenty-Four – Seattle

The only duty they could find for him after he returned from diesel school was in the engine repair shop at the Seattle base. He had always said he'd never settle for shore duty, but now he didn't care. He did his work and when he was on liberty roamed the streets of Seattle or drove his Volkswagen bus around the area, sometimes camping and hiking through the Cascades. He had no communication with Claudia or Patty.

Slowly, the pain solidified like old picnic food left behind, flattened, tasteless, ignored.

The world hadn't changed, not really. Some people experienced life differently for a while, and hoped that it could become better. The counterculture faded, the edges of it torn by bitterness and violence, the light gone out.

Months later, he got a large envelope in the mail. It was postmarked New York City, but there was no return address on it. Inside was an unsigned piece of artwork, a thick cardboard with an ink drawing of a woman's face—that looked remarkably like Claudia. The board had a coating on it, and tiny scratches over the image revealed the white board underneath, creating a subtle shading in the drawing. A single teardrop was shown suspended at the corner of one eye.

A friend he showed it to pronounced it a "scratchboard" drawing, and admired the technique. Mack bought a frame for it and hung it next to his desk.

Twenty-Five – Seattle, Some Years Later

Mack retired after 25 years in the Coast Guard. He had a healthy nest egg saved up, and was content to work part-time at various marinas. He sometimes dreamt of NOIA, and sometimes of a blind young woman and her sister. He had never married.

One day he had been lolling about a yacht club near Seattle, chatting with boaters, admiring the boats, when he spotted a craft moving slowly into the jetty—an old military-looking boat, which he recognized instantly. Eighty-three feet long, painted white with a blue trim stripe running the length of the gunwale. Some kind of deck house had been built over the stern deck, extending from the wheelhouse to cover the hatch to the engine room. A faint cloud of black smoke followed the boat as it approached the public dock.

Mack walked over to the dock and watched as people appeared on deck to tie the boat up to the fuel dock.

Where the twenty-millimeter gun mount had once stood was a wading pool, with deck chairs surrounding it. Round port holes had been cut into the hull at intervals. The old radar globe had been replaced by modern antennae, along with a cluster of other navigation instruments. Large, comfortable captain chairs were mounted on the flying bridge.

A gray-haired man waited until the boat was secured to the cleats, then swung up onto the dock. The tide was in flood, and soon the deck of the boat would be above dock level. The man nodded to Mack then entered the fuel station office. On deck were two women, one young and one middle-aged. They were sun-browned and bare legged.

Mack strolled over to the boat. "Nice boat," he said to them.

The older woman smiled at him. "She's actually pretty old."

"I know," he said. "I used to sail on one of these."

"Really?" She shaded her eyes from the sun in order to see him more clearly. "I think she was once a Coast Guard cutter."

"Yes," he said, "they built a number of them during the Second World War."

The young woman tilted her head. "And you were actually on one of them? You're not that old!"

"Not during that war," he answered. "I was in during Viet Nam."

The older woman came over closer. She was attractive, her hair beginning to gray, her body as lithe as the girl's. "You want to buy her?"

"What?"

"She's not very fast, and she drinks a lot of gasoline."

"Some of them had diesel engines."

"Not this one."

"I was an engineman. I know those old buckets." Mack laughed, but felt a familiar tug in his midsection.

"Daddy's trying to sell her," the girl said. "We want something newer—something faster."

Mack's mind was in turmoil. "Mind if I look her over?"

"Please, come aboard!"

Other than the portholes in the hull and the cabin behind the wheelhouse, the boat still looked as it did fifty years before. Inside was a different story. The added cabin was outfitted like a luxury yacht, all wood paneling and bright brass fittings. There were sleeping quarters for eight or ten people altogether, with stairs replacing the old ladders and the forecastle remodeled into an elegant bedroom. The old galley was now a proper kitchen and dining area, stretching back into what had been the skipper's quarters. A door opened aft, to another stairway to the main salon.

The gray-haired man appeared as they explored the vessel. "We tried to keep her looking the way she did as a cutter," he said. "She has grand lines."

Mack grinned. "I would have loved to serve on her this way. She's a regular yacht."

"Found her in a yacht club in Florida. She'd been neglected for years."

"I just liked her looks," the woman said. "Proud."

"Do you know her history?"

"I've got papers somewhere," said the man.

Mack looked at the two women. "You don't have a very big crew for this size boat."

They all three laughed. "My boyfriend said he'd crew for us, but he abandoned us for a fiberglass hull."

The woman looked at her daughter. "Sally's feeling deserted."

"He was a jerk," Sally said.

"That 'fiberglass hull' was another woman," said the man. Sally looked down at her feet.

"We're on our way to San Francisco Bay," said the man. "A fellow in Sausalito might be interested in buying her."

Mack introduced himself.

"Sam Whitney. Used to be in finance, always loved boats." He turned and gestured. "Miriam and Sally."

"You're on your way to California. Where from?"

"Alaska. It's still cold in Anchorage. Soon as we get refueled, would you join us for dinner? Be about an hour."

"Sure, thank you." Mack felt something tug at him, an old, familiar feeling.

He helped with the lines when refueling was completed, and Sam expertly piloted the boat to an open slip.

Miriam had prepared an excellent meal of polenta and mushrooms, and Sam poured an expensive pinot noir. "You wouldn't want to crew with us down to Sausalito, would you?" He laughed, then added, "Kidding—but we could use an extra hand."

Mack shrugged. "I'm between jobs right now. I wouldn't mind."

"Wonderful!" said Miriam.

Sally smiled. "We want to get down to the Cayman Islands this winter." It sounded to Mack like an invitation.

"We'd pay your fare back to Seattle from Sausalito," Sam said.

Mack understood that as a small reservation, that he wasn't being offered a permanent job, in spite of what Sally said. "Have to store my car," he said, "and close up my apartment."

"Can you leave tomorrow morning?"

The End

Hood Canal

One

Flying over the Hood Canal Bridge near Port Gamble, he turned southwest and dropped to five hundred feet. The evening sun disappeared behind the Olympic Mountains. It took his eyes a couple of minutes to adjust to the dim light in the gorge. Nothing looked familiar to him until he had passed Dadob Bay and picked up highway 101, down to the right along the shore. A car was going south, its headlights already on.

In that moment, he was forty years younger, driving that old Ford away from Port Townsend, going around the Canal because he didn't have money for the ferry. The back seat had been filled with everything he owned—which wasn't much. The gathering gloom had reflected his mood. He hadn't known where he was going, other than *away*.

Now he was retracing that trip in the Cessna. He wasn't sure why, except to capture, if he could, who he had been and why he had made the decision to leave her. He lowered the flaps and throttled back until he was pacing the car, watching its headlights appearing and disappearing through the trees along the road. Without intending to, he allowed the airplane to descend until he was only a hundred feet above the water. At that speed, the nose was high and he couldn't see much directly ahead. He was simply following the shoreline and its highway.

There were more houses than he remembered. A lot had changed, no doubt, in those years. He himself had changed; it seemed he was a different person altogether. He had lived several lives since then, raised a different family, left again, finally settling for something less, in which nothing was expected of him.

Hood Canal

Hood Canal isn't really a canal, but a long, narrow inlet from Puget Sound, a fjord sixty-five miles long, a mile or so wide. To the west is the Olympic Peninsula; to the east is Kitsap Peninsula.

The lights of the power station appeared ahead—that's what he remembered clearly from that evening as he had driven south along the shore of the Canal. In the shadow of the mountains beside the dark water, incongruous boulevard lights lined the road, as though they were in a city. They marked the massive building that furnished electricity for miles around all the way to Tacoma. Boulevard lights that spoke of civilization, of a quiet competence that made the world predictable and comfortable. Even out here, miles from any city, a token of permanence and solidity.

Solidity that was missing in his mind so long ago as he had driven the old car along the dark road and came suddenly upon those lights to remind him that there was a world, somewhere, in which people knew who they were and what they were supposed to do with their lives. Suddenly, it had seemed, away from his family and out of the military, both of which had given him a ground from which to try out that mysterious opportunity to live on his own, but which he had squandered for lack of clear vision; suddenly he'd been on his own. And he'd blown it. His skipper had reminded him that he needed his permission to marry, even though he did not withhold it. His own father had suggested in a letter that it wasn't a good idea with so little experience in life, even though he didn't tell him what to do. It took almost three years for him to come to the realization that he'd not been prepared to be an adult.

His airplane this night represented all that he had lacked back then. He was proud of the little Cessna as many men were proud of their cars, as a symbol of having arrived in that mysterious civilization, carrying him wherever he wanted to go, above all the crowded roads and traffic, holding him comfortably above all the rest. No longer did he cringe in the presence of others, feeling inferior, even invisible. It had taken most of those forty years since ...

A sudden awareness caught him. He flicked on his landing light to see the surface of the water just yards below his wheels. Throttling up, he pulled back gently on the yoke, feeling beads of sweat on his forehead. Even yet, he thought, he was not always so safe in the little cabin. He had to watch where he was going. He forgot the power station and its boulevard lights and the mountain road along the shoreline. He'd seen it again; that was enough.

Climbing to eight hundred feet and turning east, he looked for the lights of Tacoma Narrows Field that extended almost to the edge of a cliff overlooking the Sound. As soon as he saw it, he turned south across the water so that he could approach from the cliff side. It made him a little nervous, knowing that his touchdown had to be on the runway—landing short could be sure death against the cliff. But better that than landing toward the south, where overrunning would launch him into the air only to fall into the cold, dark waters. He smiled at these fears. The Cessna knew how to do it. He contacted the tower and requested permission to land on runway 34, then turned into the landing pattern.

The Tacoma Narrows Field was the closest lighted field to where he was going. In daylight, he would have chosen the little Port Orchard field, just a few blocks from her home. But it was only a twenty-mile cab ride from the Narrows.

Two

"I expected you earlier," she said after a tentative embrace. "When you called you were only over Ellensburg. You said you'd be here earlier."

He smiled uncertainly. "I think I got cold feet," he said. "I wanted to go down Hood Canal first."

"Hood Canal? Why?"

"You know that power plant, down at the bottom of the Canal? I remembered it from driving that way, a long time ago. I guess it represented something to me, and I wanted to see it again."

She shook her head, not comprehending. "Your dinner is cold, she said. "I'll warm it up."

He watched her move about her kitchen, marveling at the simple fact of her existence. Forty years—she was no longer the two-year-old, golden-curled child he had been remembering all these years. Only the hair seemed the same. Now more than twice as old as her mother, the girl he had married back then, she was a stranger to him—and yet she wasn't.

Pulling a wine bottle from the refrigerator, she showed it to him and raised her eyebrows in a question she didn't need to voice. He nodded. Words came hard for both of them. She put the bottle and two glasses on a low table next to a sofa. "Come," she said, "sit down for a minute."

They kept looking at each other without meeting eyes. Nervous, tentatively sizing each other up, they didn't know what to say. How to bridge forty years in small talk?

"How's your mom?" He had to ask. He really didn't care. That girl he had left behind with their child no longer fit into his world. There had been other women, several, in the years since then. Even other children, also now a part of his past.

"She's fine." Simple answer, not answering at all.

"I don't know what to say," he said.

She sipped her wine. "I'm glad you're here."

"Yes. It's been too long."

"Too long." Setting her glass down, she looked at him, a direct, almost challenging look. Then she lowered her eyes. "I was afraid you'd changed your mind."

"I was so glad when I got your letter," he said, "I've been looking forward to seeing you. But the closer I got the more scared I got. I wanted to get in touch with that night—the night I left. I thought I could explain to you …"

"Why did you drive all the way around Hood Canal?" she asked.

"No money for the ferries." The statement was almost meaningless after all those years and the bridges built since then. He remembered again that dark night, not only the darkness of the drive but the darkness of his heart, fleeing from a life he didn't know how to live.

After a long silence, he said, "When I first saw that power plant, way out there in the wilderness that night, all the lights around it, it was like there was hope out there somewhere. I guess it had an effect on me."

"I still don't know why—" She stopped, and looked down. "I know, I know, Mom isn't the easiest person to live with."

He reached over and took her hand. "I'm not either," he said, holding her eyes. "We were both too young."

She looked away, and took a sip of wine.

A timer rang in the kitchen. "Let's eat something," she said, getting up and moving away from him.

"You haven't eaten, either?"

She simply looked at him, then began dishing food from a casserole onto two plates. "I hope this is still good."

They carried their plates back to the table by the sofa. He felt tied up inside, unable to think or to feel. This wasn't what he had wanted it to be, a reunion, a warm reconnection, a restoring of family. He felt her distance from him, a thin edge of civility that could at any minute burst into blame. She was the adult, accusing him by withholding the reassurance he wanted. He felt shame and loss. They ate silently.

"It's too late, isn't it?" he said, looking over at her. "It's been too long."

She carefully put her fork in her plate, and then covered her face and sobbed. He wanted to put his arm over her shoulder but couldn't. He couldn't risk her outright rejection.

Taking a deep breath, he finally said, "I'm sorry." Then he choked up and couldn't go on.

She straightened up and wiped her face with the back of her hand. Still not looking at him, she said in a voice husky with emotion, "When I found out—when I finally made Mom tell me who you were—I had to find you. I don't know what I expected. Well, I was afraid you wouldn't even answer my letter. But I had to find you."

"When I got your letter," he said, "it was a shock. I'd given you up so many years ago, I never thought I'd see you again. And then I started a reply; it was stiff and formal; I think I was on my guard. I guess I didn't know why you wrote, and I was kinda nervous."

She looked at him, her eyes cold. "You thought I wanted something from you?"

"I didn't know. But I couldn't send that. I deleted it and sent you what I did."

They had exchanged a dozen messages since those first ones, feeling each other out, trying to find out what a relationship could look like after all those years. She needed roots—discovering that she had been adopted by her father had left her suddenly adrift. Not that Wayne wasn't good to her. He was all she had ever known as a father. Until her discovery, she accepted him with his faults and his idiosyncrasies, just as she did her mother. She'd left home to attend college, married and settled in this area not far from them.

"All those years," she finally asked, "did you ever think about me?"

"Of course I did. I didn't think I had a right to."

"You gave me up." Her voice was hoarse.

"At the time, I thought it was best for both of us. Your mom was remarried, and I'd been trying to get her to send me some pictures of you."

"Why didn't you fight for me?" It was a challenge, and it made him feel small and ashamed.

He sighed. "I don't know," he said. "I didn't know how to go from there. I was not very grown up myself. I thought it would just complicate your life, I guess."

"Complicate *your* life, you mean."

"Complicate my life. Yes."

"Then—when you were grown up—what did you think?"

He stared at the fork he still held in his hand. "I guess I wanted to pretend you didn't exist. I didn't know how to put you into my life. When I thought about you, I felt guilty. So I didn't think about you."

Her voice was hoarse again. "If I had known you existed when I was seventeen, you'd probably have found me on your doorstep."

"That's a tough age for a kid—and for a parent." He hadn't wanted to generalize. He wanted to be real to her, honest and open. During the long flight out from the Midwest, he kept telling himself that if their reunion were going to mean anything at all, he had to be straight with her and insist she be the same.

Right now it didn't seem that the second part was going to be a problem. "If one of my girls were adopted," she said, her voice carrying an edge of anger, "I'd be sure she knew it and also knew that we *chose* her. I can't imagine keeping a secret like that from a child."

He ate in silence. What if her mother had kept him in touch with his daughter? His life would not have been the same. He accepted her adoption request because at the time he was in the midst of another relationship, one that might not be able to accommodate another child in his life. But also—and he had mentally flagellated himself for this many times since—he didn't know how to be an absentee parent. It felt too complicated. Like a juggler trying to bring another ball into his performance mid-throw. Just as he had begun to feel grown up and able to function as an adult, it was all he could do to maintain his balance. It was a different life.

He'd told himself that others have been through the same dilemma. With all the divorces nowadays, a lot of children have been left dangling—unintended victims, "collateral damage," having to grow up torn between their parents who couldn't stay together. He could rationalize his reluctance to stay connected because it seemed she would be better off. And, of course, so would he.

He started to say something about not being able to influence her mother, that she had made her own decisions. But it seemed petty and self-serving.

"I know," she said, almost echoing his thought, "it was Mom's decision. It had to be. That's how she is, how she's always been."

They finished their food. She stood up and took the plates to the kitchen. "More wine?"

He nodded and she poured.

"I'm glad you found me," he said finally.

Her voice was barely above a whisper. "Did you try?"

"No."

They sat in silence.

"I wish I had." Even to him, it sounded weak.

"When?"

It was obvious to him that she wanted a sign, anything that would tell her that she meant something to him. "As soon as I got back home," he said. "As soon as I got back to Indianapolis, I thought, 'What have I done?' I missed you then."

She looked at him, her eyes glistening.

He looked down, sipped his wine. "When did you first know about me?" he asked, aware that he was almost mumbling.

"Six months ago. I *told you*—as soon as I knew, I had to find you."

They were silent for a few moments. Then he asked, "Where's your family?"

"Roger took the girls to his folks' for the night. I thought it would be easier for us to get acquainted."

"Yes."

She went to a bookshelf and brought back a framed photograph. "Here's the family," she said.

He looked at the photo of her and Roger and the two teen-aged girls. Smiling through wet eyes, he asked, "Do they know about me?"

"Of course. I told them as soon as you said you'd come. Roger knew, of course—he helped me find you."

"Chris knew about you," he said, "I don't know, a long time ago, but you didn't become real until your emails." He looked down at his hands. "Maybe not to either of us."

"How was she—Chris—about you coming here?"

"She encouraged me. She said I should have done it years ago."

Another long silence.

Then he said, "I should have."

Her voice was hoarse with emotion. "Yes, you should have!" She stifled a sob. "But you should have *wanted* to!"

He sipped his wine.

"Part of me," she said, her voice calmer, "feels that you should have. And a part of me feels that I want you to want to. They're two different things. I want you to *feel me!*"

He set his wine glass down and turned to face her. In a near-whisper, he said, "I feel you right now."

They leaned toward each other and embraced. Finally, she pulled away and stood up. "I need a Kleenex."

She returned with a box. "You have other children. Do they know?"

When she looked at him, he nodded.

"Do you have pictures?"

He opened his bag and brought out an envelope of photographs. "That's Rachael," he said, pointing, "Jennifer and Leland."

"That's Chris?" she asked, touching another photo. When he nodded, she said, "and your dog."

"Tasha."

"I like dogs."

"You have dogs?"

"Woody and Kisha. They went with Roger and the girls."

The tension he felt eased a little bit, talking about other people, anything but *why he had abandoned her*. He breathed deeply.

Finally, he had to say it. "Your mom and I would never have made it."

She looked at him steadily. "I can't imagine the two of you together," she said. "You are so different."

"Especially after forty years."

"Ever, I think. I've tried to ask her about you, but she won't talk about it. I don't think she would ever have told me if I hadn't asked her point-blank."

"How did you find out?"

She looked away. "Little things over the years, things people said to me, or things I heard, they just added up after a while. So I asked her."

"Does your dad—your stepdad— know you know?"

She shook her head. "He lives in Oregon. I haven't seen him since I found out."

"Will you tell him?"

"I don't know." She played with the envelope lying on the table. "I have to sort out how I feel." Looking up at him, she said, "This is pretty new to me."

"It's new to me, too."

"But you've known all my life!"

Her sudden vehemence startled him. "Not *this*," he said. "That was a different life. You were two years old. That was not you!"

She burst into tears. When he put a hand on her shoulder, she pulled away. After a time, she reached for a Kleenex. "But that was the me that you left." Her voice was flat.

"That wasn't even me," he said. "That was just some kid who didn't know who he was. He didn't have a clue about having a wife and baby."

She looked up at him. "Does anybody? Kids get married every day without knowing how. They get pregnant without knowing what it's going to mean—forever."

"Did you plan to have your first baby?" When she looked at him sharply, he put up a hand. "I know. That's not the issue, is it? We all get faced with big things, even before we're ready. Now, I know—I think I know—what one does when the shit hits the fan."

"*Is that what you think of me?*" she almost shrieked.

He stood up, shaking. "I need to use the bathroom," he said.

Out of her presence, he took several deep breaths. In the mirror he saw an old man. *This was a mistake,* he thought. He sat for a long time, trying to understand what was happening.

In their emails, everything had been respectful, careful of each other's feelings. He had wanted to come here, to see her, to somehow create a relationship with her. He wanted a link to that long-ago person he'd been, who had run from a situation he didn't know how to deal with. Guilt had been a familiar to him all those years. He knew he should have stayed and worked things out, not to stay with her mother but to stay with her, because she was a part of him.

It had been easy to forgive that kid. He did what he had to do. But the girl he had left was not alone. They had created another person, one who had to live her life with whatever parents she was given. He should have been there for her, taken her hand when she stumbled, cuddled her on his lap when she cried.

He remembered watching his other children grow up; he had done those things with them. How could he not have done them with her?

And here was the nightmare. It was *she,* this middle-aged woman in the other room, confronting him with his worst nightmare. He could see them as two different people, but she couldn't. She was still, inside, that two-year-old with the blond curls, surrounded by a mature woman who had lived a whole lifetime without him, who had faced her own terrible choices and collected her own memories.

The confused nineteen-year-old still sat inside him, surrounded by an old man who wanted to resolve something that couldn't be resolved.

He went back to the living room, where she sat, looking at his photographs. She looked up.

"I'm sorry," she said sadly.

"I didn't know it was going to be so hard," he said, sitting beside her. "I didn't mean that. I didn't mean *you.* When your mom told me she was pregnant, I didn't know what to do. That's what I meant."

"I know. I'm sorry."

"Neither of us knew what to do."

"At least you got married."

"Was that the best thing to do?" He shrugged.

"Better than an abortion," she said, then looked up at him and smiled wryly. "We wouldn't be sitting here talking like this right now."

"I hate the idea."

She turned toward him and asked in a small voice,. "Do you?"

"This may be hard for both of us. But there was a hole in me until you came along to fill it."

She embraced him, put her head on his shoulder, and whispered, "That's what I wanted to hear."

They held each other for a long time.

Later, she led him to the guest room. "You can sleep late if you want. Roger and the girls will probably get here after eleven."

"My plane is at the Tacoma Narrows airport. Could you drive me down in the morning? I will fly it up here to your little airport. I'm sure the fees are cheaper."

She laughed. "Of course."

He set his bag down next to the bed. "We agreed," he said, "on a couple of days."

She smiled.

He cleared his throat. "A little while ago I was wondering if I should leave sooner."

"Not this time," she said, giving him a quick kiss on the cheek. "Good night."

Three

He lay awake for a long time, thinking. It was still hard to reconcile this situation, this time, with the time of that drive down Hood Canal forty years ago and who he was then.

As she had pointed out, almost none of us are prepared to be adults in this culture. As children we anticipate "growing up" as some far-off goal, and we fantasize about the things we expect to do and have. Our childhood homes are simply launching pads, to be left behind as we fly into the world. Some of us without wings.

He remembered a book he'd read by Diane Ackerman, in which she had described the attempt of a young bird to fly from its nest. She had watched the unfortunate creature struggle to do what it was born to do, and finally, gently, she had lifted it back to the nest, where its next attempt was successful.

How he wished that he could have had that helping hand when he was suddenly on his own! Not just for his sake, but for hers. He had deprived her of the very thing he lacked.

And yet, here she was, fully formed and beautiful, a mother herself—someone who would be there for her own offspring as they poised on the edge of their nest. They would never wonder what the world was like, for she would be there with them, for them, a gentle hand to lift them up when they fell.

Her mother, that very young woman he had left, had somehow managed to raise her into the mature woman she was now. Perhaps, he thought, the human female is somehow equipped by nature, in spite of a lack of support, to prepare her offspring for life.

Why, then, had he been so bereft of a capacity to launch himself? His own childhood was stable and relatively serene. He could not claim trauma or chaos in his early years, or a lack of responsible elders. It seemed simply that he cast himself adrift.

Countless others have always found themselves on the rim of the nest and succeeded, however tentatively, to attain flight. Was it just luck that separated him from them?

Luck, and perhaps a need for something even more: love. He remembered keenly those first weeks of finding himself walking the streets of the world without another's hand in his—a parent, a sibling, or a friend—and feeling lost.

Her mother had happened along, probably herself just as lost, just as keenly needing something to steady her in that precarious perch on the edge of the nest. They had given each other something.

And then the child.

Parenthood, the part of being an adult that has always carried the most significance. What those two young people needed most was the thing that family traditionally provides: guidance and support in bringing another generation into being.

He had failed the test.

He slept fitfully, dreaming sometime during the night of headlights along a dark road, of needing to escape. And then there were the boulevard lights, the lamps of security, of competence.

Four

When he awoke, it was daylight outside. He could smell food cooking.
She smiled when she saw him. "You did need sleep," she said.
He watched her prepare his breakfast, a mother doing what mothers do, knowing what needs to be done, competent and practiced. "Roger usually cooks breakfast," she said.
As they ate eggs and potatoes, she went on talking, as though this were an ordinary day, as though he were not a stranger who happened into her life after forty years. As though he were not responsible for her very being in this world.
"We can go get your airplane," she said, "and be back before Roger gets here with the girls."
"And the dogs," he said, smiling.

They exchanged eye contact, and something more, maybe even, finally, acknowledgment.

He'd read someplace recently about mirror neurons, that part of the brain that registers what others are thinking or feeling, and that respond in kind, all without our awareness. That *click* that sometimes happens even between strangers.

They didn't talk much on the drive, eventually turning onto the road leading to the Tacoma airfield. She waited in the car for him to check out at the terminal, then walked with him to his Cessna.

"Beautiful," she said.

"Yes," he said, walking around the airplane, wiggling parts of it, checking the wheels. "My pride and joy."

It hit both of them at the same time: *pride and joy— a machine?* And then their eyes met again, this time without the flow of whatever it is, strangers looking *at* each other, wondering what the other was thinking.

Then she said, "I'd love to go up in her sometime."

"Of course."

"When you get back to Port Orchard."

He noticed her reference to the gender of the airplane. He often used that pronoun himself, but couldn't bring himself to do it now. "We could go up right now," he said.

"No, then we'd still have the car here."

"Right."

He turned and embraced her briefly, then climbed into the Cessna. Opening the window beside him, he said, "I can find the field, if you can pick me up there."

She simply smiled, and waited while he started the engine. Shielding her face from the prop stream, she stepped back, but didn't leave.

Hood Canal

"Watch the tail," he called over the noise, and she looked around and backed farther away.

Putting on his headset, he announced his intentions to the tower. Then he turned toward her and nodded.

She watched him taxi out to the end of the runway and take off, and then she walked back to her car.

He was waiting for her on a bench next to the little Port Orchard hanger when she drove up.

"Roger and the girls are home," she said when he climbed into the car. Turning to face him, she said, "Are you ready for this?"

He sighed deeply. "Are we okay?"

"We've made a start," she said, "haven't we?"

When he nodded, she slipped the car into Drive and eased out of the airfield.

The End

Donald Skiff

The Smile

The Smile

One

Pop! Pop! Pop! Three quick flashes of the strobes accented the sweet guitar *arpeggio* in Eric Clapton's "Wonderful Tonight" playing on the PA.

In the dim light at the edge of the studio set, Wayne looked up from his camera monitor. "Ask them to hold position, please," he said to Annie, the floor girl next to him.

She touched her headset, and her words interrupted the music. "Hold positions, please," she said. Eric Clapton continued playing, as though nothing had happened.

Wayne put a hand lightly on Annie's shoulder as he slipped his shoes off. The two exchanged quick smiles, and he stepped onto the heavy paper of the set.

Leaning close to the coffee-colored woman in the brown wrap, he said quietly, "You have a nice smile."

Trying not to move the position of her head, she turned her eyes toward him, the unspoken question flicking across her face.

He grinned at her. "Sorry," he said. "That wasn't fair, was it? I just meant it went away just before the exposure."

"I'm sorry," she said.

"Are you okay?"

She smiled. "I'm fine."

"Try one more?"

She nodded.

Waving at the other women on the set, Wayne stepped back into the shadows to his camera. "Okay," he said to the floor girl.

"Positions," she said into her headset. Eric Clapton had already finished his track.

Pop! Pop! Pop!

Wayne zoomed in on the image on his monitor, studied it for a moment, then said, "Okay, wrap it up."

He turned around to look at the suits in the back of the room watching their own monitors. Charlie, in the middle of them, nodded.

"It's a wrap." Annie's voice came out of the big speakers on the edge of the set.

Wayne walked back to the group of men. "Okay?" he asked.

"Good work," said one of them.

Charlie shook his hand. "Excellent," he said. "Have a drink with us?"

Wayne smiled and shook his head. "Too early in the day," he said.

Returning to his camera, he unplugged the cables and lifted it off the tripod. "Thank you," he said to the girl with the headset. Glancing at the now-empty set, he asked, "What's her name?"

She touched the screen on her tablet. "Kayla." She glanced quickly at him. "Pretty," she said simply.

"Yes."

Annie removed her headset and wound the thin cable on her hand.

Wayne stowed the camera in its case and rolled the tripod to the side of the room.

She hesitated. "Last name Sharma," she said.

He smiled at her, picked up his gear, and left the studio.

Later at home, Wayne sat on the sofa with his tablet in his hands. He accessed the modeling agency that they had used that day and searched for "Kayla Sharma." Her page came up at once, and he studied the head shots of her. Then, switching to his camera stream from

The Smile

the day's shoot, he compared his photos of the woman with the agency's photos.

She had a wistful smile that had captivated him immediately and that he had missed when he saw the first shots of the last set. Her skin was light enough that the gaffer had no trouble balancing her skin tones with the other models. Wayne didn't usually pay a lot of attention to the models he photographed, beyond what was needed for the assignment. There were so many beautiful women. It had been a lot of years since he gave up panting over the talent in his business.

He was meeting Charlie for dinner at the Bistro. As he entered, he saw that Charlie had in all likelihood been there all afternoon. Slumped on a bar stool, Charlie grinned at him and swung his overweight body off the stool. He turned to finish his drink on the bar, then floated toward Wayne.

"Are you going to be able to eat anything?" Wayne asked.

"No problem." Charlie slurred the last word,

"I hope your wife knows where you are."

Charlie just grinned. Friday night dinner had been a tradition for the two of them for years.

"TGIF," said Wayne, following the hostess to a table.

They ordered their meal and then sipped on wine. "I've never met anybody who could outdrink you, old man," Wayne said.

"In this business, you have to learn how."

"You drank with your clients all afternoon?"

Charlie grinned. "Those chickens. They quit after two drinks. By that time, I knew I wouldn't be able to work anymore—besides, it's Friday!"

"How's your liver doing?" Wayne couldn't help worrying about his friend sometimes.

240

"C'mon, Aunt Millie!" Charlie laughed. Then his face became serious. "Actually, I did have an Aunt Millie. She died a year ago."

"You were close?"

"Yeah. She always got on my case for drinking, but she made a joke about it."

"What'd she die from?"

"Some kind of woman thing. Cancer, I think. She took care of me when my folks split up. I was about eight."

"So you don't want me to nag you."

"Janet does enough of that." Charlie was smiling, but he wasn't amused.

"Your wife wants you to lose weight, too, doesn't she?"

"Leave it alone, Pal."

"Okay. Sorry." Wayne sighed. "I just keep thinking of all the things I ought to be doing to take care of myself. I guess it rubs off."

"We're cool, Bro."

"Okay, let's change the subject. You know that dark-skinned woman in the last shoot today?"

Charlie guffawed. "I saw you go up and whisper to her!"

"Strictly professional," Wayne said. "She had stopped smiling."

"Cute girl."

"Reminded me of a girl I used to know."

"Here, or in India?"

"I was over there about twenty years ago, on assignment from a magazine." Wayne leaned back in his chair.

"I hear a story coming on," said Charlie.

"We were in love. I saw her in a market one day, and I was hooked. She liked the way I talked—" Wayne

The Smile

switched to a down-home accent— "like I used to down in Lou'v'lle."

Charlie's face lit up. "I remember when you used to talk that way!"

"Naw, you never done it."

"Anyway, 'bout this chick."

Wayne looked off to the side. His memory absorbed him. "Her mother was dead-set against me."

"Her folks probably had her husband all picked out for her."

"Something like that. Anyway, Kayla has a smile like she had."

"So, when are you and Kayla getting together?" Charlie signaled the waitress with his wine glass.

Just then their food arrived, and both men turned their attention to dinner.

After their coffee, they made their way to the parking lot. "You okay?" asked Wayne.

Without saying anything, Charlie stepped up on the curb beside the pavement and walked, arms extended, the length of the narrow strip. At the end, he stepped off, glanced back at Wayne and continued toward his car.

Wayne got into his own car and eased out of the lot, punching up a Pink Floyd album, very loud. Driving home, he thought about young brown-skinned women.

Two

"Come to America with me," he pleaded.

She tilted her head, allowing her long, black hair to drift across her bare arm, and looked sadly at him. "Wayne," she said, "I can't! You know I can't."

He stroked her hair, following its curves down to her arm. "I have to be in New York on Friday," he said. "At least say you'll let me call you."

"Of course. At work, not at home."

He had never called. By the time he got to New York, there was another assignment waiting for him in Singapore. He still carried her picture in his wallet after all this time, and for years intended to call her.

The magazines kept him busy, sending him around the world for local color to accompany travel and fashion articles. Occasionally he participated in fashion shoots in glamorous locations. He enjoyed photographing women. Eventually, the regular fashion photographers requested him on their assignments, and he began getting assignments on his own. Traveling with the models was a treat, even though their high-strung art directors usually made everybody tense when they got to their locations. Then, more and more, he traveled alone, meeting the rest of the people at the site. Often, he was the only American present. Beautiful girls come from all over.

Twelve-hour flights became a drag, and Wayne took fewer and fewer overseas assignments. Then he encountered a bug, some kind of intestinal parasite, and spent several years remaining close to home and his doctor. For the past five years, he'd worked mostly for local agencies, and settled into a life style, as he said, "appropriate for my age." He dated occasionally, seldom with models. "I'm too old for those chicks," he told Charlie.

"Don't forget your biological clock," said Charlie. "You better find your one true love pretty soon, or you won't have anyone to take care of you in your old age."

The Smile

Charlie was middle-aged, like him, and had two kids in high school. His wife taught school and nagged him about his weight.

Three

"Can you give us another couple of days?" Charlie's girl friday asked him on the phone. "Same client, different catalog."

Wayne thumbed his phone. "It'd have to be Thursday and Friday this week. I've got another shoot in Boston next week."

"That'll work for us. Lemme get a confirmation from the client."

On Thursday morning, Wayne showed up at the agency. Charlie and the clients were waiting in the conference room, looking through the layouts for the shoot. Their AD was the same, but the account execs were different.

"We'll be shooting singles this time," said the AD. We liked the expressions you got on the girls last week."

One of the girls turned out to be Kayla. At the camera, when Wayne gave a little sigh, Annie looked at him. "Did you ask her out?" she asked in a near whisper.

Wayne shook his head.

The shoot went well. Kayla remembered to smile, and to smile again at him as she left the studio.

Four

"I don't usually date models," Wayne said. The waiter had just brought their drinks.

"Why?" Kayla asked.

He looked at her. Even more beautiful in her street makeup, she showed a little dimple beside her mouth. "The truth?"

"The truth."

"Beautiful women intimidate me. Probably something from my adolescence. I never feel good enough."

"You're very good looking yourself," she said.

He grinned. "You're what—like, twenty?"

"Nineteen, if you must know." She was smiling at him. "You're not that old."

He waved his hand to dismiss the compliment. "That's not it, really. We're just having dinner. But when we walked into this place, heads turned." He raised his hand to ward off her response. "Don't get me wrong. I am truly happy that you agreed to come out with me. It's not just your looks—you know how you look and how you affect people. How could you not?"

"You were nice to me. I wanted to know you better," she said.

"Same here."

"So," she said, leaning back and smiling across her white lady, fingering the edge of the glass, "what's the problem?"

He sighed. "For nineteen, you seem very mature."

"Thank you." She sipped her drink.

"Last week, when I told you that you had stopped smiling," he said, and swirled the ice cubes in his gin and tonic, "I felt—disappointed, I guess."

"I'm sorry. I didn't mean to change my expression."

"No, that's not it. I mean personally. You reminded me of someone who had that same smile, a long time ago."

"Long lost love."

"Yes."

The Smile

She made a half-serious pout for a moment, then asked, "What was she like?"
"Beautiful. Long black hair. I wanted to bring her back to New York with me."
"Oh? Where was this?"
"Bombay."
Kayla looked surprised. "Mumbai! That's where I'm from! Well, sort of. I was born here, but my parents came from Mumbai."
Wayne smiled, and pulled from his wallet a badly frayed and faded photograph.
When Kayla looked at it, her eyes widened.

Five

Anusha sat with her tea, wondering what her daughter was upset about. The girl had phoned late last night, almost in tears. "May I come to talk with you after work?"
"Of course."
It was probably a man. It's almost always about a man. Anusha remembered how upset she used to get about men in her life. *American men are so different from us.* Sometimes they are sweet, but in the end, they also need to satisfy themselves regardless of how a girl feels.
When the doorbell rang, she let Kayla in and gestured toward the teapot on the table.
They sat opposite each other across the table, cross-legged on cushions, and Anusha poured tea. Kayla used to object to that position, saying that it felt demeaning. Anusha thought it simply more graceful. But with Kayla's short American skirts, it did look uncomfortable.

"Ma, I have to ask you a very personal thing," Kayla said after a time.

Anusha waited.

"I was talking with a man last night," and she blushed. "I don't know him very well, but he has been very sweet to me."

Anusha sighed. "You are so bold."

"No, really, we met where I was working, and he asked me to have dinner with him. He was very polite."

"But Chitralekha, you were so upset when you called." Anusha used Kayla's Hindu name when she was speaking intimately.

"He showed me a photograph—a very old photograph that he carried in his billfold."

Anusha could imagine what kind of photograph it was. She frowned.

"He said it was taken in Mumbai, many years ago."

Her mother waited, watching the expression on her daughter's face.

"It looked like you," Kayla said. Then, after a long pause, "It *was* you!"

Anusha had difficulty breathing. She finally said, "Who did he say it was?"

"Someone he loved." Kayla was watching her mother closely. "Could it have been you?"

Anusha blushed, but said nothing.

"Please, Ma. Tell me."

"What did you say to him?"

"Nothing! What could I have said?"

"It is from the past. Do not dwell on it." Anusha took a deep breath, and sipped her tea. She frowned.

"But Ma!"

"He could have found the photograph someplace, any place. You don't know where it came from."

The Smile

"He said he wanted to marry you and bring you to New York with him."

It was all Anusha could do to keep her composure. She rose and took the teapot to the kitchen.

Kayla followed her. "Does Papa know about him?"

Her mother turned to her, anger showing in her face. "You don't know anything! You just saw a picture—it wasn't of me!"

"It was! It looked just like—" and she went to a bookshelf and brought back a photo album. "It looked just like you did when you and Papa married." She turned pages until she found what she was looking for. "See? I know what you looked like then!"

Anusha shook her head.

"You weren't wearing Hindu clothing. You were dressed like Americans, but it was you." Kayla put a hand on her mother's arm.

"I don't know how to convince you," Anusha said quietly. "But why did it upset you? When you called last night I could hear tears in your voice."

Kayla hung her head. "I don't know. It just felt important. You've never talked about other men in your life." She looked up. "Since you and Papa divorced, you've seemed so lonely."

Anusha pressed her lips together, as if to prevent something from escaping from them. She put her hand on the handle of the kettle. "Do you want more tea?"

Her daughter sighed. "No, I'd rather have a drink of liquor."

"You are not old enough to drink," said Anusha. "Does the place where you were eating dinner serve alcohol to minors?"

Kayla smiled. "They were very gracious there. I had a cocktail, a white lady."

"A white lady—is that what you are trying to be, a white lady?"

"Mother! It's just the name of the cocktail. It's quite sweet. It has lemon juice in it and a sugar syrup, and gin."

"You make yourself vulnerable when you drink alcohol," Anusha said, "and men take advantage of you."

"He was sweet. He never took advantage of me. He's older ..."

Anusha's eyebrows raised. "Older?"

Kayla smiled, her head down. "He's your age, I think."

"Oh, Chitralekha!"

"Ma! It's not what you think! He was a perfect gentleman."

"What did he say about this photograph he showed you?"

"He just said that she was beautiful, and that he had wanted to bring her with him to New York."

Anusha turned her back on her daughter and returned to the sitting room. As Kayla followed her, she sensed something else.

"Ma."

They sat down on the sofa. Anusha didn't answer. Kayla watched her face. "Ma."

When her mother turned her face to her, her eyes were glistening.

"Ma. There's something else, isn't there?" Kayla put a hand on her arm.

Anusha looked down.

"Ma, were you pregnant when you married Papa?" The question was asked quietly and gently, but it had the force of a blow. Her mother turned her face away.

"Ma, is Wayne Gunderson my biological father?" It was the question she had needed to be answered since dinner last night. "Ma, it's okay. I just need to know!"

Anusha buried her face in her hands. Kayla put her arms around her. "Ma, it's okay!"

After a long while, Anusha straightened up and, looking straight ahead, said, "God is punishing me!"

"No!"

"Your Papa must never know." The words came out flat and emotionless.

"Ma, of course! Ma, I love you! Papa never needs to know."

Anusha looked at her daughter. Then, in a low voice devoid of feeling, she explained her situation twenty years ago, caught in the traditional culture, swept up in a love that went far beyond such things, pulled between family and passion, even momentarily believing that she could escape to a new life, and yet knowing that she was her mother's daughter. Her husband had been selected for her. She had let Wayne go, even though she suspected that she was carrying his child. Nobody would ever know.

"I am a terrible person," she said.

"Ma, no! Ma, he is a very kind man. It's only that he has carried your photograph in his billfold for all these years, out of love for you." Kayla wrapped her arms around her mother.

As they sat there, Kayla murmured into her mother's shoulder, "I won't tell him, Ma, if you don't want me to. I want to—I want him to know who I am. But if you will feel awful, I will keep your secret." She pulled away to look at Anusha. "Papa will always be my Papa."

They embraced each other for a long time.

Six

PING

Wayne looked at his phone, puzzled. It said only, "Havnt heard from you busy?" He didn't recognize the sender: "Chitralekha".

"Why don't these people use real names?" he muttered. His first impulse was to ignore the text. But the more he thought about it, the more curious he got. *Somebody I know, somebody I've not seen recently.*

He replied, "Sorry don't recognize your name."

Immediately came the response: "Kayla"

It had been several weeks since their dinner, which had left him uneasy. The girl had seemed shocked when she saw the photo he showed her, but they hadn't discussed it, and it was getting late. He drove her to her apartment, where they promised to "stay in touch." She'd given him a quick kiss on the cheek.

Wayne thought that probably the photo had reminded her of someone she knew, but of course it was twenty years old and badly worn from being in his wallet all those years. Still, remembering that night brought a funny feeling to him. He hadn't thought of the woman in years, and had pulled the photo out of its hiding place just because Kayla had a smile that reminded him of her. He'd been a little embarrassed, like a schoolboy surprised in a furtive look at a neighbor.

But she wanted to connect with him again.

He thumbed a reply: "Meet for lunch?"

"Sure. Where. When."

Appearing in public with a beautiful young— young!—woman on his arm felt a little daunting. Wayne was past the age of wanting to flaunt his ability to attract young females, and besides, he'd grown tired of the typical level of conversation with young models. He chose a neighborhood restaurant closer to Kayla's apartment than his own, or to Madison Avenue. "Give me half hour," he texted.

"Good."

The taxi made good time, and he was early, so he waited near the doorway to the restaurant. As she stepped out of her cab, she threw him a bright smile. She wore a dress of mostly white with bold purple swirls that showed off her coffee-colored legs and purple shoes. Wayne couldn't resist a silent *wow*.

He took her elbow and guided her into the little restaurant. There weren't many tables, and no customers waiting.

"I've been thinking about you," she said, sipping white wine.

"Oh? How so?" He felt that familiar tingle of excitement. Beautiful women just have a special power to reduce a man to something between jello and expensive ice cream on a hot day. He remembered that he'd told her the last time they were together that beautiful women intimidated him. He was much more comfortable peering through the viewfinder of a camera, protected from the blaze of beauty. He felt his face get hot.

"You looked wistful when you showed me the photograph. Have you been pining over her all these years?" She had a faintly mischievous smile on her face.

"It was a long time ago." He couldn't tell her how strongly she affected him. He deflected her curiosity by talking about her modeling career, how she saw her future.

They finished their lunch—sans liquor—and promised they would continue to stay in touch. She made sure that he said he would call her soon.

That afternoon Wayne met Charlie for their usual Friday TGIF.

"How's your love life?" Charlie asked as they waited for their cocktails at the bar.

"Still non-existant. How's yours?"

"Goes up and down, as usual," Charlie said. "You been dating that brown-skinned model?"

Wayne grinned. "If you'd asked me yesterday I'd have said no."

The bartender brought their clean martinis, and both men sipped. "Ah, nectar of the gods," Charlie sighed.

"The kids have the idea that a martini should be sweet, or fruity—or full of olive juice."

"Chocolate!"

They both laughed and took another drink from the sparkling glasses.

The hostess approached them with an invitation to take a table. "Great broiled salmon on special," she said.

As they made their way with their drinks to the table, Wayne observed, "You either have to go to your table before you've had more than a sip of your martini or finish the drink first so you don't spill it."

Charlie took a large quaff from his drink as they followed the hostess. Wayne just shook his head.

It was early, and their waiter arrived almost as soon as they sat down. "Give us a few minutes," Wayne said to her.

"Okay, Pal," said Charlie, grinning. "If I'd asked you yesterday—"

"Had lunch with her today."

Charlie propped his chin on his knuckles, waiting.

"She called me this morning, out of the blue."

"Aha! You got a nibble."

The Smile

"Don't know why, for sure. She just asked me a lot about that photo I carry."

"What was her name—the gal in the photo?"

"Anusha."

"You told me Kayla was surprised when she saw it. She say why?"

"No, and I was afraid to ask."

"Cause she might know, uh, Anusha?" He stumbled over the name.

"I got to thinking," Wayne said, "she could even be related to her."

"That smile."

Wayne grinned. "Brought back a lot of memories."

"Okay, then," Charlie said, looking at the ceiling, "let's see—you say Kayla's nineteen."

"What she said."

"Born here, but from Indian parents."

"I tried to do the math. I don't remember exactly when I was with Anusha. About twenty years ago, I think."

Charlie laughed out loud. "Ha! She's your daughter!"

"No. Anusha couldn't have gotten pregnant. She was on the pill. She'd have told me, anyway."

"Yeah. That would have been a scandal for her family."

"But it gives me a funny feeling."

"What if ..."

"Yeah."

They ate their meal and talked about other things, but every once in a while Charlie just looked at Wayne and grinned.

Seven

The next week, Wayne dutifully called Kayla, and she invited him to her apartment for dinner. "Roommate's out for the weekend," she said.

Her apartment was fresh and clean, with modern furniture. She seemed comfortable with cooking, telling him to "watch how traditional Indians do food."

He sipped a drink as they chatted.

"What did you think of India when you were there?" she asked.

"What I saw—I didn't travel around much. I was on assignment, mostly in Bombay, and I was pretty busy."

"Hope you like curry."

"Sure. Not too spicy, though."

She grinned at him. "You'll get used to it."

Pulling warmed naan from the toaster oven, she sliced it and spooned a chutney over the slices. "Fig and ginger," she said. "Very mild."

"Good!" he commented with his mouth full.

Kayla began heating a large skillet, and extracted from the refrigerator a plate of balls of dough. "As soon as the chapatis are done," she said, "we can eat."

She began flattening the chapatis with a rolling pin and placing them in the hot skillet. "Would you please dish out the pulao and masala into those two bowls and put them on the table?"

Wayne followed her instructions, and poured water for them both.

In a few minutes she placed a basket of the thin bread, covered with a napkin, on the table and sat down. Smiling at him, she pointed to the bowls and said, "This is vegetable pulao, and this is paneer butter masala—it's cheese. Please help yourself."

He grinned. "I recognize the paneer."

The Smile

As she offered the basket of bread, they smiled at each other.

Wayne picked up his glass and saluted her. "Smells wonderful!"

"If I were my mother, there would be a dozen other foods on the table as well. I'm pretty Americanized."

Wayne had a sudden impulse to say, "I remember your mother's cooking," but stifled the urge.

He tried to see this young woman as just another young woman he'd recently met, without a history that he knew of. It was difficult, especially after Charlie had spent the evening teasing him, insisting that she was his daughter.

Kayla's smile kept intruding. "I should have asked you if you liked Indian cooking before sitting you down to eat it," she said.

"This is wonderful."

"Not too spicy?"

He made a face, then grinned. "No, it's great."

"You said you hadn't traveled much in India."

"No, I didn't have time that trip," he said. "I always meant to go back."

"For her?"

He felt his face become hot, and he sighed.

"I'm sorry, that was rude, wasn't it?" She reached a hand across the table to touch his.

How can I talk about Anusha? he thought. *I should never have showed her the picture! What if she's related to her? What if Anusha is actually her mother? Those people are so ...*

"I'm sorry," Kayla said quietly. "I embarrassed you, didn't I?"

Wayne took refuge in his food. "This is delicious," he said, smiling.

"Wayne, I don't mean to pry into your life. I'm just trying to get to know you better."

"Why?" He tried to say it gently, without judgment.

"Ever since that first time you spoke to me, in the studio, I've thought that I could be comfortable with you." She raised a hand. "I don't mean romantically. Maybe just the opposite. You seemed so—so considerate."

"Do you have a boyfriend?" Wayne wanted to shift the conversation away from himself.

"Not at present," she said. "I date occasionally, but I'm not looking for any kind of serious relationship."

"Yes, you have a long time to learn what you really want from life."

"I enjoy modeling. I don't very often get assignments where I have to look seductive, and that suits me fine."

"You have great features," he said. "I like the line of your cheekbone—and of course, your smile."

"Thank you. You've seen a lot of models, haven't you?"

"I feel like a voyeur sometimes," he said. "Peering at pretty faces through a viewfinder."

She smiled. That smile. "If you weren't getting paid to do it, would you like it as much?"

He raised his eyebrows. "Wow. That's a personal question." A knot formed in his midsection.

"I'm sorry! I didn't mean it like that! I'm not trying to psychoanalyze you. Just curious."

He grinned. "There are two sides to every photograph. I could ask you if you'd want to pose for people if you weren't getting paid for it."

"Touché. Okay, I can answer you—in a way. I enjoy posing for some people, when it's clear that we're both trying to get a certain effect. Some photographers, though, feel to me as though they're leering at me. Depends on how they act, how they direct me."

"Fair enough." He leaned back in his chair. "But—"

"You didn't leer at me," she said sweetly.

Even as he spoke, he felt his face redden. "Didn't I?"

She shook her head.

"Sometimes I think I do. I told you that beautiful women intimidate me. Behind that, maybe I'm leering."

Kayla tilted her head. "Really?"

"I don't know," he said. "Sexual attraction is complicated. I make an effort to be professional."

"I'd never guess that you were working at it." She smiled.

"Thank you."

They were silent for a few minutes, finishing their meal.

"You know," he began, "I went to a nude beach one time, on the French Riviera. At first, I was really uncomfortable. I was afraid to look at the women, it was so arousing. But after a couple of days, it just felt *normal*."

"I don't think I could do that."

"Most of my work as a photographer gets routine. I can photograph women in swim suits or whatever, and I just concentrate on the task. Somewhere in the back of my mind, I'm sure," and he laughed, "is an ogling teenager. What I'm aware of is, 'here is this pretty woman and my client is paying me to show her at her best' and there's nothing personal going on. It's all composition, light and shadow."

"Tell me more." She sipped her drink. "This is fascinating."

He grinned. "Not yet. First, I want to know when you first thought you'd want to model."

Kayla stood up and began clearing the table. "Do you want tea or coffee with your dessert?"

"Coffee, please." He helped her set out some pastries and cups for the coffee. Then he leaned against the wall and watched her move around the kitchen area. "A recruiter get to you? You're a natural—you have the looks and the grace."

She smiled without looking at him. "A friend suggested I try. He took some head shots and gave me suggestions for applying."

"What did your parents say?"

"Ma hated the idea." She looked up at him. "She's beautiful herself, but she's very shy."

Wayne felt an apprehension well up in his chest. Memories flooded through his brain. Anusha, dressed American style, with short skirt and high heels. She'd been working for a foreign corporation, doing ordinary office work. When he saw her on weekends, though, she wore the traditional sari and sandals, and a bindi—that red dot—on her forehead. He'd met her family, or part of them, and felt awkward in her home. They had treated him politely, but he felt like an intruder. Her mother clearly didn't approve of Anusha spending time with him outside of their domain.

"Have you worked only with that one agency?" He wanted to shift the conversation away from her family.

"They've treated me well," she answered. "Some of the girls make really good money."

They sat back down with their coffee and sweets. Wayne had relaxed, maybe even a little bit more. He tried to be careful of what he was saying, avoiding the thoughts that kept trying to work their way into the conversation. Dangerous thoughts.

"Ever think about doing something besides modeling?

The Smile

She nodded. "This is like professional athletics—one's career time is limited. I'm just starting. I don't know what else I'd be good at."

"College?"

She shrugged. "I just got out of high school. I want to work for a while before I get back into a classroom."

"College is expensive," he said. "Saving your money?"

She laughed. "You sound like my mother!"

"Sorry. Just thinking."

"Ma has always regretted not going to college. She got married and then after I was grown up enough to leave alone she got jobs as secretary and bookkeeper, typical women's work."

She was beautiful enough to be a model, herself, he thought, but stopped himself from saying it. "I guess it's hard, even for professional athletes, to put away money when it's coming in."

"She reminds me, all the time!"

Something was shifting in him. Whether he believed Charlie or not, Wayne was feeling very father-like toward this young woman.

"You haven't married?" Her question took him by surprise.

"No. Came close a couple of times."

"But she couldn't come with you to New York."

His face hot again, Wayne tried to think of something to say that didn't have to do with Anusha. Finally, he half-invented a story. "I grew up in Kentucky," he said. "There was a girl when I was in high school—not much younger than you are. I would have married her in a minute."

"But she had other ideas." Kayla smiled at him.

"Yeah."

"No current prospects?"

"No."

"Nobody you're even interested in?" She was teasing him.

He almost said something about *that smile,* but immediately quelled the thought and shook his head.

She had a mischievous grin on her face. "How do you see *your* future, Wayne Gunderson?"

Red-faced once again, Wayne pursed his lips and thought. "Nobody's asked me that for a long time," he said. "Well, Charlie did a couple of weeks ago."

"Charlie's the account man at the studio?"

"Yeah. He's been married for years, and he thinks my biological clock is running out." Wayne laughed.

Her face grew serious. "Is it?"

He laughed again. "No. But I don't think I want any children—at my advanced age."

She looked down, and almost mumbled, "I think you'd make a good father."

Wayne watched her silently.

After a long time, he said, "I have to be up early in the morning." He pushed his chair back.

Kayla didn't move, but met his eyes. Finally, she also rose, but remained on the far side of the table. Her eyes looked sad.

Wayne thanked her and moved toward the door. "It's been a very nice evening," he said. "For me, anyway."

"I loved having you here." She followed him. "Next time I'll do something more elaborate—show you what Indian food is really supposed to be like."

On the taxi ride home, Wayne felt regret about the evening, guessing that Kayla had wanted him to say something more about the woman in the photograph.

Why didn't I follow up with Anusha? But how could I? She was very clear that she couldn't leave her family. Maybe later, maybe she would have changed her mind.

The Smile

"Shit," he said aloud. The cabbie glanced at him in the mirror, and he smiled.
"You didn't kiss her?" The fellow was grinning at him.
"How'd you guess?"
"The look on your face. I see it a lot."

Eight

It was two weeks before he heard from her again. He had put off calling her, kept telling himself that he had probably hurt her by leaving so abruptly.

He was in Boston on another fashion shoot on the waterfront by the *Constitution,* setting up his camera and monitors when his phone pinged.

"U free nxt Sat for dinner?"

He put the phone back in his pocket without responding, and asked a gaffer to move his light in closer. The two models talked to each other, laughing as they waited for the set to be completed.

He looked at each one closely in his iPad, studying her face and the way she smiled and talked.

"What's the sigh for?" Annie, his assistant, asked at his elbow.

Wayne turned and grinned at her. "Thinking about something else."

"Someone else."

His grin disappeared.

"Your face is so readable!" She adjusted her headset and said into it, "We all ready?"

The models looked toward them and nodded. The gaffer raised a thumb. The account exec and director nodded toward him.

Wayne moved his camera three inches to the left. He felt his phone vibrate in his pocket. "Yellow suit," he said, "turn very slightly toward your partner."

Annie repeated the command into her microphone.

At the end of the shoot, Wayne pulled his phone out of his pocket.

"Say yes!" was the message.

He thumbed a reply, wondering if he could continue to deflect her questions.

Nine

When he phoned Kayla to arrange details, he protested that it should be his turn to treat her to dinner. She just laughed.

"You didn't get an authentic Indian dinner," she told him.

When he rang her bell he had mixed feelings about the evening—anticipation, and apprehension that he might say the wrong thing and complicate not only their relationship but her relationship with her family. His hand was shaking as he pushed through the door to the stairway.

Upstairs, The Smile greeted him when she opened her door. She wore a sari and a red bindi on her forehead. Aromas of curry and masala flooded from the apartment, and another scent that Wayne only half remembered. Something was interfering with his breathing. He slipped off his shoes.

Leading him through into the living room, she turned suddenly and said, "Wayne, I want you to meet my mother, Anusha. You may remember her."

Wayne stopped breathing. The woman rising from the sofa across the room appeared as from a soft fog,

The Smile

smiling that same smile. She reached out her hand to him but touched his only momentarily. "Hello, Wayne," she said. "It's been a long time."

Later, he couldn't remember what he said to her, only that her perfume made him remember that last time he had seen her, with her black hair falling over her bare arm.

Kayla, seeing his face blanch, exclaimed, "I'm sorry! I didn't mean—I wanted to surprise you!"

"Excuse me," he said, looking around the room for a place to sit. His knee was shaking. Finding a chair, he grinned. "You certainly did that."

Kayla went to him and touched his shoulder. Her mother returned to her seat.

Wayne finally looked up and smiled. "I'm sorry. Not a very good way to greet an old—"

"You look good, Wayne," Anusha said softly, deflecting his word.

"I thought—," began Kayla, "I thought this would be a treat for both of you." She kept her hand on his shoulder.

He looked in her face. "I guess we both guessed, didn't we?"

Anusha smiled at him. "I wasn't sure," she said. "I thought that if you weren't the Wayne I knew, that we could simply have a pleasant evening—for Kayla."

"I wasn't expecting—" Wayne began.

Kayla hung her head. "Poor Wayne! I'm sorry."

He looked at Anusha. Her hair contained a bit of gray at the temples, but she was the same beautiful woman he had carried in his billfold all these years. All he could manage to say was, "I meant to call."

"I know," she said. "It was impossible."

"Ma is—" began Kayla.

Anusha shook her head at her daughter, frowning slightly, and said, "Not now, Chitralekha." Then she smiled at Wayne. "We've both lived many lives since then, haven't we?"

Her grace softened him. His impulse to flee the room faded. "Yes," he said simply, looking from Anusha to Kayla. Then he looked back at Anusha. "It's good to see you again, Anusha." He felt his tight shoulders relax.

Kayla moved toward the kitchen. "We all need a drink!"

Anusha hurried after her daughter. Wayne heard their voices, but couldn't make out what was said. He took a deep breath and looked around the room. The question—the big question—came to him and was pushed away. *She's the same Anusha,* he thought, *and Kayla is her daughter—her smile. That's all.*

"I know you like gin," Kayla said, returning to the room gracefully carrying his drink as though she were floating. "There. Didn't spill a drop!"

To his unspoken question, she added, "It's a white lady. I hope you like it."

The tart liquid felt warm in his throat. He was tempted to down the whole thing in a gulp, but paused with a sip. "Delicious."

Anusha had remained in the kitchen. "Wayne," Kayla said softly, concern showing in her voice, "I'm sorry. I should have told you."

He managed a grin. "You are full of surprises."

Kayla's face pouted, then she smiled. "You are too, you know. When you showed me her picture, I was stunned."

He lifted his glass slightly. "Are you having one, too?"

"Yes." She went into the kitchen and returned with another drink, gliding as before.

"You are very graceful," he said. "Both you and your mother."

Kayla smiled, and sipped from her glass. "Ma won't drink until after we eat." Then she sat near him. "She is making the whole meal," she said. "I helped some, but she insisted."

They had finished their drinks, saying little, when Anusha appeared in the doorway. "We should sit," she announced.

Wayne looked at his hands. "May I wash?"

Kayla gestured toward the bathroom.

The table looked like her family's tables so long ago. Anusha hovered over them and served everything. Finally, she took her own seat.

"It's just like I remember," Wayne said.

"I gave you a fork and spoon," laughed Kayla, "so you can eat the way you want."

He tore a piece of chapati and dipped some masala. "I'll try," he said. "I'm a bit rusty at this."

As the meal progressed, Wayne relaxed more. Kayla got up and poured water for them all. Then, sitting down, she lifted her glass. "To old friends."

Wayne touched Anusha's glass, then Kayla's. "Thank you, Kayla."

"I thought, since you liked my smile, that you'd like the original."

Wayne's and Anusha's eyes met. "It doesn't show up very much in the photograph," he said, "but I've never forgotten it."

Anusha smiled and looked down.

Kayla was watching them both. "How did I—" she began, then stopped when Anusha caught her eye.

"Your daughter is quite graceful in front of a camera," Wayne said. "She's a very natural model."

"I've tried to persuade her to go to school." Anusha put her hand on Kayla's. "She's very smart."

Wayne grinned. "She certainly is." Then he looked at Kayla. "What would you want to study?" He was aware that the conversation was stiff.

"You've asked me that before. I don't know yet." She glanced at her mother. "Maybe fashion design?"

"You're certainly getting a lot of contact with designers," Wayne offered after taking a bite of food.

"Yes, it's interesting to see all the designs they come up with."

"You could do better," her mother put in. She looked at Wayne. "You've been a photographer for a long time."

He nodded. "Never really wanted to do anything else. Maybe eventually getting a portrait studio of my own. Kind of settle down in one place."

"Sometime would you do my portrait?" Kayla smiled at him. "Not these fake fashion shots—and I don't need any more head shots."

"Love to," he answered. "It would be hard to see you objectively, though, in terms of light and shadow. I'm too involved with you personally."

"You are?" Kayla's face had an impish smile.

"What does a portrait photographer look for?" Anusha was trying to guide the conversation away from where it seemed to be headed.

It's getting too personal, Wayne thought. *She doesn't want her daughter hooking up with a guy old enough to be her father.*

That thought stopped him. He'd almost forgotten Charlie's prediction. The possibility intruded in his mind. He managed a smile. "You look for character," he said, almost pedantically. "The personality, reflected in ordinary expressions. The thing that makes a person real to others."

The Smile

"My smile?" asked Kayla.

"Well," he paused and took a breath, "that's the problem. I know there's more to you than your smile—it has such a strong emotional effect on me." Suddenly uncomfortable, he glanced at Anusha.

She met his eyes.

"Uh." He stopped, and looked down. "Kayla and I have become friends," he said vaguely.

"Nothing more," Kayla added. She looked at her mother. "Proper friends."

Wayne felt his face become hot. "Yes," he said quietly. When he looked up, Anusha was smiling at him.

They finished the meal quietly. Wayne didn't know what to say to either of them, but his earlier tension had relaxed.

"I have to go out for a few minutes," Kayla said unexpectedly.

Both Wayne and Anusha looked at her questioningly.

"My friend Barbara needs me to help her with something." Kayla screwed up her face. "I'd promised before our dinner was planned. I shouldn't be long—she lives just upstairs."

"Chitralekha," Anusha began.

"I'm sorry, Ma. I'll be back in a few minutes. Besides, you two must have a lot to talk about."

Anusha looked concerned. Wayne wondered what Kayla was thinking. The tension in his gut began building again.

As she rose and went toward the door, Kayla turned and said, "Promise you won't leave until I get back!"

Wayne didn't respond. He watched her go through the door, then turned back toward Anusha.

"She's being very rude," her mother said. "I had no idea she was planning this."

He smiled and sighed. "Your daughter has a mind of her own."

"Yes." She looked steadily at him.

After a long, uncomfortable silence, she rose and went to a cupboard. "Will you have cognac with me?" Turning toward him, she waited for a reply.

Wayne nodded.

Anusha smiled—that smile—and took a bottle and two snifters from the cupboard.

He followed her into the living room, still not sure what to say to her.

"Kayla says you have not married." She poured the liquor and handed him a glass.

"No." A sudden sadness overtook him.

"I'm glad you didn't call me. It would have been very hard."

"My work kept me busy. You did marry."

"Yes. Ramesh. A friend of my family."

"When did you come to the States?"

"Actually," she said, "right after we married. He came here to attend graduate school. Columbia." She saw him glance at her left hand, and put it into her lap. Holding her right hand out, she said, "It would be on this hand. I no longer wear it."

To his unspoken question, she nodded. "We are divorced. Four years."

"I don't know what to say to you," Wayne said.

"You don't have to say anything, Wayne. I am happy in my life." She smiled, and gestured toward the door. "Chitralekha is my life."

"Chitralekha." He managed to smile.

"It means as beautiful as a picture."

"She is, isn't she?" His smile broadened. "Or a photograph." He was thinking of Kayla's modeling.

Anusha sipped from her glass.

The Smile

Wayne's face became hot. The Question sat there, waiting.

She held his eyes. "Yes."

"Anusha—" He couldn't say the words.

She simply nodded, almost imperceptibly, and he knew the answer.

"Why didn't you tell me?" His voice, barely above a whisper, broke on the last word.

"I didn't know until after you had gone."

A long moment later, he asked, "Does she know?" Before she could reply, the next question formed and was asked: "Is that why she left us alone?"

"She didn't tell me. It would not surprise me."

Wayne finished the drink.

"Wayne," Anusha said quietly, "You don't need to do anything. You don't need to say anything. I thought you might want to know—that's all."

He looked at his empty glass and shook his head. *My God*, he thought, then said, "Charlie guessed."

She looked at him quizzically.

"A friend. I told him about you."

"We have each lived many lives since then," she said, then paused. "I told no one."

"It must have been hard for you."

She shook her head and smiled.

Just then Kayla came through the door. Before saying anything, she looked from one to the other. "Barbara feels better."

Anusha rose without looking at her daughter, went into the dining area and began clearing the table. Kayla went to Wayne and touched his hand. "Is she angry?" she whispered.

Although his heart was pounding, he shook his head, then picked up his empty glass. "I'd like a bit more." He struggled to breathe normally.

She immediately took his glass, and with a questioning look, turned and poured more brandy. Handing it back to him, she looked into his eyes without speaking.

"Will you have one with me?" he asked.

She picked up her mother's glass and drained it.

"Wayne—" she began, then stopped, and sat on the sofa.

They looked at each other for a long time without speaking. He took a deep breath. "You said Barbara is feeling better."

She lowered her head, then looked up at him sheepishly. "Did you have a good talk?"

The clatter of dishes in the kitchen told them that Anusha was keeping busy. Wayne nodded. "You knew."

"She admitted it right after our first dinner. I had to ask her. I had to know."

"How do you feel?"

"It's been a roller coaster," she said. "At first I blamed you. Eventually, she explained it to me. It was impossible." Kayla looked at him steadily. "You didn't know. But what if you had?"

He opened his hands in a gesture of helplessness. His voice was a hoarse whisper. "I would have stayed in Bombay."

"It was impossible."

He shrugged.

Kayla covered her face with her hands, then dropped them. "I don't know how to feel. I don't know what I feel!"

"I don't either."

"It's up to you two." Anuasha had returned unnoticed. "I would not have told you," she said to Kayla. "But now you know."

Then she turned to Wayne. "I trust you, Wayne. Please don't hurt her."

The Smile

Unable to speak, he shook his head.

Anusha had an empty brandy snifter in her hand. She went to the carafe, poured a small amount in the glass and then sat in a chair.

The three of them sat silently for a long while. Wayne finished his drink. Kayla looked from one to the other. Then suddenly, she burst into tears, burying her face in her hands.

Wayne went to her and placed a hand on her shoulder without speaking.

After a moment and without moving his hand, he looked at Anusha. "You cried your tears many years ago."

She nodded with a slight smile. "Many tears."

Kayla looked up at Wayne, her face streaked. After a long silence, she said, "I don't know how to think of you. I have my Pa."

"Of course you do," he answered.

"I don't want him to know—ever." She faced her mother.

"No," said Anusha. "He can't know."

Wayne cleared his throat. "I understand. But—"

The two women looked at him, waiting.

He took out his billfold and drew the photograph from it. Handing the picture to Anusha, he asked, "What do I do with this?"

She looked at the photo for a long time, then looked up at him, her eyes glistening. "She was a child."

He shook his head. "No."

"I'm not a child," said Kayla.

He smiled at her briefly, but he felt closer to tears.

"It's just a photograph," Anusha said softly. "An old photograph."

Kayla looked at her mother. "No," she said. "It's still warm from his body."

Emotion welled up in Wayne's throat. He took a deep breath to push it back down. Taking a seat across the room from the two women, he stared at a small bronze sculpture on a table near him.

Anusha rose and came to him. Lifting his chin so that she could look into his eyes, she said, "I'm not her, not anymore."

He tried to withdraw his face from her hand, but she persisted. He finally closed his eyes, and she let go.

Looking down at the floor, he managed to find his voice. "I know."

She gestured around her. "This is new," she said, "new for me. We are not who we were twenty years ago."

"But Ma!" exclaimed Kayla, her voice trembling. "What about me?"

They both looked at her.

"I am not Wayne's fantasy." She pinched her arm. "I'm real. I came from you both. You're my mother." She looked at Wayne. "You're not my father—I have my Pa. But I'm part of you. I'm part of you both!" Tears were again streaming down her cheeks. "You were real, then. Your love was real. You can't deny it. You can't deny me!"

Anusha took her hand and pulled her to her feet. Embracing her, she said, "Yes it was real." She looked at Wayne. "I dreamed about you for years. Maybe you caused my marriage to go bad. I don't know."

He looked at her without speaking.

"Ramesh was a good husband. He never knew what you meant to me. We just drifted apart. Something changed in me, after that." She picked up the photograph. "I'm not this girl, this girl that you've kept warm in your pocket all these years. If I could be—if I could be, for Chitralekha, I would."

The Smile

Kayla disengaged from her mother's grasp and gently sat back down.

Wayne took another deep breath. "You're right. I've kept a ghost in my pocket. It's kept me from letting myself be with other people. I'm more comfortable peering at them through the viewfinder of my camera. I see that you're not the woman in my pocket. Maybe you never were."

Anusha smiled.

"That's not fair!" Kayla almost screamed the words. "That means I'm nothing!" She covered her face again.

Wayne stood up and went to her. "I'm sorry, Kayla. Will you let me hold you?"

She stood and melted into his embrace. Anusha put her hand on Kayla's head. "Chitralekha, my baby," she crooned. "It was real. You were conceived in love." She looked up at Wayne. "Maybe I was never that ghost in your pocket, but I was real once, and you were real, and I was glad this baby came out of that reality."

Kayla lifted her head and kissed her mother, then Wayne.

The three of them disengaged slowly, letting their hands be the last touch. Then they all sat down quietly. Wayne handed Kayla his handkerchief, and she wiped her stained face.

"This isn't the end, is it?" asked Kayla softly.

"No," said Wayne.

"No," said Anusha, and she smiled at Wayne.

Donald Skiff

The Kerchief

The Kerchief

One – Current Time

Lewis felt a pressure on his wrist. Opening his eyes—he couldn't quite turn his head—he got a glimpse of red hair.

"Oh, you're awake," she said gently. "I'm just taking your pulse." Her fingers were warm on his wrist, and he didn't want her to let go.

You're new," he managed to say. The tube against his nose bothered him, and he reached for it. She moved the tube a little, and he could see her smile.

"I'm Rayna," she said. "Celia is off today."

Something tugged at his memory.

Rayna checked his catheter bag and tucked his blanket under him. "Are you warm enough?"

"Yeah."

"We'll have breakfast up for you in a minute," she said, bringing his water straw close to his lips. "Just a sip," she instructed.

"You remind me of somebody," he said.

"Somebody nice, I hope."

"Long time ago."

"Want to tell me?" She put a hand on his.

He looked at her hair, fringed in light. "Kerchief," he said.

Two – About 1950

Calderson grinned at Lewis as he bounced the rattling forklift over the threshold of the loading dock doors. Taking his hands off the wheel for a moment, he made bouncing motions with his hands at his chest. Lewis turned and watched him roll past, expecting him to say something, but he just barreled on into the holding room, the electric drive motor whining. Lewis punched in and headed for the bag factory.

It was bright and airy in the bag factory, a big change from the machine shops he had worked in before. At one end, the twin tubers formed multiwall bags—like sugar comes in—from rolls of paper. Conveyors carried the cut tubes to the sewing machines, which closed the bottoms with tape and stitching. Working off the conveyors from the sewing machines, balers gathered bags and pressed them into bundles, tied them with twine and stacked them on skids for packing and shipping. All the machines were noisy; if you wanted to talk to somebody, you'd have to yell.

Lewis signaled to Mitch, the head baler, that he was ready to work, and he received just a hand wave in response, pointing to the baling press he was to use. He noticed that several of the balers had their heads together, laughing.

On the other side of their conveyor, the super and his sidekick were huddled near one of the sewing machines, talking to someone. Lewis got a glimpse of color: a woman, dressed not in jeans and T-shirts like all the other women in the factory, but in tailored slacks and a colorful blouse. A kerchief was tied over her red hair.

"New sewing inspector," yelled Billy in his ear.

They watched until Mitch, himself grinning, waved them back to their presses. This was not an ordinary female factory worker. As Lewis passed Billy's press, he heard something to the effect that Calderson "would get into that by the end of the week."

For the remainder of the shift, most of the male workers in the place spent more time watching the new inspector than tending their machines. Even Solly, the mechanic, perched on top of one of the tubers with a

The Kerchief

wrench in his hand, gazed down at the woman in the yellow blouse. The balers had the advantage of working just across the conveyor from the sewing machines, where they could feast their eyes on the newcomer as they picked up stacks of bags. The woman, after some demonstrations by the super about what to look for in the bags coming out of the sewing machines, moved from machine to machine, peeling back the top bag in each stack to make sure the stitching was perfect.

Lewis was on his last day shift, and would work swing beginning Monday. On his way home, he thought about the red haired woman and wondered what a classy gal like that was doing in a factory. The next week, he caught a glimpse of her at the shift change, and then she was gone. "She only works days," Billy told him. "She's got kids in school."

Lewis was beginning to like his work. When he started a month ago, he went home after his shift with hands bloody from the baling twine, and shoulders and back hurting like hell. But gradually his hands calloused and his muscles grew, and he found that the baling job required only a minimum of attention. Pick up, stack, press, tie, toss onto the skid, over and over for hours at a time. His mind could be elsewhere, and that suited him. Occasionally, one of the machines broke down or they had to change paper rolls, and the whole line became quiet. The balers, separated from most of the other men in the factory by their conveyor and the sewing machines, took advantage of the break and talked among themselves.

All country boys, working at the only place in town where they didn't have to have an education, their talk was about farms and pigs and milking and women. They joked about the women who worked at the machines, country folk like themselves, and speculated about their chances with them. There was a bigger turnover among the women than the men, pregnancy being the principal reason. For all of them, future prospects were more of the same.

One benefit of swing shift was getting off work at 1 A.M. Their families would be asleep but the local bars would be open until 2:30. Lewis joined the other balers and sometimes one or two of the machine operators, who were usually older and not so given to carousing. At first, he entered those places with some caution, but as his arms and shoulders filled out from the heavy work, he found that he was no longer afraid of trouble. He never sought out a fight, but simply lost his fear. Getting hurt in a brawl was no big thing. You patched yourself up and went on with your life. And the guys looked out for each other.

Her name was Raye, he found out when he again began working day shift. He hadn't seen her except at a distance since that first day. He'd had to be at his station before the previous shift of balers could leave, and he could see the other workers only in passing. She had a different kerchief over her hair and her clothing was less noticeable, although she never wore jeans. She smiled at him once as they met across the conveyor belt, he about to pick up a stack of fertilizer bags and she reaching to check a corner of the top one. He smiled back, and caught a whiff of cologne. Like all the other men, he watched her whenever the chance arose.

Even though he hung out with the guys most of the time, Lewis always felt different. A couple of times he happened to mention some topic that was outside their shared experiences, such as how the war in Korea seemed to be going or asking where was the closest place that he might buy a camera, and was met with silence. They all knew there was a war going on, of

The Kerchief

course, but they didn't want to talk about it because even thinking about it might cause them to be called up in the draft. They didn't have money to spend on such things as cameras—their cars needed brakes instead.

They were all weekend mechanics, working on their old cars, good with their hands and learning what they needed from each other. Lewis was there, too, trying to keep his old Ford running. He kept seeing other things, though, like the way a tree was silhouetted against the sky, or a cat sunning herself next to the house. He lived alone in an old shack he rented on the edge of town, and on weekends he wandered the streets of the little town, looking at things and, when moved, capturing a picture. On payday he took his film to the old guy who ran the photo studio on Main Street. Lewis admired him, the only man in town who wore a full beard and sported a beret when he was outdoors. When Lewis got his prints back they talked about photography.

One day on the line, as he gathered up a stack of bags, Raye touched his hand and caught his eye. "You're the quiet one," she said, just loud enough for him to hear. He grinned and held his ears as if to say, "Nobody can hear you in this place."

At the end of the shift, he was in line waiting to punch out when he saw her outside, sitting on a bench. As he passed her on his way to the parking lot, she motioned for him to sit with her. He sat down, but couldn't bring himself to look at her. He set his lunch box down between his feet.

"I tried to catch you the other day," she said, "but you were in a hurry to leave."

"Oh," he lied, "I didn't see you." Out of the corner of his eye he now saw her smiling at him.

"So what's a fellow like you working in a place like this?" Her voice was deep for a woman, and smooth.

Lewis frowned. "What do you mean?"

"You're not like the other men here." She reached over and pulled his chin toward her. "Can you look at me, Lewis?"

He grinned shyly. "I guess so," he said. He felt embarrassed just sitting on the bench with her. He could smell her cologne and felt the warmth of her thigh not quite touching his.

"Tell me—what do you have planned for this weekend?"

He shrugged. "Nothing much. Maybe take pictures."

"You're a photographer! I knew you were different."

Something changed. Lewis looked at her eyes. "Do you take pictures, too?"

"I love to! Would you take me along with you? I don't know enough. I'd like to learn."

He guessed that her words were not as spontaneous as he had thought. She was coming on to him. The idea made him nervous. She seemed so sure of herself, so sophisticated. The talk in the men's shower room about her had built her up into some kind of femme fatale, and Lewis felt totally inadequate around her. The only girl he had ever tried to get to know better back in high school was even more shy than he was, and that didn't turn out well. Eventually even she got bored with him.

"Sure," he said, "but I can't teach you noth—anything. I just shoot what I see."

"Where do you get them developed? That photo studio downtown?"

When he nodded, she said, "Well, let's go out and learn together. My children are with their father this weekend, and I'd love to spend a day just looking at things and taking photographs." She looked around to see if anyone else were in earshot. "This town doesn't have much else to do, does it?"

281

The Kerchief

They agreed that he would pick her up at home on Saturday morning and they'd spend the day taking pictures. He was relieved when their conversation ended and he could go to his car. Part of him was excited, but another part of him was terrified of this woman. She was older than he—how much, he wasn't sure—and was completely at ease with herself.

On Saturday, he found out that she was separated from her husband, an army officer at the base. She lived with her two small children and came to work at the paper mill "because I was going crazy in this little town." She and her husband had come from the East Coast to this place where he was preparing to ship out to Korea. They were both college graduates, and had lived in large cities all their lives. "I would have left this town and gone back home," she told him, "but I couldn't take his children so far away just before he has to go to war." She looked down at her hands. "I couldn't do that to Wayne."

"Why'd you split up?" He immediately regretted his question. "I'm sorry."

"That's okay," she said. "We hadn't been doing well together for a long time. He loves his children, but he and I just don't get along. He lives at the base."

Lewis stopped the car at one of the bay overlooks, and they walked around, aiming their cameras at things. She didn't want him to photograph her, however. "I don't take good pictures," she said.

Eating lunch at a restaurant in a nearby town, they talked sporadically. He admitted that he felt different from the other workers in the bag factory, and someday wanted to go to the city.

What do you want to do?"

"Go to school," he said. "Study photography."

She smiled. "I could tell that you were cut from different cloth. You don't laugh at the awful jokes the other men tell. You're polite. A woman can trust you."

Lewis had been raised by his aunt after his mother had abandoned him and run off to Arizona with a man. He never knew his father. His aunt had treated him like a son, making sure he went to school and cautioning him about hanging out with the wrong crowd. He never knew anybody who loved him except her and one of his teachers in high school. Mrs. Eberhardt had loaned him a camera when he was a senior so he could take pictures for the annual, and ever since then he had known what he really wanted.

Aunt Minnie, it turned out, wasn't too sure about his spending time with Raye. "You'll get yourself in trouble," she said the next day when he told her about his experience. "She says she's separated from her husband, but you don't know what's really going on with 'em."

"She's not like the people at the bag factory say about her," he responded. "We just talk."

"That's how people get themselves shot." Aunt Minnie turned her attention to something on the stove.

Orders at the bag factory became slow, and they finally shut down the swing shift. Lewis thought sure he would be laid off, but he was one of the lucky ones. He liked the day shift better anyway, since it gave him more chances to see and talk with Raye. He didn't miss the late-night bar hopping with the guys. One day when he was on break in the shower room, some of the men began teasing him about Raye. He hadn't realized that everybody seemed to know about the time they spent together. Afterward, he felt even more separate from the

The Kerchief

other guys. They all assumed that he was, or would soon be, sleeping with the pretty new inspector.

Actually, it hadn't occurred to him. Not that he didn't find her attractive. He just didn't have the nerve to even consider it. The warm feeling he was developing toward her had little to do with sex. The two of them spent most Saturdays driving around the countryside, taking pictures and talking about things he had only read about in high school.

One Saturday, she asked him, "Do you like music, Lewis?"

He nodded. "Don't know anything about good music," he said. "All you get on the radio around here is Western music. Get kinda tired of that."

"They teach you music in school?" She was looking at him with a kind of smile on her face while he drove the old Ford. She'd turned around, with one knee up on the seat, facing him.

"Yeah, some. They had a orchestra, but I couldn't afford to buy an instrument. We learned to sing in music class and read music a little bit."

"Turn around," she said suddenly. "Let's go back to my house. I want you to hear something."

Lewis was taken aback. Things were changing, and he wasn't sure what it meant. When they met, he had only picked her up in front of her house. He'd never seen the inside. Flowers grew behind a low fence in the front yard. This time she led him through the front door.

It was an old house, painted white, more like a cottage than the big old brick houses so typical in the town. Raye told him she had rented it from another officer at the base who had already been shipped out to Korea. To Lewis, it wasn't luxurious, but still much better than homes he had lived in. In the living room the most dominant piece of furniture was a large console phonograph. Next to it stood a bookshelf filled with phonograph records in albums like the ones he had seen in music class at school.

"Do you know any of that music?" she asked him.

He shook his head, opening the albums one by one, reading the titles on the twelve-inch records. "I've heard this one," he said.

Raye took the record from its sleeve and looked at it. "Night on Bald Mountain." She opened the phonograph lid and put the record on the turntable. "I love the Russians!" she said as she started the turntable.

"Mrs. Randolph played that for us one time," he said, "and she made us close our eyes and picture the scene." Lewis laughed.

"What did you see?" Raye was smiling at him.

"I saw this big old mountain, and ghosts and things floating around."

As the music finished, Raye took the record off and pulled another one, this time from a flat cardboard envelope. "Now," she said, handling the disc carefully by its edges, "you're going to hear something special."

Making an adjustment to the turntable, she placed the disc on it and set the needle down. Beautifully full and clear orchestral sound came from the speaker, without any clicks or static. Lewis grinned broadly at her.

"And they get twenty minutes on each side!" she exclaimed.

He took the sleeve from her and began reading the description. "It's like you're right there!" he said,

"Have you ever been to a concert?"

He looked at her and smiled. "Only the high school orchestra."

"We will have to do that."

The Kerchief

His look was a question he thought he knew the answer to, but was too shy to ask.

"Go to a real concert," she said, "in Seattle."

Life had changed for Lewis. He had found a friend—more than a friend—who took his mind out of that small town, with its bars and talk about farming and the price of corn and gossip about local women and girls.

The men he worked with noticed it, too. He was not included as much in their talk during breaks, and he noticed grins on their faces whenever Raye was nearby, and knowing looks in his direction. While he felt isolated from his peers, thinking about Raye and the world she represented to him more than made up for it.

Their conversations ranged from world affairs to history and literature, and especially to music. Photography became less important as a shared activity and more as a reason to spend time together. Often, they simply sat in her living room and drank beer and listened to classical music. He learned the different sounds of composers such as Mozart and Schubert and Sibelius. She taught him about the different eras of music, from the baroque to the romantic and beyond.

One Saturday afternoon, they were sitting and listening as usual, when they heard a car stop outside. "You're going to meet my children," Raye said, getting up from beside him on the sofa and switching off the phonograph.

Lewis wished he were someplace else. She turned and extended a hand toward him. "C'mon," she said. Taking his hand, she led him to the front door, where she let go to open the door.

Outside, Lewis saw two children, a boy and a girl. Behind them, coming up the walk, was a man in uniform. When the man saw Lewis, his eyebrows went up a little, but he made no further indication.

"This is Billy," Raye said, her hand on Billy's shoulder. "Billy, this is Lewis. He's a friend of mine."

Billy shyly extended a hand, and Lewis, not knowing what else to do, shook it gently.

"And this is Ginny," Raye said. Ginny smiled at Lewis, who smiled back.

Behind them, the soldier extended a hand. "Wayne Gunderson," he said to Lewis.

"Lewis works with me," Raye said. "We were listening to Appalachian Spring."

"That Koussevitzky LP is the best I've heard," said Wayne.

Lewis smiled, but his discomfort showed in his face.

"The kids haven't eaten since noon," Wayne said to Raye. Then he turned and went to his car. "See you," he said, and closed the door.

For the next few minutes, Raye was busy fixing food for the children, who behaved as though nothing unusual were happening. Occasionally, they glanced at Lewis. Lewis retreated to the sofa and pretended to read the recording jacket.

When Raye finished in the kitchen and approached him, Lewis stood up. "I guess I'd better go," he said.

She laughed. "I'm afraid our little concert is interrupted. It's not going to be quiet enough around here anymore today. We can pick it up another time." She walked with him to the door.

"I'll see you at work," he said.

She laughed again. "That wasn't too uncomfortable for you, was it?"

He smiled, but didn't reply.

Driving home, Lewis was aware that he was beginning to breathe again. He thought of Aunt

The Kerchief

Minnie's words about "getting shot." And yet, her husband had been very polite to him. In the culture Lewis had grown up in, a situation like that would almost certainly have resulted in a fight. Or worse.

The next day he stayed home and finished a novel he'd been reading off and on, about submarines. It was an action story, not about warfare but about civilians who had acquired World War Two submarines for exploring the oceans. After he'd finished it he went to the public library to check out more books, but it was closed. He stopped at the grocery store on the way home and bought beer.

Thinking about Raye—how new and exciting it was to be with her, but how nervous he was being discovered with her. She had acted as though it were nothing, that she was simply introducing him as a friend. It was more than that, he knew. He felt guilty even though nothing wrong had happened between them.

He drank three bottles of beer instead of eating, and was soon dreamily fantasizing about Raye, about making love to her in that living room with "Romeo and Juliet" playing on the phonograph.

The next morning, Lewis took his camera with him, but his destination was Aunt Minnie's.

She wasn't shocked. "I'm surprised that he didn't shoot you," she said.

Lewis tried to explain that his friendship with Raye was just that. "But meeting her children and her ex-husband felt weird."

"It *is* weird!" she said. "You may think that she's just a friend, but it's not like you were going out taking pictures with a school buddy. How old is this woman?"

Lewis admitted that he didn't know, for sure. "Probably about thirty."

"It ain't right," she said. "You should be going with somebody more your age." Aunt Minnie set her coffee cup down on the table with a bang. "She's using you!"

"She don't belong here," he said.

"You're right—she don't belong here. She don't belong here fraternizing with young boys!"

"I'm not a boy, Aunt Minnie!" Lewis was exasperated with the conversation. "You don't understand."

"Oh, I understand. It's you that don't know shit!"

Lewis gave up. He went into the living room and turned on the television. There was nothing but religious programs on all three channels, and he didn't want more of that, so he turned it off and sat brooding.

Aunt Minnie came into the room and sat beside him. "I'm sorry I yelled at you, Son." She didn't often call him that.

"I know," he said, not looking at her.

"There's lots of pretty girls for you around here," she said. "I just don't want you to get hurt."

Lewis didn't answer.

"I know what she sees in you," she said. "You're a real hunk. You done built up your body working in that bag factory, and any girl'd be tickled to death to get you." She took his hand in hers. "But what do you see in her?"

He looked at her and squeezed her hand. "She's like fresh air, Aunt Minnie. She knows all this stuff, and she's lived all over, and she likes good music just like me. And we talk about things that I can't talk about with anybody else in this hick town!"

Aunt Minnie's face dropped. She let go of his hand and didn't say anything for a long time. Then she said, "We're not good enough for you, huh?"

"Aunt Minnie, I didn't mean you! You're like my own mother. I talk about everything with you."

The Kerchief

"But let this city girl—she ain't a girl anymore—let her start telling you about the big wide world out there, and all of a sudden we aren't good enough for you in this hick town?"

Lewis let go of a deep sigh. "I need to get away from here, from this town, from that bag factory. I want to go to school."

"You been to school!" she said. "And they didn't even teach you how to hoe a garden."

"I don't want to know how to hoe! I want to take pictures for magazines, or have a studio like old Mister Svensen downtown. I want to go to hear music in Seattle. Raye said she'd take me to a concert down there."

"We ain't city folks here," Aunt Minnie said, her voice showing her discouragement. "You ain't city folks, either, Lewis. Your mom grew up down in Chimicum. Your dad came from Forks."

"I don't care!" Lewis stormed out of the house, grabbing his camera on the way.

Driving on 20 alongside Discovery Bay, he stopped at the overlook by Eaglemount, and just sat in the car, thinking. He hated to have Aunt Minnie mad at him. She'd been the only mom he'd ever known, and he grew up worshiping her. But she was stuck in this country—it was all she knew. He knew there was more, and he wanted to find it. But where would he go?

As he sat there, he noticed how the sun filtered through the trees, and how the bay in the background shown, with tiny whitecaps dotting its expanse. He got out and snapped several pictures.

The next day, Raye was standing close by the conveyor belt, and her face brightened when she saw him. Lewis suddenly knew that he was in love. The first chance he got, he went over near her. It was too noisy to talk to her, so he just stood there, the conveyor between them, and grinned at her.

The conveyor suddenly stopped. Somebody was yelling at him. He realized that his bags were piling up at the end of the conveyor. Mitch was waving his arms. Lewis moved to the pileup and pulled bags off the belt. The stacks had scattered all over the floor. Mitch came over and helped him sort through them, grouping them so they'd stack in the baling press.

Mitch was furious. "You got to pay attention!"

Lewis pressed and tied the bundles as fast as he could, and soon the conveyor started up. He could easily keep up with his stacks, but it required steady effort. Once, he glimpsed Raye over by one of the sewing machines. She was watching him. His face turned red.

At lunch break, the two of them sat outside at one of the picnic tables. Her lunchbox was pink, with pictures of flowers on it. Lewis opened his plain black lunchbox and took out his thermos.

"You should have seen your face," she laughed. "You had bags all over the place!"

"Mitch told me I had to stay away from you," he said. "He said you're a bad influence on me." Lewis grinned at her.

"I *am* a bad influence on you," she said, her eyes twinkling.

He looked down at his sandwich. "That was scary, Saturday."

Raye's expression changed. "Why scary?"

"I didn't know what your husband was going to do."

"What would he do?" she seemed mystified. "We're not together anymore. He's a civilized gentleman. An officer."

Lewis shook his head. "I was expecting him to come at me."

The Kerchief

She laughed. "He's not a cave man, Lewis. He doesn't tell me what I can or can't do. He knows how I hate it here."

"I ain't afraid of him," he said. "Long as he doesn't come at me with a gun. But I don't want to fight in front of you—and your little kids."

Exasperated she said, "Quit thinking like a hick."

That hurt. Lewis turned his attention to the peach he was eating.

She put a hand on his arm. "I'm sorry. I didn't mean that."

"S'true," he said. "I am a hick. I come from the sticks."

"You're not! You're a sweet man, and you just have to get out of this place and learn how civilized people act."

They finished their lunches and walked back into the bag factory. "Lewis," she said, "don't make any plans for this weekend.

He looked at her. "Why?"

"I'm going to take you to a real concert in Seattle. Well, not in a concert hall. There's an outdoor concert at Green Lake on Saturday night, in the park. You'll love it!"

Lewis felt better that afternoon, but there was still a little nervous feeling in his gut when he thought of Raye's husband and children.

Raye drove them in her car to Seattle on Saturday, expertly navigating through the two ferries at Port Gamble and Kingston. Lewis was willing to let her make all the decisions because he felt out of his element. He didn't know what was going to happen. When she suggested they pick up food to take for a picnic as they listened to the concert, he readily agreed. She had stored a couple of folding chairs in the back of her car, and a blanket to spread out for their picnic.

When they arrived, she found a spot on the lawn close to the orchestra stage. "They're playing Gershwin and Cole Porter," she told him. "We want to sit over here on the left so we can watch the pianist better."

She had brought wine instead of beer, and produced two wine glasses from the trunk of her car, carefully wrapped in a towel. They were nearly finished eating when the orchestra began setting up their instruments. His head slightly fuzzy from the wine, Lewis was fascinated by the preparations. He and Raye exchanged glances.

Finally, the orchestra began tuning up, and the two of them collected their picnic materials and blanket, then set up the folding chairs.

Lewis had never heard such sounds! Even though there were people talking occasionally around them, and they could hear trucks on the nearby streets, the clarity of the instruments entranced him.

He remembered hearing Gershwin's *Rhapsody in Blue* in recordings at school, and even once at a concert by the high school orchestra, but never had he heard it played like this! His head swam with excitement—and with the effects of the wine. For the second time in a week, he thought he was in love.

It was dark by the time the concert concluded, and they carried their supplies back to the car. Raye carefully wrapped the wine glasses before tucking them into a safe corner.

She maneuvered the car out of the parking lot, following a long line of cars. "What did you think?" she asked him.

"It was wonderful!" he replied. He couldn't stop grinning. They talked about the different pieces that

The Kerchief

had been played, and Raye offered historical information about Gershwin and Porter. "My mother actually watched George Gershwin play at one of his radio broadcasts," she said. "He had his own program on NBC."

"That instrument at the beginning of *Rhapsody in Blue*," Lewis said, "what was that?"

"A clarinet," she said.

"But I've never heard it played like that!"

"It's a glissando—that means gliding."

"How did he do that?"

She smiled at him. "I don't know."

"You don't know? I thought you knew everything!"

They both laughed.

A few minutes later, Raye said, "I don't want to drive all the way back tonight. Besides, the ferries will have probably stopped running by the time we get to them."

He looked at her, his forehead wrinkling.

"Okay," she admitted, "I made arrangements for us to stay in Seattle tonight."

"Where?"

"At a hotel." She looked at him and smiled.

Lewis's heart thumped in his chest. He took a deep breath and let it out slowly.

"Don't worry," she said, "we won't meet anybody we know."

By the time they had parked next to the hotel, Lewis was trying hard not to shake. But his body seemed to belong to someone else.

Raye went to the trunk of the car and pulled a small suitcase from it. Handing it to Lewis, she said, "It'll look better if you carry it."

In the lobby, Lewis avoided looking at the desk clerk. Raye signed them in and turned toward the elevator, followed by Lewis, who was by this time feeling like a dog on a leash.

At the door to their room, Raye handed him the key without saying anything. At first, he didn't know what she wanted him to do, but then he set down the suitcase and opened the door.

Inside, she turned to him. "You didn't really want to drive all the way home tonight, did you?"

Lewis shrugged, not able to speak, and Raye laughed. "Relax, Lewis!"

He didn't know what was expected of him. She opened the suitcase and brought out a full wine bottle. "There will be a corkscrew in one of those drawers. We'll have to use their glasses—I didn't think to bring ours up."

She also pulled a nightgown from the suitcase, then closed it and set it on a rack by the door. "You open the wine for us," she said, "and I'll freshen up." With that, she went into the bathroom and closed the door.

Lewis stood still for a moment, overwhelmed, then opened drawers in the two nightstands before finding a corkscrew. Fumbling with the tool, he managed to get the cork out of the bottle in two pieces. Then he sat on the edge of the bed, bottle in hand, and waited. He heard water running for a while.

Raye appeared in a smooth yellow nightgown that flowed to beneath her knees and revealed her shoulders. She stopped, smiled, and tilted her head. "Do you approve?" she asked softly.

He just grinned.

She moved close to him and began unbuttoning his shirt. Then she stopped and looked into his face. "Lewis, have you done this before?"

He shook his head. He was still holding the bottle of wine.

The Kerchief

A slight smile on her face, she continued undressing him. "I'm sure you'll want to shower before we go to bed, won't you?"

"Yeah," he managed.

"Bring the glasses from the bathroom when you come," she said, pulling his undershorts down to his ankles.

Lewis turned red, aware of his erection just inches from her face.

She smiled and stood up. "I'll pour the wine if you'll get the glasses now."

The warm water felt good on his body. He'd been sweating ever since they came into the room. When he was finished and dried off, he wrapped the towel around him and went out of the bathroom. "I don't have a toothbrush," he said.

Raye pointed to the suitcase. "There's one in there." Then she said, "And get rid of that silly towel." With that, she peeled the nightgown off her shoulders and let it fall to the floor. They stood, staring at each other for a moment before she picked up the glasses of wine and held one out to him.

"We're going to make your dreams come true," she said softly.

In the morning, they packed up and left the hotel. "Hungry?" she asked, pulling out of the parking lot.

Lewis's head was full of thoughts and feelings and memories, and he wasn't sure where he was anymore.

They stopped at a House of Pancakes for breakfast. The sun was bright, and as they started to enter the building Lewis saw Mount Rainier in the distance. He stopped. "It's so close!" he said.

She smiled and opened the door.

Later, driving north on 99, Raye was talkative, chattering about inconsequential things, but Lewis felt overwhelmed by their experience. She'd been gentle with him, guiding and encouraging him, but later he had that same dog-on-a-leash feeling. It wasn't what he had fantasized.

The intensity of his own orgasm was not new to him, not since he had begun to experiment with himself years before, but nothing had prepared him for how she might experience the same thing. In fact, he was shocked. At the height of it she had seemed oblivious to him, absorbed in her own private sensations.

On the Kingston ferry, they stood on the top deck and let the wind sweep their faces. When Raye looked at him, he grinned, not knowing what to say.

He didn't tell Aunt Minnie about the trip. He almost slipped and said something about the music, but caught himself. All weekend, he played the memories over and over in his mind, like a movie. Lurking somewhere behind them was an unsettled feeling. He wanted to talk about it, but there was nobody he could trust with it.

All week, as they sat together at the picnic table eating their lunches, they avoided the subject. Occasionally, Raye touched his hand gently, then withdrew. Lewis could feel eyes on them. He wondered if their guilty secret showed on their faces.

Not hers, he decided. This was not her first time, not by a long shot. To her, it was probably just another fling. *A conquest?* he wondered, echoing Aunt Minnie. He felt just a tinge of resentment.

Every night in his bed, however, he replayed the movie in his head and masturbated.

The Kerchief

On Saturday, when Raye suggested music, he said he needed to go to the library instead. Her face showed something other than disappointment—surprise? Apprehension?

In the library later, he was browsing the photography books when one of the librarians approached him. "You've been reading novels," she said, and held out a book. "I think you might like this writer." The book was *Opus 21* by Philip Wylie. "It's not a novel, but he has a new novel just out, called *The Disappearance*. It's kind of science fiction. If you like, I can reserve it for you."

Lewis thanked her, and spent an hour at one of the tables, reading the book she'd handed him. The author's style rather shocked Lewis, but his point of view was very close to Lewis's own—except he'd not had the courage to express it.

He wondered how the librarian had guessed that he would like that author. Wylie would certainly not be widely read in this town. It reminded him of the few teachers he'd had who had seemed to give him more attention than they did other students. It was another reminder that the world was bigger than this town.

The next week at lunch, he mentioned Philip Wylie to Raye, and told her about the librarian. "You probably know him, right?" he laughed.

"I read his *Night unto Night*," she said. "They made a movie from the book, but Hollywood usually doesn't do well adapting philosophical novels."

Lewis hadn't seen many movies. Aunt Minnie had taken him to a couple when he was a kid, and he'd watched a few about World War Two. He liked Westerns and movies about flying. Mostly, he'd rather read books.

He read every book about photography that the library had. Old Mister Svensen showed him how he developed films and made prints, and Lewis hoped that he might be permitted to do some of his own.

"First thing you have to do," the old man told him, "is get yourself a good camera. You can't do much with that camera you're using. And get a tripod and a light meter."

Otherwise, Svensen seemed reluctant to give Lewis much information. His business wasn't exactly thriving, and training somebody to compete with the little business there was seemed not to his benefit. "Maybe when I get ready to retire," he said, "I'll teach you so you can buy my business from me."

That might be one possibility, Lewis thought, but it meant staying in this little hick town. He dreamed bigger dreams.

The escapade with Raye wasn't repeated. Part of him still wanted to enjoy the intensity and the passion, but something held him back—her family responsibilities, perhaps, even—and he couldn't put this into words—her tendency to control things. Lewis was rather a passive person, but in his fantasies he was different. Quiet but powerful, like John Wayne or Gregory Peck.

Lewis and Raye continued their Saturday afternoon "music lessons," playing the great music and talking about it. Lewis valued these sessions, and loved the quality of the new Long Playing records. Raye even bought several albums from a store in Seattle, having them mailed to her.

Her interest in photography, however, gradually waned. Lewis thought that perhaps she had pretended an interest in the beginning so that they could do something together. Since they'd been staying home instead for the music, Lewis got to know her son and

The Kerchief

daughter. They were instructed to not interfere with the music, mostly staying in their rooms to watch television cartoons. Lewis became a regular guest at their dinner table, soon becoming comfortable with the very bright children.

He didn't encounter Wayne Gunderson any more. When he asked Raye about it, she said simply that Wayne had been shipped overseas. "Please don't tell anyone," she said. "There will be gossip." Lewis wondered how the gossip could get any greater than it already was.

One Saturday, in the middle of a "music lesson," Lewis asked Raye to turn the phonograph off. "I need to tell you something."

She stopped the music and looked at him quizzically.

"I'm leaving," he said.

He couldn't read the expression on her face. She came back to sit beside him on the sofa.

"I'm going to a photography school in Seattle. I might get a scholarship to help me, but they've accepted my application."

Raye got up and went into the bathroom, returning with a handful of tissues, wiping her eyes. "You didn't tell me you were even thinking of that," she said. She was obviously trying to control her emotions.

"I've known for a long time that I don't belong in this town," he said. "And when I met you it just made me even more aware of my difference. You made me see that there's a bigger world out there than I could even imagine."

She dabbed at her eyes. Sighing, she said, "Of course you don't belong here. That's what attracted me to you. I've loved what we've had here—especially the music—

and I've loved watching you blossom. Yes, that's the word. Blossom."

"I'm going to miss you."

"Me, too." She straightened up and looked directly at him. "First, though, you have to tell me what happened to us after Seattle."

"What do you mean?"

"You know what I mean. You were so lovely and passionate that night, but then you pulled away." She continued to look into his face, waiting for a reply.

"I don't know," he said, looking away.

"Lewis, look at me! You haven't kissed me once since that night!"

He sighed. "It was wonderful, ..." he began.

"But what?"

"Thinking back on that night, I thought that maybe you're too much for me. I didn't feel like I had any choices."

She frowned, and started to say something.

"No, wait," he said. "It was like, well, like it was your party. I didn't know what you wanted me to do, until you told me or showed me. All evening. Once I had the feeling like I was a poodle on a leash."

Raye burst into tears, burying her face in her hands.

"Raye, it's not like I wasn't enjoying it—I really was. I loved the music on the lawn, and the little surprises you planned for us. But afterward, the next day, I felt like, I don't know, like something was missing. I think it was me."

He let her sob, putting a hand on her shoulder and sighing.

Gradually, she quieted, and sat up, wiping her face. Then she turned to face him. "Why couldn't you tell me?"

The Kerchief

He shrugged. "I don't know. I wanted to please you. I was afraid I'd hurt your feelings."

"Well you've done that," she said, her voice hoarse.

They sat, silent. After a while, a door opened and little Ginny cautiously came out. "I thought you were asleep," she said."

"No, Ginny," said Raye. "We're just talking softly."

"Are we going to eat soon? I'm hungry."

"Oh my god!" Raye looked at her watch. "We are definitely going to eat soon!"

Lewis stood up. "I better go," he said.

Raye stood and leaned her head against his chest. "Let's talk more," she said quietly.

"Yes." He turned and walked out.

Sitting in his car in front of her house, shaking, Lewis thought about what had been said. He felt nervous—it was hard for him to breathe—because he had hurt Raye, and she might not care for him anymore. Another part of him felt strong. He had spoken honestly, "stood up for himself"—as Aunt Minnie used to say to him—without blaming Raye. Or at least, trying not to blame her.

His decision to go to school was his own. He thought about telling her when he first wrote to the school, but then he waited to see if they would accept him. After their trip to Seattle, he felt distant from her, although he had tried to let go of that. He could see her differently now—Aunt Minnie was right; Raye was using him. She wanted him to be different from what he was. She wanted him to be a man with her, but at the same time a boy that she could control.

She was also giving him something that he needed—an acknowledgement of his difference from the men around him. He had built up his body in that industrial work, and found a new confidence in himself. But that didn't touch his other side, the side that liked to read, that liked classical music and photography. She had given that to him, that other part of him.

It was time for him to live as that new person that he had become.

Lewis put the car into gear and drove home, where his books waited for him.

On Monday, he gave his boss notice that he was quitting. Mitch told him that he wasn't surprised. Balers usually didn't stay long anyway, but he could tell that Lewis didn't really fit there.

At lunch, Lewis and Raye were quiet. They agreed to see each other again on Saturday so that they could continue the conversation in private. Raye seemed calmer about his decision.

"You're right," she said in his car on Saturday. She had a neighbor watching the children so she and Lewis could have privacy. "I wanted you," she said, "and I guess that's always on one's own terms. That's why relationships are so hard—we each need things from each other, and they're not always the same. You were easy." She smiled at him.

"I loved how you were with me," he said, returning her smile. "I felt taken care of, like you were one of my teachers. You *were* my teacher, actually."

Raye lowered her head and then looked up at him. "You were a wonderful lover."

"I'd never felt like that before," he said. "I always thought sex was just—" He opened his hands and shrugged. "I was so nervous and excited at the same time!"

She put her arms around him. "You're going to make some woman a great husband," she said, her mouth

The Kerchief

close to his ear. Then she separated from him and took his hand in both of hers. "I love you, Lewis—as a friend." She kissed him on the lips.

They stared into each other's eyes for a long time.

Three – Current Time

"Long story," he said.

Rayna patted his hand. "I'll go get your breakfast, and you can tell me—okay?"

Lewis drifted away again. The smell of food woke him.

"We have eggs this morning," Rayna said. "I got your catsup, too."

"How'd you know?"

"Celia told me." She scooped up a small amount of scrambled eggs with red dotting the top and fed it to him. "Kerchief," she said, "remember?"

He managed a smile. "You knew her?"

"You were just about to tell me," she said. "You just said 'Kerchief.'"

"Confused," he said.

"Tell me what you remember." Rayna held his orange juice so he could sip from it.

He closed his eyes.

It was a big, dark studio, with broads and spots on rolling stands, and a young couple sitting on stools in the center. His view camera sat on a heavy tripod, and he rolled it into place.

"Set your main light first," said Anthony, the instructor, from the shadows and Lewis switched off all the lights except the main. Approaching the models, he thrust a meter in front of their faces.

"F-eight," said Anthony. "Adjust your light to get an F-eight reading."

Lewis moved the main light a little closer and took another reading.

"Okay, now set your fill light."

Lewis was suddenly overcome with emotion.

Seeing his silent tears, Rayna changed the subject. "Celia told me you were a photographer," she said.

"All I ever wanted to do," he said.

"I've seen your pictures in the book down in the lobby. You do beautiful work." She wiped his chin and stepped back so he could see her. "Do you remember the kerchief you started to tell me about?"

"She made me go to school," he said.

"The kerchief lady."

He nodded. "She had hair like yours."

Rayna half-sat on the edge of the bed and held his hand. "How did she make you go to school?"

"She made me want to," he said. "She seduced me." He grinned weakly. "and she made me be—somebody—a man."

Her eyebrows went up.

"A mentor, I guess," he said. "She showed me the world. But then I had to stand up by myself. If it hadn't been for her, I might not have done it."

"So you turned out pretty well?" Rayna smiled at him.

"Always wanted to thank her."

He squeezed her hand feebly, and closed his eyes. "I need to sleep."

Rayna quietly stood up and left the room.

The End

Touching

Touching

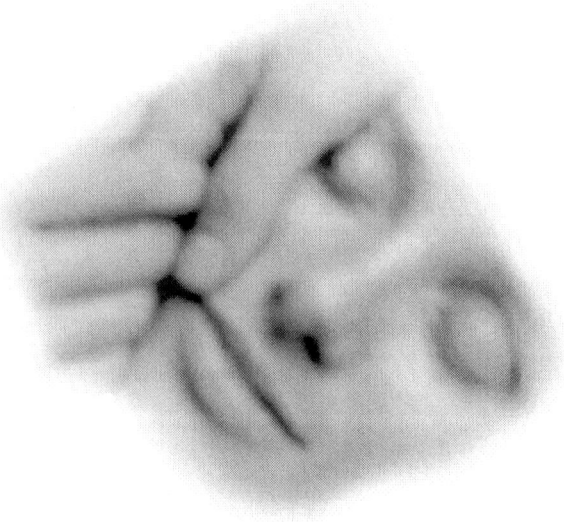

The bathroom door was ajar. Doug pushed through it and moved unsteadily past her naked body as she leaned against the vanity, applying mascara.

"'Scuse me," he mumbled sleepily. "I couldn't hold it." Leaning over the toilet and supporting himself with his hand against the wall, he looked over at her, amused at the similar angles of their bodies.

"'S'okay," Laurel said, still looking into the mirror. She dabbed at her cheek with a pinky.

He sighed, finished his task, flushed and closed the toilet. As he moved past her again, he stopped, turned and embraced her, cupping her breasts in both hands. "Morning," he said against her neck.

"Morning," she said, the little brush suspended in front of her face. "Now please leave."

He backed away, small hurt lines appearing on his forehead. "I thought you liked to be touched."

"I do," she answered, "but not in front of this mirror."

He stopped in the doorway and turned. "I like to look at us," he said. "You used to."

"Fifty years ago I liked my body."

"I still do." He pulled the door closed behind him and returned to the bedroom to dress.

Later, at the breakfast table, he looked at her. "I'm disappointed," he said.

"So am I."

"We're still us," he said. "Time only changes the outside of us."

"I know." She rested her chin on her knuckles. "It's not your body that people admire about you."

"You don't think that fifty years ago were your best years, do you?"

"No," she said, "but those were the years I felt good about my body."

"You're disappointed that you've lost your youth?"

She frowned. "For you, youth means strength and vitality. For me, it's sexual attractiveness."

He sighed. "You think I no longer find you sexually attractive?

She smiled. "I believe you do," she said. "But I don't."

"Then I'm not doing my job."

The smile faded. "Your *job?*"

"Part of my responsibility as your mate is to make you feel as good about yourself as I feel about you."

"Why should that be your responsibility? Isn't it up to me to find meaning in my life?"

"Don't you?"

"Not sexually." She stopped, aware of his reaction. In a small voice, "I just don't feel sexy anymore." She looked down at her hands.

"That's not my responsibility."

She looked up. "You just said ..."

"I didn't say I was responsible for you feeling sexy." He stopped. "Okay, maybe I could have a little influence—"

She looked at him without speaking.

"Okay," he repeated, "I want you to feel sexy—although I'm not sure exactly what that means—because when you do you respond differently to me."

"How do I do that?"

"You make *me* feel sexy," he said. "Even when I can't get it up, you make me feel like there's something physical going on between us."

"What's going on?" she said, a faint smile beginning around her mouth.

He got up from his chair and circled the table. "Exactly this."

Doug pulled into a parking spot and shut off the engine. Opening the window, he placed the speaker inside, They sat there silently for a while, waiting for the movie to start.

They had met the previous weekend at a party, and spent most of the evening in a corner talking. When he suggested that they attend a drive-in movie, she agreed.

While their conversation at the party had been easy and delightful, tonight left them with few words.

He turned toward her and touched her cheek. She smiled and turned to face him so that he could kiss her. His hand wandered down the front of her blouse.

"No," Laurel whispered.

"Why not?"

She pulled her face away from his. Still smiling, she said, "Too soon."

Coming out of the store, Laurel shifted her bag to her other hand, and took Doug's hand.

She had suggested they meet for lunch, after which she wanted to shop for a gift for her aunt. They were beginning to relax with each other, especially in public.

They walked down the busy street swinging their arms between them.

Alone, however, they often found themselves a little bit tense. Physical attraction had come to dominate their relationship. Neither had learned yet the multimedia languages of negotiating this thicket of youth.

Touching

Holding hands in public was making a statement, both to the world and to themselves. It was short of commitment, yet claiming, the slightest bit, possession.
She looked up at him and smiled with her teeth showing. He squeezed her hand.

"I hate pantyhose," Doug murmured as his hand moved up her thigh. "You wear short skirts and short shorts, and show off your legs. But it's 'Don't touch!' like those glass cases in the jewelry department. It's a tease!"

"It means you have to ask first," Laurel said. The tone of her voice didn't say, 'no.'

"Reaching the top of a nylon," he said, his hand exploring farther, "is such a nice soft feeling!"

She pushed his hand back down to her knee. "I need time," she said. "You get turned on quicker than I do."

"You used to."

"It was new." She wasn't looking at him.

He turned to face the windshield. "I don't know what you want."

"I don't know, either," she said. "I just want to feel like more than my body."

He sighed.

"Touch my face," she said. "Look at me."

They were dancing very close, to soft music. Flitting spots of light roamed the dark hall from the silver ball hanging in the center of the room. Doug's fingertips touched the small of her bare back. As they began to explore higher, Laurel took her arm down from his shoulder and pushed his forearm down.

"Behave," she said seductively.

"You can't be serious," he said. "Your back is inviting me to touch it."

"No, it's inviting you to look."

"How can I look without touching?" He backed away enough to gaze at her cleavage. Meanwhile, his right hand guided her around the room, his fingertips tasting her skin.

"You are incorrigible." Same tone of voice.

"Let's go out to the car," he said.

"We came here to dance, remember?"

"I want to dance inside you."

"Behave."

The song ended, and they made their way back to their table holding hands.

The party was loud, but contained inside the house. The two of them slipped through the French doors to the pool side, giggling.

"It's cold out here!" Laurel laughed, letting her gown fall to the pavement. The blue light from the quiet pool danced on her skin.

"Greg said the water's warm," Doug said. Hurriedly undressing, he reached over and unhooked her bra. They stood looking at each other, shivering and grinning, and then held hands as they jumped into the

Touching

water. As they broke the surface, she started to shriek but stopped when he covered her mouth with his hand.

"It's not so bad if you keep moving." He embraced her,

"We don't have towels!" she laughed, and pulled away to swim toward the edge of the pool.

A few minutes later they emerged from the pool to find their host standing near the door holding towels, laughing at them. "These'll cost you," Greg said.

"Anything!" she said, grabbing a towel from him.

Doug opened the other towel and wrapped it around her trembling body. She reached up and kissed him.

With one finger Doug traced her spine all the way from her necklace down to where it disappeared between the mounds of his pleasure. Laurel lay still, smiling at him.

Then she pushed him to roll onto his back. "My turn," she said, and kissed his cheek.

Then, "Oh, my goodness—already?"

Laurel reached out, her hand searching for his. Finding it, she clutched it with all her might. Arching her back, she wailed. Doug took her hand in both of his, and nestled his face against her shoulder.

"Push!" yelled the nurse.

He gripped her hand tightly, and felt as though he were going to faint.

                                                            * * *

The theater was dark except for the flickering screen. The music was ominous.

Doug's hand slipped down between her thighs. Laurel squeezed his hand between her legs. Neither of them took their eyes from the screen.

They let the warm water stream over them for the longest time, holding each other tightly. Then Laurel reached for a bar of soap, rotated it in her hand, replaced it and lathered his back, allowing her hand to explore his crevice. Between them, she felt him grow powerful.

Doug bent over to taste a breast, the shower still splashing over them both. She moved her soapy hand to his neck and pulled him against her.

"I want the light out," Laurel said, pulling the sheet up to her throat.

Doug obediently switched off the light, then reached under the sheet to stroke her body. She moved against him.

Neither of them spoke, their hands doing all the communicating.

Touching

In the packed subway, they stood next to each other, their bodies touching intimately. Laurel looked up at Doug and smiled. The car undulated on its tracks; they undulated together. Through several layers of clothing, they could feel each other's body, reminding them of last night's delights.

&—&

"Don't touch me!" Laurel said, sobbing.
"I'm sorry!"
"You couldn't wait for me? Kristen, for god's sake? That bitch!"
"You were gone so long."
"But—Kristen?" She dabbed at her eyes and looked challengingly at him. "You told me you just had dinner."
"We got plastered," Doug said, looking away.
"How can I let you touch me and not think about you touching *her?*"
"I would never confuse the two of you. She's skinny."
She suddenly laughed. "That's what I've been telling you all these years!"
"You have a perfect body."
Soberly, she said, "Used to have."
"We both used to have."
She lay still, looking at the ceiling. "I could never do that with anyone else."
"I didn't think I could, either."
They were silent for a long time. He reached over to her, tentatively.
She suddenly turned toward him. "Are you bruised?" She giggled. "From all those bones?"
"Made me appreciate you even more." He touched her belly.

"After the fact," she said, her voice gone flat. "Didn't notice it beforehand, did you." It was not a question.

He withdrew his hand. "I'm sorry."

"Bet you are."

"I had to tell you, though," he said. "I couldn't live with myself otherwise."

"Maybe you'll have to for a while."

"What d'you mean?"

"You're grounded, Buster!" She turned away from him and lay still. Then a muffled, "Long as I can stand it."

He sighed.

"Can we just cuddle?" Doug asked quietly.

After a minute, Laurel turned to face him. "Are you okay?"

"Yeah. Just don't have any juice tonight."

She studied his face. "It's okay, Sweetie. Sometimes I don't feel like it, either."

"Why didn't you say something?"

"I like to feel you."

They allowed silence to drift over them.

"We're getting older," he said finally, turning to look at the ceiling.

She put a hand on him. "It's not so bad."

"I'm disappointed."

"Yeah."

He continued to look at the ceiling. "Next step separate beds?"

"Not while I have anything to say about it."

Turning toward her again, he fondled a breast. "Still feels wonderful."

Touching

"I love to be entwined with you," she said with a chuckle. "Feeling our legs all tangled together, every inch of us touching each other."

He pulled her closer. "Skin against skin."
She reached down and felt his growing confidence. "Yes," she said quietly. "Sometimes that's enough."

The End

Donald Skiff

Do-Over

Do-Over

Track One

    Ernie carefully set the needle down in the middle of the LP. Then he put his finger on the disc and rotated it backward until a sudden silence told him that he'd found the start of the track. "Easier," he said to me, "than trying to stop the record exactly there while it's playing." Turning on his microphone, he announced the next song.
    Sitting next to him drinking a beer, I'd been enjoying talking with him about old times while he played music for the reception.
    "I just had this funny feeling," I said.
    He started the music and looked over at me without saying anything.
    I shrugged. "You know, déjà vu?"
    "Yeah."
    "Like wanting to find that exact place in your life when you could have done something different? And had a different life?"
    "You mean, like the road not taken?"
    "Yeah. A lot of stuff in my life just sneaked up on me, and I didn't have any say in what happened. But there were a couple of places when I, like, flipped a coin, thinking it probably didn't matter what I chose, anyway. So I picked."
    He grinned. "Or you let the girl pick for you."
    "Hmmm. Yeah, maybe."
    "Like, that time you showed your girl the condom you had stashed in your billfold, and she wanted to see it and then she threw it in the bushes. You told me about that."
    That night came back to me vividly. I'd felt that sinking "Oh, no, what did you do?!" and wished I'd never pulled it out of my pocket. I was showing off, making my

move, and she raised the ante. If I could have put my thumb on the record and just backed it up to the quiet spot just before...

She had explained that she "didn't believe in those things." I wasn't sure what she was telling me, but maybe that's the place where I could have pulled up sharp on the reins—and lived a whole different life.

It wasn't a bad life, actually. After three kids, four cars and two houses later we agreed that we probably weren't meant for each other anyway. She finally went off with some out-of-work philosophy professor, and eventually I found the love of my life.

But if I had taken the road not taken, as Ernie put it, I've wondered what life I would have had instead of the one I had. Those twenty years that they call the best years of your life are when you prove to yourself and if you're lucky you prove to the world that you're somebody to be reckoned with. You know, college and all that. I didn't know I was throwing it all away that night when I didn't rein up like John Wayne, making my horse hop on all fours to stop things right there where they were. He wouldn't even have had to say, "Whoa." He knew that he was changing the course of his history from this to that. And he knew why.

Yeah, I know, I was just a kid letting my dick tell me what to do. She didn't say, "I don't do that," or even, "Not until we're married." I'd heard those things before. In those days, you knew that some girls did it and some girls didn't. But she said, "I don't believe in those things," meaning the condom.

John Wayne would have said, "Whoa, Baby. Let's not tempt fate. Are you ready to have babies?" He'd have put it right up there.

Do-Over

> *And she would have looked up sheepishly, and asked, "Are you sure you want this relationship?" Or something like that—the old commitment thing.*
> *And he'd have ridden off into the sunset. And lived a different life than I did.*

Most of my life—the first half, anyway—I often had this feeling that my one true love was someplace else. Got me into a lot of trouble sometimes. Like, how do you know? How do you know you made the right decisions when you locked yourself into something—or some*body*.

I always thought Ernie locked himself in, too. I could see how his girl had to have things her way. "Trapped" is not exactly it. He had his eyes open. But I've always wondered how he felt about things after a bunch of kids. Course he was Catholic, and the rules were different for them. He used to kid me about my choice back then, but he never said I should have taken a different road. It's only been lately, after we both chose our lives and lived with the consequences for years that we could be that honest with each other.

I looked at Ernie. "I guess," I said, "what I'm wondering is—if I'd pulled back right then, would I have even recognized my one true love when she came along? You know, how you learn what it is you don't want?"

Ernie looked at me out of the corner of his eye and kept talking into his microphone. "Here's another oldie," he said, cueing up the turntable and letting it play.

Track Two

Just now, looking out of my dorm room at the green lawn and watching the low sun make everything like gold, and listening to real music, I thought about the life

I might have lived if I'd gone ahead and screwed that girl anyway. Probably she'd have gotten pregnant right away, and we'd have been off on the usual merry-go-round of low-paying jobs and getting kicked out of apartments because we couldn't keep up the rent when the old car broke down. Brings a shiver to me now.

I hated English Lit, but I really dug physics, even though it took a lot of math to understand it. I got into conversations with this gorgeous girl Corrine, who was in both of my 101 classes, and she said she'd help me with my Lit assignments if I'd help her with her physics. I learned how to coach somebody without putting them down for what they didn't understand, and I learned how to admit just what I didn't understand about, like, why T.S. Eliot kept saying things in riddles. She laughed, but she didn't make fun of me. "When you use words to describe something," she said, "you can choose words that mean different things depending on how you look at them, Maybe what you're trying to say means something on different levels."

"Different levels," I repeated. I didn't have a clue.

"Okay," she said patiently, "look at what he says here." She leafed through *The Hollow Men* and found a place. After reading several stanzas to me, she said, "Notice all those words like *dry* and *dust* and even *straw?* He's describing people, but on another level he's also describing a lifeless state. *The Hollow Men* is about people who don't think—maybe most of us—when we just do what everybody else does. When we don't see a bigger picture. He's trying to get us to see more meaningfully."

"Why doesn't he just say that, then?"

She looked at me with those big black eyes that always made my knees weak. "Maybe he knew that if he did, nobody would listen. It's because we have to work at understanding him that we really get what he's saying. It's like in physics class, when the teacher actually dropped those two steel balls on the floor instead of just telling us that they would fall at the same rate even though they were different sizes and weights."

Right then I got this strong feeling that my life was set, that I could see it going along a very long, straight highway. Into the sunset.

I didn't know that twenty years down that highway I'd wonder what it might have been like if ...

How it really went, she got a job with a publisher in New York, and I went to work for Home Depot in this little suburb in New Jersey near our home. I kept sending out resumes for jobs in research, but the longer I went without that kind of job, the harder it was to get somebody to talk to me.

She got pregnant, of course, and it was nice while she was on this fabulous maternity leave, when we could have a normal family life. Naturally, I became the stay-at-home dad, and went to the park with the stroller and chatted with other parents about baby food and all that, and she became civilized.

Then one day, I looked at myself in the mirror and didn't recognize that guy. "What happened?" I asked him.

"You put your finger on that record," he said, "and wound it back to the silence..."

Track Three

"Corrine," I said, as we walked out of Lit 101, "I think we live on different planets."

She took the hint, and began dating somebody else. I met Evie, a kinda mousy girl but sharp as a tack, and we spent hours talking about nuclear physics and how the world could be made easier for everybody.

After graduation we took jobs in the same company outside of L.A. We had a great life, surfing and skiing, until she hooked up with a bronze god-type astrophysicist who wore a *gopro* camera when he rode the waves or skied down the big slopes at Aspen.

Not much point in wondering at that point how life would have been if ..., because it wasn't my choice.

Well, maybe I did have something to say about it. It just felt like, well, there are winners and there are losers, and I was the loser. I started lying on the beach with a six pack while she and her god splashed in the surf. When somebody tells you, even without actually saying it, that you're a worthless piece of shit, it's hard not to believe them on some level. So you become what they call you.

What I could have done, but didn't, was to get out and be what I had always thought I might be. Not a god with a *gopro* camera and a surfboard, but a better physicist, looking for that key in the equations on the chalkboard, thinking about how it all fits together.

Another track to find on the LP.

Track Four

"I guess it's all the same thing," I said the next day as Ernie took a long pull on his beer. "You back up the record, or you let it play out. The only certainty is, no matter what you choose, you live until you die."

Ernie shrugged. "So you let it play out," he said.

"Didn't we both?"

In my head I went back to those days when we sat in the bar on State Street talking about life. That's where

Do-Over

we met, in the Red Hawk, sitting at the bar trying to get the attention of the cute bartender. I'd make a funny comeback to something she said, and she'd laugh and turn away, and I'd see Ernie roll his eyes.

Turned out we were both new in the physics department at U of M but hadn't met each other yet. We got to talking about the politics of university life, and how we both felt there was something else inside us that wanted to come out, but never would.

"What's that thing in you?" I asked, after the third shot of Patron Silver.

"Thing?" He laughed.

By this time we were sitting in a booth at the back of the bar. The waiters all knew us, but they didn't banter much with us.

"That thing—that lump in your gut that reminds you of what you meant to do but somehow never did."

"Music," he said. "I should've gone into music."

"You play?"

"No. I can't stay with the routine of practice. It's all in my head, instead of my fingers."

"Like what?"

He took a swig from his beer. "When I was eleven years old, I was plinking on my sister's piano, and this thing came to me—how certain notes *just went together*. I spent hours at that piano, trying out different combinations—different chords. I was obsessed with it."

"So you went into physics." I leaned back and looked at him.

"Well," he said, "when I looked it up in books, it just seemed like the whole world made sense if you go at it from the right place. I figured out how musical scales are in a logarithmic progression, so when you try to transpose them up and down everything is, like 'almost' perfect ..."

"Except an octave and a perfect fifth and a perfect fourth." I had to say that, 'cause I wanted him to know I was keeping up with him.

He just grinned. "So, what's your 'secret lump'?"

That took me back a little. "I don't know," I said.

Something in my face must have shown, because he said, "C'mon. What's that thing inside you that wants to come out?"

I had to shrug. "I guess I'm still waiting to find out."

We got into a long discussion about our lives. Turned out Ernie had married young, like me, but he'd stuck with his family. Unlike me, he was committed to the long haul. He showed me photographs he kept in his wallet. Wife and kids, like everybody else. "You got a family?" he asked.

Even though I nodded, I registered something else. *My life—my real life—hadn't started.*

Track Five

I first saw her on the street, in a bunch of people waiting to go into a theater. She was flipping her long hair out from her coat collar, like in those slow-motion TV commercials. She was with some other people, but I couldn't keep from staring at her. *Is she The One?*

I kept seeing her around town. I never got the nerve to speak to her, even when I was alone and she seemed to be alone. Usually, Jen was with me. We'd be having one of our arguments, and my mind would be on a lump I felt somewhere south of my beltline.

Then, one evening I was sitting at the bar in SAVA, having my Patron Silver and waiting for Jen, when SHE came in and sat right next to me. "I'll have one of

Do-Over

those," she said, motioning toward my drink. *How did she know what it was in my glass?*

Turned out she had been standing near me when I ordered it. And she turned her face toward me and smiled.

I started to say something to her, and then the image popped into my head, *of that black record, with my finger on the edge, pushing it back around to the silence...*

The End